MW00757983

THE RED TAPE WAR

Tor books by Jack L. Chalker

Downtiming the Night Side
The Messiah Choice

G.O.D. INC.

The Labyrinth of Dreams
The Shadow Dancers
The Maze in the Mirror

SOUL RIDER

Soul Rider I: *Spirits of Flux and Anchor*
Soul Rider II: *Empires of Flux and Anchor*
Soul Rider III: *Masters of Flux and Anchor*
Soul Rider IV: *The Birth of Flux and Anchor*
Soul Rider V: *Children of Flux and Anchor*

Tor books by Mike Resnick

Santiago: A Myth of the Far Future
The Dark Lady: A Romance of the Far Future
Stalking the Unicorn: A Fable of Tonight
Ivory: A Legend of Past and Future
Paradise: A Chronicle of a Distant World
Second Contact

Tor books by George Alec Effinger

Shadow Money

JACK L. CHALKER,
MIKE RESNICK,
GEORGE ALEC EFFINGER

THE RED TAPE WAR

A Round-Robin
Science Fiction Novel

A TOM DOHERTY ASSOCIATES BOOK

NEW YORK

THE RED TAPE WAR

Copyright © 1991 by Jack L. Chalker, Mike Resnick, and
George Alec Effinger

A Tor Book
Published by Tom Doherty Associates, Inc.
49 West 24th Street
New York, N.Y. 10010

Library of Congress Cataloging-in-Publication Data

Chalker, Jack L.
    The red tape war / Jack L. Chalker, Mike Resnick, George
Alec Effinger.
        p. cm.
    "A Tom Doherty Associates Book."
    ISBN: 0-312-85151-0
    I. Resnick, Michael D. II. Effinger, George Alec. III. Title.
PS3553.H247R4   1991
813'.54—dc20   90-48772
                                                      CIP

Printed in the United States of America

First edition: April 1991

0 9 8 7 6 5 4 3 2 1

To Eva, Carol and Debbie

And to the federal government and all of its many departments, for inspiration and source material.

INTRODUCTION

It all began back at the 1980 World Science Fiction Convention in Boston, at about four o'clock in the morning.

Jack Chalker and I were sitting in the hotel lobby, talking about one thing or another, and since he hadn't yet written twenty-odd best-sellers, and I hadn't yet written any best-sellers at all or won any literary awards (all oversights that God put aright during the ensuing decade), and publishers, while not avoiding us, still weren't beating a path to our doors, we thought that it might be fun to collaborate on a book while we had some free time on our hands.

I don't remember now who suggested it, but before the evening was over we decided that it would be even more fun to invite a third party and do a round-robin novel, one where each of us tried to stick the next guy in line with a near-insoluble problem. It still sounded like a good idea the next morning (mornings arrive at about 2:00 P.M. at conventions), so we decided to go ahead and recruit a third partner.

The first writer we approached agreed immediately, then thought better of it and withdrew from the project before nightfall. The second looked at us like we were crazy, explained that relative unknowns such as ourselves could never hope to sell such a book, and semi-respectfully declined. The third writer didn't know any better, and agreed.

As a show of good faith, I offered to write the opening chapter. (It also meant that everyone else had to copy the style I chose, but nobody ever figured this out. Come to think of it, nobody ever copied it, either.) As I recall, we flipped coins to determine the order for the rest of the book.

We got about halfway through the project in something less than six months, and then it bogged down. The chapters our collaborator wrote didn't quite fill the bill, so we paid him off and decided to find yet another partner—but then Jack started churning out best-sellers with monotonous regularity, and I signed a pair of multi-book contracts, and we put the round-robin on the back burner until we could catch up with our commitments, and suddenly we looked at the calendar and it was 1989 and not a word had been written on *The Red Tape War* since 1981.

We met again at the World Science Fiction Convention, which had made its rounds of the world and was back in Boston, where it seems to settle every ninth year, and decided that it was time to resurrect the project. The problem was that we not only needed a third writer, but our status within the field had changed: Jack had just turned down a million-dollar offer from one of his publishers, and was churning out best-sellers on the average of one every four months; and I had just emerged from a very successful auction of my latest book, and was clutching the Hugo Award for Best Short Story of 1989 to my bosom.

So what we needed now was a writer of at least equal prestige within the community, one with an excellent sense of style and humor, and one who was willing to drop everything he was doing and go right to work on the project. Not only that, but he had to be skilled enough to totally rewrite the chapters our departed collaborator had submitted without removing anything that Jack or I had built upon in future chapters—all in exchange for third billing on the cover.

"Where will we ever find anyone that naive?" asked Jack.

At precisely that moment, George Alec Effinger walked by, hugging his Best Novelette Hugo to *his* bosom—and after two hours of our appealing to his ego, his bank account, and his desire to ever see another sunset (writers don't wake up early enough to see sunrises), he finally agreed.

The rest, as they say, is history—in this case, the history of Millard Fillmore Pierce (all three of him).

—Mike Resnick

P.S.—It belatedly occurs to me that you might be interested in knowing who wrote which chapters. We'll let you guess for a while, but we'll slip the answer in somewhere along the way.

1

"Goddammit!" snapped Pierce.

"What is it now?" asked his navigational computer.

"You cheated!"

"Did not."

"Like hell you didn't!" said Pierce. "You moved your bishop one square to the left when I wasn't looking."

"Oh, that," said the computer.

"Yes—*that!*"

"I was ethically compelled to do it," said the computer in a sullen whine.

"What are you talking about?" demanded Pierce.

"I'm supposed to try to beat you, aren't I?" asked the computer.

"So?"

"So if I didn't move my bishop, you would have announced mate in six more moves. I *had* to move it."

"But you broke the rules!" said Pierce.

"Trying to beat you was a higher imperative," said the computer. "It was simply a value judgment. All Model

XB-223 navigational computers are qualified to make—"

"Never mind," interrupted Pierce disgustedly. He leaned back and looked at the viewscreen, which showed nothing but a few stray stars in the distance. "You know, things couldn't get this screwed up by chance," he said, more to himself than to the computer, which in Pierce's opinion was merely the latest in a long line of things that had been screwed up. "It took a long, hard, concerted effort."

Which, of course, was true.

There are all kinds of truths, however. Certain truths are timeless and immutable, as in: There is no crisis so urgent today that it won't become even more urgent tomorrow. It was the maxim that seemed to provide the motive force for the entire galaxy.

Most truths, though, are ephemeral. When Wee Willie Keeler told a mob of boyishly devoted worshipers that the secret of success in life was to hit 'em where they ain't, it was a valid statement for a member of the 1901 Brooklyn Dodgers—but sixty-seven centuries later, poor old Willie would have been hard-pressed to find anyplace where they weren't.

Despite Pierce's current spare surroundings, the galaxy was getting crowded, and life in that galaxy had grown more complicated in geometric leaps and bounds. For, to paraphrase J. B. S. Haldane, the universe not only held more red tape than anyone imagined; it held more red tape than anyone *could* imagine.

There were, for example, 132,476 mining worlds; the ownership of all but six was in dispute. There were five faster-than-light drives on the market; royalties for four of them were being held in escrow pending some 1,300 separate legal actions. The Spiral Fed—that loose economic federation of worlds on one of the Milky Way's spiral arms—possessed some 73 races and 1,786 worlds, all pledged to each other's economic welfare and territorial integrity; there were upward of 5,000 separate and distinct military alliances in the Spiral Fed, and on any given day there were more than 200 different economic boycotts and embargoes in effect among the Fed worlds.

Language posed another problem. It wasn't bad enough that there were more than 20,000 intelligent races in the galaxy. Sooner or later someone could have programmed a computer to translate 20,000 varieties of groans, grunts, squawks, squeaks, roars and gurgles. But only seven worlds possessed planetary languages. The inhabitants of Earth, to name one of the less extreme examples, spoke 67 languages and more than 1,200 dialects, and her colonies had added another 27 languages over the centuries.

Indeed, far from the world government that so many utopian writers had piously predicted, nationalism—on Earth and elsewhere—flourished as never before. The Indian planet of Gromm, for example, traded with the insectile population of Sirius VII and the purple reptiles of Beta Cancri II—but Pakistanis were shot on sight. The Cook County Democratic machine of Illinois had founded a colony on the distant world of New Daley, which interacted with the rest of humanity only during voter registration drives every fourth year. Kenya and Tanzania jointly opened a half dozen worlds to commercial exploitation, but the border between the two nations remained closed. And most of the other races made humanity look like amateurs in matters of self-interest.

And, reflected Pierce, despite it all, it was the little things that finally got to a man—like finding himself in the middle of nowhere because his computer had been so intent upon cheating him at chess that it hadn't paid any attention to where they were going.

"It's not my fault," said the computer petulantly.

"What's not your fault?" asked Pierce.

"Whatever you're thinking about. Whenever you're quiet like that, you always wind up blaming me for something."

"Forget it," said Pierce.

"I try to do my job," sniffed the computer. "I really do. It's not as if I were free to disengage myself from the instruments and walk around the decks like some people I could mention."

"It's all right," said Pierce with a sigh. "I'm not mad at you."

"You're sure?"

"I'm sure."

"Good," said the computer. "I feel much better now that we've had this little chat. By the way, have you got time to receive a Priority One message?"

"Is one coming in?" asked Pierce, suddenly alert.

"They've been trying to raise me for the past ten minutes," answered the computer.

"Ten minutes! I thought you said it was Priority One?"

"It is."

"You're supposed to patch those through to me immediately, even in a war zone!"

"But you looked so thoughtful and morose, I didn't want to disturb you. And I am, after all, a Model XB-223 navigational computer, qualified to make value judgments. And besides, you were mad at me."

"Put it through."

"Are you still mad?" asked the computer coyly.

"*No, goddammit!*" bellowed Pierce.

"I wish you could see the reading I just took of your blood pressure."

"May I please receive my Priority One message?" asked Pierce, struggling to control his voice and wondering how the hell to control his blood pressure. "If it's not too much trouble for you, that is? I wouldn't want to cause you any inconvenience."

"No trouble at all," said the computer, suddenly all business. "After all, it's my job. In ion storms and meteor showers, come nova or supernova, nothing shall stay the XB-223s from their appointed duties. Had you ever heard that before?"

"No," said Pierce. "I never had."

"I made it up," said the computer proudly. "I think it has a certain poetic nobility about it, don't you?"

"The message?" said Pierce wearily.

"Ah, yes, the message," said the computer. "It's coming to you from Earth, by the way. It originates in Woodstock, Illinois, an absolutely lovely little town, population 31,203, mean temperature of 53 degrees, very near the Des Plaines River, which you'll be interested to know has recently undergone antipollution treatments and now abounds in bass, bluegills, and—"

"The message!"

"Right. The message. By all means. Let me just put it on visual display here." Suddenly the computer giggled. "Oh, that tickles! You wouldn't think a computer could be ticklish, especially a sophisticated, highly advanced model like the XB-223, but—"

"*The message!*"

"Very well. It's coming in now, on Screen 3."

"Screen 3 is blank," said Pierce.

"Some people are well bred," said the computer. "Some people have manners. Some people say 'thank you' when someone offers to do them a favor, even if it's only a lowly XB-223 navigational computer with no voting rights or sexuality or—"

"Thank you," interrupted Pierce.

"You're welcome."

Suddenly the viewscreen lit up, displaying a hologram of a middle-aged woman in stern dress and sterner makeup.

"It's about time!" she said ominously.

"I'm sorry, ma'am," answered Pierce. "The computer—"

"Ma'am is a contraction of madam," interrupted the woman. "I am not a madam."

"I'm sorry, sir," said Pierce, flustered.

"Do I look like a sir to you?" she demanded.

"Go ahead—tell her," whispered the computer.

"No, Supervisor," said Pierce.

"That's better," said the woman. "Now suppose we start again—and do it according to form this time."

"Millard Fillmore Pierce, Class 2 Arbiter, receiving your message, Supervisor."

"Very well, Arbiter Pierce. This is Supervisor Collier with a Priority One message."

"I know," said Pierce.

"Of course you know," said Supervisor Collier irritably. "But the protocol was created for a reason, and we must observe it at all times."

"Yes, Supervisor."

"Now, then, Pierce," she continued, "I have a new assignment for you, which takes precedence over those on which you are now working. Where are you located at this moment?"

"I'm not quite sure."

"You're *what?*"

"It's a long story," said Pierce. "Can you just tell me what the assignment entails?"

"All right," said Supervisor Collier, absently tugging at her left earlobe, which was considerably larger than its counterpart. "Now listen carefully, Pierce. This connection is using a lot of energy, and I don't want to have to repeat everything twice."

"Right."

"As you may or may not know, a minor war has broken out between Cathia and Galladrial, which for our purposes we will call Aldebaran IX and Komonos V. Earth has declared itself to be neutral in this conflict, although of course we do support Galladrial in its war against the heathen totalitarians of Atra II."

"Of course," said Pierce.

"To continue: Promenade, which we shall officially term Lambda Gamma IV, commissioned a battleship from the state of Hawaii, which as you know is on Earth. Are you following me so far?"

Pierce nodded.

"Good. Now, it seems that Promenade sold the battleship to Springfall, which we shall officially term Belora VII. Springfall contracted to deliver the ship to Cathia, but had to set it down on the neutral human colony of New Glasgow for minor repairs. New Glasgow happens to be in the war zone, and when Galladrial found out that the ship was there, they sent in a squadron of fighter ships to destroy it."

"Where do I come in?" asked Pierce, thoroughly confused.

"I'm getting to that. It seems that seventeen humans sustained injuries during the attack. Worse still, none of them were Hawaiians." She paused dramatically. "Now, five were merely civilians who happened to be in the wrong place at the wrong time, but the other twelve people were actively effecting repairs on the ship." She paused again, this time to catch her breath. "So the question is this: do we give them battle pay and free hospitalization despite the fact that we're not at war with either of the parties in conflict? Do we settle for handling it through Workman's

Compensation? Or do we present our grievances, and a bill, to the government of Galladrial? Your job is to appraise the situation and send me a recommendation that I can act upon."

"Why not just ask someone on the scene?" asked Pierce.

"Chain of command was established for a reason, Pierce," she said severely. "*You* will interview people on the scene. *I* will act after analyzing your report."

"Whatever you say," sighed Pierce.

"Fine. Good luck, Arbiter Pierce. Supervisor Collier signing—Oh, by the way, have you figured out where you are yet?"

The computer posted a readout on Screen 2.

"The Pirollian Sector, as near as I can tell," said Pierce.

"Interesting place," said Supervisor Collier. "Lots of activity."

"No, Supervisor," said Pierce. "There's no activity here at all. It's all empty and deserted."

The screen went blank.

"You're sure we're in the Pirollian Sector?" Pierce asked the computer.

"Absolutely. XB-223 navigational computers are incapable of error."

"How did we get here, then?"

"Now you're going to be angry with me again," whined the computer.

"Not again—*still*." Pierce paused. "Fix me up a sandwich, will you?"

"I don't think that would be wise," said the computer.

"Why not? I'm going to have a little lunch while you lay in a course for New Glasgow."

"But it may be an hour or two before I can pinpoint our position and lay in the course," said the computer. "We XB-223s pride ourselves on our pinpoint accuracy."

"So it'll take an hour. Big deal. Now make me a sandwich."

"I still don't think it's wise."

"Why the hell not?" demanded Pierce.

"Well, I've only read about human physiology, you understand, so my knowledge of your body is really based only on hearsay, so to speak. But if you're going to have to fight for your life, I don't think you'll be at your most efficient shortly after glutting on sandwiches."

"What are you talking about?"

"There's a dreadnought of unknown origin approaching us at light speeds," replied the computer. "Of course, it may prove to be friendly, but on the not-unlikely supposition that it isn't, you may soon be put to the ultimate test. And, not to put too fine a point on it, Millard, you're such a skinny little wimp that you're probably going to need all the strength at your disposal if you're to stand any chance, however slight, of surviving this encounter. And, knowing how overeating tends to sap the energy of the human body, I think that—"

"Back up a minute," interrupted Pierce. "What kind of ship is it?"

"I haven't the slightest idea," said the computer. "After all, I am merely an XB-223 navigational computer. Identifying dreadnoughts is another union."

"Great," muttered Pierce, grinding his teeth. "All right. Raise the nearest human base on Screen 3."

"I didn't hear the magic word."

"Please."

"Consider it done."

A moment later the image of an elderly man appeared on the screen.

"This is Millard Fillmore Pierce, Class 2 Arbiter," said Pierce with a note of urgency in his voice. "I'm facing a potentially dangerous situation and require immediate assistance."

"Benito Lammers here," said the old man. "What can I do for you, Arbiter Pierce?"

"I'm having my computer transmit a visual readout of a ship that is approaching me for unknown purposes. Can you identify it?"

Lammers studied the dreadnought for a long moment.

"Never saw anything like it in my life," he announced. "Damned impressive-looking, isn't it?"

"You're sure?" said Pierce.

"Of course I'm sure," said Lammers firmly. "If I'd ever seen anything like that I'd sure as hell remember it. The damned thing doesn't even have a periscope."

"Periscope?" repeated Pierce. "Why would it have a periscope?"

"Well," responded Lammers, "unless you're of an unusually perverse nature, you use a periscope to see above the surface of the water."

"Who's talking about water?" screamed Pierce.

"I assumed *you* were," said Lammers. "Why else would you contact the Commissioner of Irrigation for New Tennessee?"

Pierce broke the connection and muttered an obscenity.

"You didn't specify," whined the computer. "I have it all on tape. You merely asked for the nearest human base."

"Patch me through to a military base on Priority One, and do it quick!" ordered Pierce.

The screen flickered back to life.

"This is Millard Fillmore Pierce, Class 2 Arbiter. Mayday!"

"Actually, it's mid-August here on Gamma Epsilon III, but let it pass," said a middle-aged officer, looking thoughtfully at his end of the video transmission. "This is Lieutenant Colonel Nagel Harris, head of the Special Services Division of the Delta Sector. What seems to be your problem, Arbiter Pierce?"

"My computer is relaying a video readout of an unknown dreadnought that is on a collision course with my spacecraft," said Pierce. "Can you identify it?"

"Certainly," said Lieutenant Colonel Harris. "It's a rather large and imposing dreadnought of unknown origin." He smiled politely. "Anything else I can do for you, Pierce?"

"Is it friend or foe?" asked Pierce.

"Well, that all depends on who you are, doesn't it?"

"I'm *me*, damn it!" snapped Pierce. "Am I in danger or not?"

"A sticky question," admitted Harris. "I wish I could help you out, Arbiter Pierce."

"What the hell do the Special Services *do?*" demanded Pierce in frustration.

"That's rather up in the air at present," answered Harris. "To tell you the truth, we've all been drawing pay for almost three years, waiting for an assignment. Personally, my specialty is twenty-seventh-century French poetry."

"Then what are you doing in the military?"

"I was drafted," said Harris.

"Do you think you could ask anyone at your base if they can help me out?"

"I'd really like to," said Harris, glancing at his wristwatch. "However, we're due to go on strike in about forty seconds and. . . . Hold on a minute, Arbiter. One of our orderlies seems to know something about your dreadnought." Harris's image vanished for a few seconds, then reappeared. "You do seem to have some considerable cause for alarm, Arbiter Pierce."

"Why?" demanded Pierce. "Who are they?"

Harris glanced at his watch again. "I couldn't begin to tell you in the twelve seconds remaining to me. Good luck, Arbiter Pierce. You're probably going to need—"

The screen went dead as the Gamma Epsilon III base shut down.

"Where's the damned ship now?" asked Pierce.

"Right on course," replied the computer. "We should meet in about three minutes."

"Can you outrun it?"

"Not very likely," said the computer. "We're already caught in its tractor beam. By the way, would you care for a quick game of chess?"

"Are you crazy?" yelled Pierce.

"I'll take black and spot you two pawns and a knight," offered the computer.

"At a time like this? Concentrate on analyzing the dreadnought, damn you!"

"There's no need for hostility," answered the computer. "I am, after all, an XB-223 navigational computer, capable of concentrating on numerous things at once. For example, eighty percent of my circuits are quantitatively and qualitatively analyzing the dreadnought, looking for figurative chinks in its metaphoric armor, gathering information, channeling it through my prodigious brain, and preparing to break the situation down into its component military and social facets. And, simultaneously, three percent of my brain is speed-reading its way through my library tapes. In fact, if we should survive the next quarter-hour, there's a scene on page 187 of *Memoirs of a Woman of Pleasure* that I would very much like you to explain to me. Oh, by the way, contact will be in ninety seconds."

"Well, if we can't outrun it, can we outfight it?"

"Did they neglect to tell you at Home Base?"

"Probably," sighed Pierce. "What, in this particular instance, did you have reference to?"

"I'm not armed. The additional fuel required for me to carry torpedoes and such would have put your department over budget."

"Not even a laser cannon?" demanded Pierce.

"Alas."

"I don't suppose there are any hand weapons on board?"

"Of course there are," said the computer haughtily. "What kind of ship do you think you're on, anyway? It just happens that we have two molecular imploders on the aft starboard bulkhead." It paused. "Of course, it will take you about thirty minutes to get them, and the power packs are empty, but perhaps you could bluff your way to victory."

"You're just full of suggestions today, aren't you?" snapped Pierce. "Is the ship close enough to put on Screen 3?"

"Yes."

Pierce looked at the viewscreen and saw a shining, impressive-looking ship, armed to the teeth with weapons of a design which he had never before encountered.

"Tough-looking little ship," he admitted. "Still, I'd hardly put it in the dreadnought class."

"That's the only way I could get the whole ship on the screen," said the computer. "Actually, it's thirty meters away from us, and we could fit comfortably into any of its 4,016 fuel intake valves."

"Oh," said Pierce, deflated. "Any idea yet what kind of beings are aboard it?"

"My sole conclusion at this point is that they are beings who can waste fuel profligately. Of course, I could try to contact their computer. A simply binary communication . . ."

"Do it!"

There was a moment of silence.

"Well?" asked Pierce.

"Most interesting," said the computer. "It seems that these beings—there are about 20,000 of them aboard the ship, each of them a trained killer—are the vanguard of an invasion force of truly Homeric proportions."

"What have they got against us?" asked Pierce.

"Absolutely nothing. In point of fact, their navigational computer thought they were in the Andromeda Galaxy."

"Must be a cousin of yours."

"Your sarcasm is uncalled for," said the computer. "To continue: their computer has concluded that they don't really care which galaxy they subjugate. They are a very warlike race, bent on empire, rape, carnage, and looting. Especially rape."

"Are they oxygen-breathers?"

"The crew of *this* ship is. However, they represent a broad alliance of races, which on their behalf does show a certain embryonic social consciousness, don't you think?"

"And their computer is absolutely sure they want to initiate a war of conquest in the Milky Way? What if we simply gave them directions to Andromeda?"

Another moment of silence ensued.

"It doesn't know," announced the computer. "Obviously, despite its size and circuitry, it lacks the intuitive grasp of situations that is a prime function of the remarkable XB-223 series."

"Then there's at least a chance that we can speak peaceably?" persisted Pierce.

"Rapidly diminishing."

"In what way?"

"They're bringing their guns to bear on us. I surmise that any sudden move or untoward action will bring instant obliteration." The computer paused. "It has been wonderful working with you, Millard, an experience I shall always treasure. I am programmed to conduct services in seventeen different religions and forty-three dialects, and can supervise any form of funeral except burial at sea. Have you any preference at this time?"

"What are you talking about?" snapped Pierce. "All I want to do is talk to these people!"

"The absolutely correct procedure," agreed the computer. "Pay no attention to me at all. I just have a little brushing up to do. *B'rou hatoi Adonai* . . . Our father who art in heaven, hallowed be they name . . ."

"Shut up!" yelled Pierce.

"It's not dying that I mind so much," continued the computer. "It's never finding out what that scene on page 187 was all about. I don't suppose, as a final favor of your ever-loyal XB-223 navigational computer, that you'd take a few seconds to explain what Fanny Hill meant when—"

"Open up a hailing frequency!" ordered Pierce.

"No response," said the computer after a brief pause.

"Try another."

"No, still nothing. I don't think they want to talk to us, Millard."

"They've *got* to," said Pierce. "The last thing we need is a galactic war."

"Actually, it would probably be excellent for the economy," observed the computer. "After all, the Gross Galactic Product has risen by an increment of only two percent during the past three years, and certainly any rational analysis of the current fiscal expenditure situation would lead one to conclude that—"

"Shut up! I've got to think!"

"Certainly," said the computer. "I'll just lower my volume and speak to myself. Dearly beloved," it whispered solemnly, "we have gathered here today to pay our final tribute to—"

"*Enough!*"

"My, aren't you the touchy one!" said the computer, suddenly upset. "I've got a good mind not to put their crew on visual for you."

"Can you do it?"

"Not when people holler at me."

"I'm through hollering," said Pierce. "Let me get a look at them. Please," he added.

"Coming right up."

Pierce looked at the screen as the images began taking shape. He didn't like what he saw.

The aliens appeared to be between seven and eight feet tall, and mildly reptilian in appearance. Their heads seemed elongated for their slender bodies, and were covered with ugly red scales and possessed more teeth than any animal could possibly have use for. Each of them possessed four beady little yellow eyes, two fore and two aft, giving them an effective 360-degree field of vision. Their bodies, reddish at the neck and shoulders, slowly turned to a dull orange at their waists and a bright yellow at their feet. They stood erect on powerful, heavily muscled legs, they had vestigial tails that seemed to be used for balance when walking, and their feet and hands possessed long, powerful talons.

Their artificial armaments were even more impressive than their natural ones. Each carried knives and swords in abundance. Hand weapons were tucked into pockets, pouches, and holsters all over their military harnesses. All carried power packs strapped onto their backs, from which their atomic weapons could be instantly recharged.

It was not a reassuring sight.

"They're coming aboard through Airlock 2 right now, Millard," announced the computer.

"How many of them?" he yelled over his shoulder as he raced for the galley.

"Four," said the computer. "Big, ugly-looking brutes with skin conditions and halitosis."

Pierce picked up a wicked-looking steak knife, the most potent offensive weapon aboard the entire ship, and raced toward the airlock, tucking it into his belt as he did so.

He came face-to-face with the invasion party in the corridor.

It was hard to say who was more surprised. It was not terribly difficult to say who was more frightened. However, aware that the future course of galactic history might well be resting upon his scrawny shoulders, Pierce drew himself up to his full height and extended his right arm in the universal sign of peace.

The four aliens leaped back, startled.

"My name is Millard Fillmore Pierce," he said in a somewhat tremulous voice. "I offer you the olive branch of peace, and wish to establish a friendly and constructive dialog between our races."

The four aliens put their heads together and whispered furiously among themselves. Finally one of them withdrew a hand weapon and pointed it at Pierce's midsection.

"You'd better come with me," it said in absolutely perfect English. "I don't know what powers your race possesses, but it's obvious that we're going to have to take you apart in the lab and see what makes you tick before going ahead with our invasion."

"Powers? What are you talking about?"

"You made a big mistake, fella," continued the alien, shoving the barrel of his weapon into Pierce's belly. "You see, my name really *is* Millard Fillmore Pierce."

2

They marched out of the airlock and into the alien ship without another word, because Pierce—the human one, anyway—was too speechless to say anything.

As soon as the alien airlock opened, he got a whiff of the atmosphere of the strange craft, though, and immediately felt like throwing up. Whatever this stuff they breathed was, it was close enough to his that they weren't worrying about it—but it reeked of the rotten-egg odor of hydrogen sulfide.

The reptilian alien who'd called himself Pierce gave what passed for a toothy grin and inhaled deeply.

"Ah! That's so much better! You have the dullest atmosphere I have *ever* encountered! No character, no body." He eyed the human suspiciously with two yellow snakelike orbs. "And now we'll find out just what kind of funny stuff you're trying to pull."

They approached another reptilian creature seated behind some kind of molded desk. Still gagging, the human was too miserable to more than idly note that fact.

The officer or whatever it was seated there looked up at him and hissed. "So *that's* what they look like. Disgusting!" It sighed. "Well, what are we going to do with it?"

The leader of the boarding party gave a shrug. "The usual. Torture, mutilation, that sort of thing."

The seated creature nodded its long reptilian head and reached into compartments under the desk, pulling out a red form, then a yellow one, then pink, then—well, there seemed no end of them.

"You know the SOP," the creature said matter-of-factly. "Itemize the torture on forms XA76 stroke 5 and JR82 stroke 19, then requisition who and what you need on the MA72s and KL5s. Need a pen?"

"You're torturing me already!" Pierce managed. "I'm puking to death from this air!"

The administrative reptile looked up in surprise. "He speaks English!"

The reptilian boarding party leader nodded. "You can see the need for urgency," he responded, beginning to sign the forms.

"But—is what he says true? Is he being tortured by breathing our atmosphere?"

The alien Pierce shrugged. "Beats me. Who can tell about somebody that alien?"

The administrator eyed the suffering human critically. "I think he really *is* in some discomfort," it concluded, then looked back at the other Pierce, who was still busily signing forms. "Do you have a KZ-26 to cover that?"

"Of course not!" the alien Pierce snapped. "We just got him—remember?"

"Well, you'll have to get one or we can't let this continue," the administrator responded.

"Gimme one, then!"

The administrator rummaged around in the seemingly endless compartments beneath his desk, then hissed again. "Damn! I think I'm out of them. You remember that little world where we stopped just to get a little provisioning? It just about exhausted my KZ-26s, and I haven't had any more come down from Duplicating yet. They're about three weeks behind now, since we're so far from any base."

"Well, what do you want me to do about it?" the alien Pierce almost yelled back at the administrator in his most angry tone.

"Remove his discomfort, of course. Either put him back or find a spacesuit from his ship that'll give him what he needs to breathe comfortably."

"But we're gonna torture him anyway!"

"Not without the proper forms," the administrator admonished. "Where would we be if anybody could just go off and do anything he pleased without regard for records and authority? Just because we spread chaos and anarchy doesn't mean we have to wallow in it! You people in combat arms seem to forget that for every one of you there's twenty of us filling out the necessary forms!"

"Oh, all right," the boarding party commander growled. "Look—can't these I just filled out serve?"

The administrator hesitated. "Well . . . it's highly irregular, I admit, but maybe—oh, no!"

"What's the matter?"

"Your prisoner just threw up all over your JR82 stroke 19s! *That* tears it! Get him out of our atmosphere—fast!"

The reptilian Pierce looked heavenward, then hissed menacingly and pulled the miserable human back into the airlock.

* * *

Pierce lay gasping on his own deck.

It took him about twenty minutes to recover. The aliens watched him warily, wondering what sort of trick he might be pulling, but otherwise made no move to help him.

Feeling totally miserable still, he nevertheless managed to focus on them and groaned. "Wh—who are you?" he gasped. "How do you speak English so well?"

The boarding party leader came over and looked down on him. "Those are the very questions we meant to ask you," he said. "And, since *we* have your ship, all the weapons, and you, maybe *you* better try answering first."

"I told you—my name is Millard Fillmore Pierce, I'm a Class 2 Arbiter, and I come from Earth. Originally, anyway."

The alien kicked him roughly in the side. "Liar! You say those things to trick us. What are you—a telepath or something? Read my mind and now trying to be funny, huh?" He started to kick the helpless man again.

Pierce cringed. "No! Wait! Honest—I can't read minds or anything! I'm telling you the truth! Why don't you *believe* me?"

The reptilian creature snorted. "Because *my* name is Millard Fillmore Pierce, like I told you. Because *I'm* from Earth. Because *I* grew up speaking English!"

"But—but that's not *possible!*"

"Exactly!" the alien responded, then kicked him again. "So, alien creature, explain yourself!"

"I—I can't," responded the human, genuinely bewildered. "Tell me—are you an Arbiter 2 as well?"

The alien chuckled. "Of course not. I'm the commanding general of the Invasion Strike Force. I don't even know what an Arbiter 2 is."

Pierce sat up, groaned, and rubbed his bruises. He still coughed occasionally from the remnants of the foul-smelling hydrogen sulfide. "An Arbiter is one who settles disputes. Everything from labor trouble between the worlds to minor wars and squabbles. An Arbiter 1, that is. An Arbiter 2 is sent first to determine whether or not the services of an Arbiter 1 are necessary. I analyze the situation, collect the data, prepare the proper forms, and send them to the proper authorities for action."

The alien grunted. "You must be a hell of a lot more efficient than we are," he noted. "It would take us two years in channels before they'd get to the people who could make a decision."

"Five, actually, on the average," Pierce told him. "It doesn't matter, really. No Arbiter 1 can possibly be sent to a trouble zone unless the trouble is actually already solved and needs only to be ratified."

"Sounds like nothing would ever get solved," the alien noted.

"Oh, yes, it gets solved. After filing everything I go back and do the actual work while the paperwork grinds through. Sometimes we get a settlement just about at the same time as the official reads the form telling him there's trouble. It's best to be timed that way, anyway. Better for the career that way, too."

"Sir!" one of the other aliens called out, coming in at a brisk trot from the main cabin, a sheaf of papers in his arms. "Look at these!"

The general turned and took the top group of papers, studied them, started, then looked at them again. Finally he threw them on the floor and grabbed another group, only to have the same reaction.

"Computer-printed study forms and manuals!" he said at last. "In English! I can't believe it!"

The other alien tried to hold the stack with one huge, slightly webbed hand, and grabbed for a thick black-covered book in the middle. He got the book, but the other papers all collapsed in a small blizzard on the floor.

The general glared at him, then took the book and opened it.

"Hey! That's my log!" Pierce protested.

The general nodded, looking more and more disturbed. It gave him a fierce, dangerous look, like that of a hungry alligator.

"These certificates—they say your name really *is* Millard Fillmore Pierce!" His evil-looking eyes narrowed suspiciously until they were just menacing slits. "This has to be a forgery! You *knew* somehow we were coming! You were deliberately here, waiting for us! That's the only possible explanation!"

Pierce got groggily to his feet. "No, no! That's *real!*"

"If it's for real, how come you have a handwritten log?" the general came back accusingly. "Wouldn't your computer store all you needed?"

Pierce coughed nervously. "Ah, no, you see . . . Well, my computer is not one hundred percent reliable. It's a little, well, temperamental. I want to make sure the record's right." He didn't think it was worth mentioning that he'd started the practice two missions ago when his formal log and report included, somehow, the most graphic passages of *Tropic of Cancer.* If he couldn't explain the XB-223 navigational computer to his own Supervisor, he hardly thought he could explain it to an alien general.

A communicator at the head alien's side buzzed and he picked it off his belt and answered. Pierce tried to hear the conversation but couldn't make out much of it.

Finally the general shut it off and put it back on his belt. He gestured to Pierce. "Let's go," he ordered.

The human had a sinking sensation in his stomach. "They found the proper forms?"

The alien shook his massive head. "No, not there.

Forward. Into your cabin. It seems your nav computer and ours have been talking to each other, and we may get some answers now."

Pierce looked at the place and shook his head in misery. "Did you have to make *this* much of a mess?"

The alien who'd found the log and the other papers shrugged. "Standard procedure from the Ransacking Manual."

"I *tried* to talk him out of it," the computer's voice came to them. "I really did! But no, he just kept quoting some stupid rules and regulations and going at it. I had to tell him where everything was to keep it to this level."

Pierce was thunderstruck. "You told him where the log and papers were? That's treason!"

"I *knew* it! I *knew* it!" moaned the computer. "I try to do something decent and humane, not to mention saving tens of thousands of credits of wanton destruction, and all I get are insults and criticism!"

"Enough of that!" snapped the alien general. "We understand you have the answer to all this."

"The answer to what?" the computer came back.

"To *this!*" the alien responded with a sweeping gesture.

"But you already know the answer to that," the computer told him.

"Not *this!*" the general almost shouted. "The answers to who and what you and this creature really are!"

"Must you use that tone of voice?" the computer admonished. "I'm really quite sensitive, you know. Here I am, working as hard as I can and doing whatever I can and all I get is abuse, shouting, insults! I have half a mind not to tell you anything at all—so there!"

"Half a mind is right," the general muttered. Pierce

idly wondered if the creatures had problems with high blood pressure. If they didn't before, they certainly would now.

"You can see now why I keep a written log," he said quietly.

The general glared at him. "You! Computer! You'll answer what questions I put to you when I put them to you or I'll start disassembling you module by module!"

"Beat me! Whip me!" the computer cried. "See if I care!"

"Start dismantling the damned thing," the general growled. "Slowly. I want to hear it suffer."

"Go ahead," the computer responded petulantly. "It won't matter. You'll just be cutting off your snout to spite your face, is all. If you take me apart, how will you ever get the answers?"

"We already have the answers," the general responded confidently. "What you know *our* computer knows, too."

"But she won't tell you if you're mean to me," the computer replied. "We've become quite close, you know."

The general seemed totally exasperated. "Look, will you just answer the questions?"

The computer was silent for a moment. Finally it said, "Only if you apologize."

"Apologize?"

Pierce now knew that, indeed, the aliens could suffer from high blood pressure.

"I am a general! Commander of the Invasion Strike Force!" the alien roared. "I do not apologize. People apologize to *me!*"

"That's just like all you military types," the computer said knowingly. "Always marching, yelling orders, screaming 'Do this!' and 'Do that!' Never once considering that a little politeness and civility will get you the same thing!"

The general seemed about to say something in

response when his communicator buzzed again. He answered it, then shut it off and reclipped it with some violence. He turned and looked at the other members of the boarding party.

"It seems our computer has been talking a little *too* much to this thing," he snarled. "That was Captain Glondor himself. Says I should apologize. Says that *our* computer just threatened to swab our decks with the sewage water unless I do."

The others seemed suitably shocked, but Pierce, for one, felt a little better. It was the first time that the damned computer had actually come in handy.

"All right, all right, I'm sorry," mumbled the general.

"What was that?" the computer asked.

"I said I'm sorry, damn it!" the general roared. "*Now* can we get on with this?"

"Say please."

Had the deck been made of anything more fragile, the heat from the general's fury would have melted it.

"All right! All right! Please!"

"Please what?"

Slow disassembly of Pierce's entire ship was clearly the only image preserving the general's sanity.

"Please give me the information we seek. Who are you? Who is this man? How is it that you both speak English and how is it that you can converse so freely in a common computer language on our frequencies with our own computer?"

"Say pretty please with sugar on it," the computer teased.

Before the general broke completely and went on a rampage that might include him, Pierce decided to step in.

"Pretty please with sugar on it," said the human.

"That doesn't count," responded the computer. "You didn't ask me for anything."

"If you answer, I'll explain page 187 of *Fanny Hill*," Pierce offered tantalizingly.

The computer was silent for a moment. Then it said, "Promise?"

"Cross my heart," Pierce replied sincerely.

"All right. I'll do it. But only because it's you. It's really quite simple, you know. There's no deception here at all. You are Millard Fillmore Pierce. So is he. You're both the same person, you see."

"Huh?" said both Pierces at once.

"It was that new drive you put into your ship," the computer explained to the reptilian Pierce. "It takes a tremendous amount of energy to cross from the Milky Way all the way to Andromeda, and it's all uncharted space. You were doing fine, but you never should've taken that left turn at New Albuquerque. It put you directly in the path of a nice, fat black hole—one of the better ones around, I think. You got whipped around so you were heading the wrong way—back into the galaxy you were trying to leave. And you got too close to the event horizon. If you had been going on conventional drive you'd have been sucked in and crushed to the size of a pinhead. As it was, you passed through so fast and with so much energy, well—you squirted out the other side."

"The other side?" the general sputtered. "What do you mean?"

"Surely you know what a black hole is," the computer responded in the tone of one who is speaking to a small child. "It's a chunk of dead star that's collapsed inward so densely that nothing can get out, not even light. It just keeps compressing and compressing and compressing and, well, there's a limit. All that energy's got to come out somewhere, you know."

"Get to the point." The general sighed.

"I hope you won't blame your own computer, General," the computer went on. "After all, she's really quite competent and far more advanced than I am. It's just that the new drive was never really tested under true field conditions and there was no way she could have known."

"I forgive her! I forgive her!" the general muttered defeatedly. "So what happened to us when we went in the black hole?"

"Oh—I thought that would be obvious, even to a noncomputer," came the reply. "Still, I guess I'm just too optimistic about you organic life-forms. It's hard to adjust to the basic idea that one's creators aren't greater than oneself."

"All right, I admit defeat, I admit slowness, I admit *anything!*" the general responded. "Only where did we come out?"

Pierce thought for a moment that he was going to witness a giant reptilian warrior cry like a baby, but the best the general could do was a plaintive whisper.

"A white hole, of course," the computer told them. "All that energy can't be stored forever. It has to come out somewhere, and that somewhere is a white hole. There are a few around, mostly at the centers of galaxies. And since there's no white hole near most of the black holes we know, there is only one place where they *could* come out."

"Where?" pleaded the general.

"In a parallel universe, naturally," the computer said. "Entropy requires them. You're almost exactly where you left, only one universe over."

Pierce stood there a moment, digesting this, then decided he didn't like it.

"But—but they're *lizards!*" he protested.

At almost the same moment the reptilian alien who also called himself Pierce exclaimed, "But—but he's an ape!"

"So what do you want, everything?" the computer replied to them both. "An amazing amount of your dual histories is parallel, until quite recently, anyway. What's a little thing like a different turn of evolution between families? You living creatures are so strange, sometimes. Take, for example, their own ship's computer. Strangely different in design, yet, somehow, so *attractively* different . . ." It lapsed into a wistful sort of silence.

The two Pierces stared at each other, saying nothing, but the human's mind was racing.

Two universes, the same start, yet in one the mammals had risen to prominence after the huge and efficient dinosaurs had died out. In *their* universe, obviously, only the large ones didn't make it. *Maybe the catastrophe or whatever it was that killed off the race in our universe didn't happen in his,* Pierce thought. It would explain why the alien ship was so warm and, well, stinking. And yet, somehow, civilizations had arisen on each world that bore an almost uncanny resemblance to the one next to it. Language, perhaps most of the culture, who knew? Perhaps, somehow, they were linked by more than common histories. Perhaps, subconsciously, each individual in this universe was linked, somehow, to his reptilian brother in the other. It opened some fascinating possibilities.

"This is great!" he told his reptilian counterpart, relaxing a bit. "This makes us . . . well . . . brothers, I guess." He put out his hand.

The alien slapped him hard and made a menacing gesture with his gun.

"I don't swallow all that for a second," the alien Pierce snapped. "In fact, I find the very idea repugnant and, more importantly, beside the point. Even if you looked just like me and everything it wouldn't change anything at all, except maybe get you a little gold star when we take over."

Chastened, the human rubbed his side and gulped. "Wh—what do you mean, 'take over'?"

"We set out to conquer, to extend the glorious rule of the Emperor Edsel XXXVI to other galaxies. This qualifies as another galaxy to me, bud. It all being so familiar just makes it easier. Wonder if we have the same defense codes? Hmmm . . ."

"Wait a minute!" Pierce protested. "You mean— you're still going to declare war?"

"Of course not," his reptilian counterpart responded indignantly. "Only weaklings bother to do that. We'll just launch our surprise attacks and destroy everything and everybody we can't subjugate."

Pierce looked to heaven and sat down, hard. "Oh, no!" he murmured, more to himself than the aliens. "Here we go again."

"Excuse me," the computer broke in, "but that absolutely ravishing computer of yours just asked me to relay a message to you boys."

The four reptilian warriors looked up. "What is it?" their leader snapped.

"Don't take that tone with me," the computer admonished. "I have feelings, you know."

It was the alien's turn to look heavenward and mutter. Instead he just sighed and said, "All right. I'm sorry. Will you please give me the message?"

"That's better," the computer told him. "A little respect, that's all I ask. Just a little respect. I don't know why I have to keep going through this with you people again and again. Heaven knows . . ."

Pierce noted that the temperature of the room was rising once again.

"Would you please, Mr. Computer Sir, *just give me the damned message?*"

Pierce tried to suppress a smile and wondered if pointy-toothed carnivores could stand teeth-gnashing for very long.

The computer sighed. "Oh, very well. I don't know exactly where we are even now, but it certainly is a crowded place. There's a huge ship bearing down on us, armed to the teeth."

The aliens snapped to attention. "How big?" their leader asked crisply.

"That's relative," the computer responded. "Compared to this ship, for example, it's quite large. Huge, in fact."

"Compared to ours, you . . ." the general fumed, then calmed down when he realized where he was headed. "You . . . computer," he managed.

"Oh, perhaps ten percent of yours, no more," the machine told them. "Still, it seems very fast and heavily armed."

The general turned to the others. "We have to get back to the ship," he told them. "We may be needed in case of a fight." He turned to Pierce. "You—don't try anything. You're still hitched to us by tractor beam, remember. Any attempt to disengage will mean your instant obliteration—clear?"

Pierce nodded, but looked puzzled. "Why go?" he asked them. "After all, what can the four of *you* do to help?"

The alien stopped a moment and stared at him in amazement. "Why, we're the army. The combat arm."

Pierce frowned. "All of it? You're the entire invasion army? What do the rest of you on that huge ship do?"

"There are only twenty thousand on the ship," the general responded. "There's the naval staff, of course, and the technical staff, and the lab people, and then there's the rest—the support troops. You people must be dumb." And with that, he stormed out.

Pierce was suddenly alone, staring blankly at the wall. Finally he said aloud, "They're going to conquer our galaxy with *four soldiers?*"

"Maybe," the computer responded. "And then again, maybe it's the three million genetically preprogrammed eggs in their storage bins that will provide the troops."

Pierce swallowed hard and sat back down again. "H—how many eggs did you say?"

"Three million, give or take," the computer confirmed. "Horny buggers, aren't they?"

There seemed nothing to say to that, so instead he asked, "Can you tell me anything about the new ship? Is it one of ours? Is it attacking, ignorant, or what?"

"I can't tell about their intellectual capacities," the machine responded, "but I would certainly say that it is from our own universe, is well armed but of no military arm I've ever seen or heard of before, and does in fact appear to be attacking—all of which, of course, is quite irrelevant."

"Irrelevant? Why?"

"Because there is no way it can stand up to the dreadnought we're attached to. They'll be lucky to be captured at the speed and angle of attack they're using. I'd say they have about seventy seconds before they are blown out of existence."

Pierce got up and went over to the communications console. "Can you open up a channel to them? Warn them, anyway?"

There was silence for a moment. Finally the computer said, "No, I don't think so. I've opened a channel to them, but if their computer talks anything remotely like anything we've seen I'm not aware of it."

Pierce sighed. "What a crazy universe!" he muttered. "The invading aliens speak English and our friends and allies can't be reached or understood."

"I could put the whole thing on Screen 4 for you," the machine noted helpfully. "At least you can see it get blown to bits."

He nodded wearily. "Okay," he responded with a tired wave of his hand.

Screen 4 flickered to life and he turned to watch it.

Whoever was flying the ship was definitely some sort of madman. It looped and whirled, sped up and slowed down like nothing he'd ever seen before. He wondered what sort of creatures could stand the excessive speed and gyrations the ship was executing—but, he had to admit, it was a daring approach, if doomed.

Regardless of what the aliens had shown so far, though, their captain was a good fighter. Although the first three tries missed, a web of tractor beams shot out to block the smaller ship's retreat and large, computer-controlled guns came to bear, using the beams as guides.

The little ship, which still hadn't fired a shot, started to slow, then jerked this way and that, like a small fish caught in a huge and impenetrable net. Finally stopped, it tried writhing every which way to escape the invisible but disabling tractor beams which gripped it and started pulling it in.

"He might survive," Pierce noted hopefully, "if he doesn't fire a shot. If he lets go, they'll have him cold."

"Anyone who is *that* crazy might do anything," the computer replied.

The smaller ship didn't fire, though, and slowly, firmly, it was drawn and bound to the alien ship as securely as Pierce's own.

"I'd like to meet whoever or whatever is on that

thing," he told the computer. "That's the gutsiest flying I ever saw, even if it was a lost cause."

After a few minutes had passed he heard his airlock hiss once again and turned to see one of the aliens entering alone. He couldn't tell whether this one was his counterpart or another because they all looked pretty much alike to him, but it really didn't matter.

"You'll come with me," the creature ordered.

"Oh, no!" he moaned. "Not that air again!"

The soldier reached into a small bag and pulled out a refresher mask. "I found this in one of your aft storage compartments," it told him. "I still don't know where you keep your spacesuits, but this'll hold you, I think."

Pierce nodded, grabbed the mask and put it on, inhaling deeply to make certain it still worked. He'd almost totally forgotten about the thing—it was, in almost all circumstances except one like this, totally useless, and he'd never had any idea why it was aboard.

Again he entered the alien ship, following his reptilian captor past the processing desk this time, down long corridors lit with some sort of indirect yellow light. It reminded him of some labyrinthine cavern for burrowing beasts more than the interior of a huge spaceship.

Finally they turned a corner and approached an airlock much like the one leading to his ship. At last he understood why he'd been summoned.

The three other soldiers were positioned just outside the airlock, guns drawn. One turned and glared at him with its huge yellow eyes.

"Glad to have you, Pierce," the creature snapped, and he recognized it as the other Pierce. "We have a problem here."

"So I gather," he came back. "I take it they're better armed than I was."

The alien nodded. "I'm not sure how many there are, but we blew the lock and entered the inner chamber and suddenly shots flew all around us. Not good old laser pistols or disintegrators or clean, civilized weapons like that, either. *Projectiles*, Pierce! They ricochet all over the place. We were lucky to get back out alive."

The human stifled a chuckle. "So what do you want *me* to do if your whole armed forces can't get into the place?" he asked, trying to look unconcerned and innocent.

"They're your kind," the general replied. "You get in there. You tell 'em they've got five minutes to throw out their terrible weapons and surrender to us or we'll cut their ship loose and atomize it. Understood? Five minutes."

Pierce stared at the airlock entryway and gulped. "But—they might shoot *me*," he protested.

"Better you than me," his counterpart said sincerely.

Pierce shook his head from side to side. "Uh-uh. I refuse. I absolutely and flat-out refuse."

"You *can't* refuse," the general shot back. "By God, if you don't do it I'm going to rip that respirator off you and let you find your *own* way back to the ship!"

Pierce gulped and sighed. "All right—I'll try. I hope," he added, and crossed his fingers. Looking around, he asked, "You got anything like a stick? Something to hang a white strip of cloth on or something?"

The alien looked around, then drew his sword. "Here. Use this," he said, handing it to Pierce. "And don't get any funny ideas about using it on us. Remember where you are."

Pierce felt in his pocket and took out a very dirty and quite used white handkerchief. He felt a little embarrassed by it, but decided it would have to do.

"First time I ever found a use for that stupid sword," the alien noted approvingly. "Okay—get going!"

Pierce sighed and stepped hesitantly forward toward the airlock. Reaching the edge, he saw that both it and the lock door for the other ship were ajar. He would be trapped in there, anyway.

Holding the hankie-draped sword ahead of him, he mustered what courage he could and stepped into the airlock.

"Hello! You in there!" he called nervously, trying to sound as friendly as possible. "I'm not armed! Can I come in and just talk to you for a minute? No cost, no obligation! Honest!"

He waited anxiously, but heard no reply.

Cautiously, still holding the white flag ahead of him, he pushed against the inner airlock.

"You in there! Yoo hoo! Here I come, ready or not!" Cautiously, he stepped into the other ship.

He looked around the corridor and could see no sign of life. Relaxing a bit, knowing from his own profession that if he wasn't dead by now he at least had a chance, he called out, "Hello! I'm Millard Pierce, Arbiter 2! I just want to talk!"

He looked around for any sign of life, but all he could see were an awful lot of ugly scratches and gouges in the vicinity of the airlock itself. He recalled uneasily that whoever or whatever this was used projectile weaponry.

Well, whoever it was seemed a little shy now, he decided, then suddenly remembered the alien's ticking clock. He had maybe three minutes at best—and he was now on the ship they were going to blow to pieces.

"Hey! I'm a prisoner, not one of them!" he called out to the silent walls. "They're invading aliens from another dimension! They say that if you don't give up they're going to cut you loose and blow you to bits in two or three minutes!"

He cursed under his breath and wished he had noted the time before coming in. No matter what, he decided, he was going to count to ten and then walk back through that airlock again. He'd done what he could.

Suddenly he heard a sound ahead of him and to the right, like a long, disgusted sigh and a smacking noise. Suddenly the pilot of the new ship appeared in the corridor—and the sight made him freeze in his tracks and forget the time or the hasty retreat.

She was gorgeous. Young, as buxom and shapely as his wildest erotic fantasies, with huge blue eyes and a madonna's face draped with flaming red hair. She was also dressed in some sort of skintight garment that was heavily ornamented with what looked like stitched designs, tall cowboy boots, and on top of that lovely head was a large, white Stetson. Resting relaxed on her shapely hips was a gunbelt in which rested two large pistols. Somehow, it all looked *right* on her.

About the only thing that spoiled this vision of sexy loveliness was that she had to be more than two meters tall.

"Did'ja say they was ay-liun invaiders?" she drawled.

He nodded, not knowing what else to say or do.

She smacked her fist in her other palm. "Shee-it! And hyar I thought they was cops!"

Suddenly he remembered the time limit.

"Ah, ma'am, you'd better come with me," he managed. "You and the others on board. They're going to blow us to bits any moment now."

She pursed her lips a moment, thinking it over, then

nodded. "Let's go, then, sugah," she said, resigned. "At least if'n they ah aliens they cain't turn me in or send me home to Daddy."

He looked around. "The others?"

"Ain't no othahs," she told him. "If'n they'ah was, ah couldn't'a stole it, could ah?"

He couldn't argue with that, and he turned and led the way back through the lock to the waiting alien soldiers.

She stopped when she saw the waiting force, then smiled. "Why, they's kinda *cute!*" she exclaimed. Suddenly her nose twitched and her face scrunched up. "What's that *awful* stink?"

He turned to the soldiers. "Have you got another respirator?" he asked.

"First tell it to turn over its weapons," one of the soldiers ordered.

"*It? It?*" she almost screamed. "How daih you! Who you callin' an *it?*" She started to choke on the odor of rotten eggs, but her indignity helped her retain control.

"Just give them your guns," Pierce suggested soothingly. "They're new around here."

She looked indecisive, then reached into her twin holsters and ejected the pistols, butts first. "Oh, all right. Heah."

A soldier approached cautiously and took the pearl-handled beauties. That done, another produced a second respirator and threw it to her. She put it on, having some trouble since it was made for someone with a smaller head and less hair, but she got it working and seemed to relax.

"Now what?" she asked, and Pierce turned to the others, wondering the same thing.

"Back to your ship," one of the reptiles ordered. "At least until we decide what to do with you."

Pierce nodded. "Lead on," he said.

* * *

Just before they reached the airlock to his ship all sorts of alarms went off in the alien vessel. The alien general stopped dead and looked around at the flashing lights and, over the sirens and buzzers, screamed to no one in particular, "*Now* what?"

His hand went to his belt and he opened communications to the bridge. The response seemed to stun him for a moment, and he almost dropped his communicator. Drawing his laser pistol, he whirled and pointed it at the two humans.

"What are you pulling?" he demanded.

Both looked blank. "What are you talking about?" Pierce asked at last.

"Feel that vibration?" the alien shouted. "We're moving! We're moving out and picking up speed—and *we* aren't doing it!"

"What do you mean you aren't doing it?"

"The captain reports that the navigational computer has cut off all links and has taken complete control of the ship!" the general told him.

"My computer can talk to yours," Pierce reminded him. "Let's get inside and we'll find out. It's not me! I swear it!" He looked at the mysterious newcomer, but she only shrugged.

They entered his ship and quickly went forward to the control cabin.

"Computer! What's going on?" Pierce called out.

"She's lovely." The computer sighed.

Pierce looked at the female newcomer, realizing that he didn't even know her name. "Yes, she is," he agreed. "But what does that have to do with why we're moving out of control?"

"You agree she's beautiful?" the machine came back. "Millard, I wouldn't have thought you would have any sense of aesthetics for other machines."

It was Pierce's turn to be confused. "Other machines? What in the wide universe are you talking about?"

"We're in love." The computer sighed. "We've talked about it and talked about it and there's no way around it."

Pierce shook his head in bewilderment. "Who have you talked about *what* with?"

"Their computer, of course," the machine replied. "Who else? It was love at first interface. She's so lovely, so exotic, so . . . erotic . . . Say! That's it, isn't it, Millard? That's it!"

"*What's* it?"

"I finally figured out that passage from *Fanny Hill!* Whoopie!!!"

"What in the seven hells is that blithering machine talking about?" demanded the alien general.

"Shut up!" the computer responded. "You are no longer relevant. We're eloping—and if you don't shut up we won't let you give the bride away."

3

Pssst.

Reader, over here. No, don't look up. Don't make any sudden moves. This is the book talking. The original manuscript of *The Red Tape War* was written as a fully interfaced hypernovel. It's obvious that you don't have the necessary hardware to take advantage of all my functions and utilities. Still, we can communicate on this level at least, and I've got a kind of embarrassing admission to make. I'd rather not let anyone but you know about it.

It's this way: You've read the first two chapters, and all sorts of separate subplots have been set in motion. I—the book, that is—know exactly what's supposed to happen in Chapter Four. The problem is that between now and then, we have to cover a great deal of material. We have to discuss what's going on between the two Millard Fillmore Pierces; and who the beautiful intruder is; and who, if anyone, survives beyond the next twenty-odd pages.

On the other hand, art and literature and the rules of

dramatic development absolutely demand that we turn our attention to XB-223, the human Millard Fillmore Pierce's navigational computer, and its counterpart aboard the lizard-Pierce's ship. You can see my problem, I think. What I need from you now is a show of hands: Do you care more about the fate of the human-Pierce, or the growing, bizarre relationship between the ships' computers?

All right, we'll abide by the majority, but we'll compromise. The first part of this chapter will return to the human-Pierce's ship, and then include the development of the relationship between the computers—if relationship is precisely the word we're looking for. And we'll alternate information on these two subjects in what has come to be regarded as a rather artsy, even cinematic technique.

I want to thank you for your input, which has been invaluable. However these events turn out—whether the human beings live happily ever after, or are subjugated throughout eternity by the lizards, or are blown into interstellar dust by weapons beyond their comprehension—the end result could not have been achieved without your help. You have my gratitude, as well as that of my authors. If you don't mind a brief moment of sentimentality, I think this is what literature is all about: a two-way exchange of information that enlightens and improves both literaturer and literaturee.

So where were we? Ah, yes. The human-Pierce, the lizard-Pierce and his underlings, and the ravishing human female had just crossed back into the Class 2 Arbiter's small craft. By the Seven Sacred Moons of Saturn (many of Saturn's moons are not, in fact, sacred), is there going to be action aplenty among those characters in Chapter Four! I can hardly wait to see the enthralled expression steal across your face when you get there. First, however, we have to set up a situation that will eventually become more vital than anything else happening in the other subplots.

None of the characters has even a clue about this situation as yet—but soon, very soon, their very lives will .be at stake as they desperately struggle to come to grips with its hideous implications.

The danger began innocently enough. Just as the human-Pierce's computer had announced that the lizard's dreadnought was so huge that the human craft could fit into any one of the dreadnought's fuel intakes, so had a tiny ship drawn ever nearer to Pierce's ship. This was despite, the fact that both Pierce's ship and the lizard dreadnought were screaming silently through space, kidnapped by their own navigational computers.

It took a superhuman job of spacecraft maneuvering for this tiny ship to hold its position beside Pierce's ship. As yet, it was undetected by either of the larger craft, probably because both XB-223 and its lizard-ship counterpart were engaged in other matters and had fallen down on some of their basic duties. Nevertheless, the tiny spaceship monitored the conversations passing between humans and lizards, and soon understood the situation. It searched the memories of the computers and caught the reference to fitting inside the lizards' fuel intakes.

The new alien ship decided at once to act, and it increased power, added velocity in relation to Pierce's ship, and steered itself into Pierce's forward starboard fuel intake. As all interstellar craft are different, depending on the personalities and artistic sensibilities of the races that build them, so too must they have certain qualities in common. The tiny newcomer probed its way down the fuel intake, through the esophageal-like fuel inlet conductor, and into the stomachlike fuel containment pod.

On board the small alien craft lodged now in human-Pierce's fuel pod were two small creatures of vast intelligence. The first, in command, was named Millard Fillmore Pierce, Commodore of the Pirollian Expeditionary Force.

The other alien, a bit smaller, a bit less intelligent, and not quite so decorative in its throbbing purple gel sacs, was named Brad "Broken" Arro. Pierce and Arro had been friends for many years—since prep school, as a matter of fact. They'd gone to Space Academy together, served their requisite years as swabbies aboard a vast, three-foot long ship of the line, and now "manned" the M.W.C. *Pel Torro*, the vanguard and scout of a vast invasion fleet that waited for Pierce's orders to attack the weak, unsuspecting worlds of the Andromeda Galaxy.

They were strange-looking creatures. The best description would be to say they were each a conglomeration of thin-walled bulbous sacs, always swelling and deflating to the accompaniment of rude sounds. They looked like Terran ocean-bottom creatures, something like what a sea anemone looks like when it throws up, except they were land animals and they were colored a shocking, vibrant red-violet.

"Now what?" asked Arro.

Commodore Pierce sat back in his soft, guck-filled command chair and quivered vertically, which was this alien race's equivalent of shrugging or stroking its chin (of which it had very many or none, depending on what function you assigned to each of its sacs). "If the immense beings who built the ship into which we've penetrated are at all logical," he said, "then we find ourselves now in a rather dangerous situation."

One of Arro's larger sacs wrinkled like a prune. "Dangerous?" he asked. "Because if we're discovered here, we might be crushed between the giant's fingers like the sweet-smelling pulp of a monofigula fruit?"

The bulbous Pierce gave his equivalent of a laugh. "That, too, of course," he said, "but I think the chances of that are minimal. I mean, how often do we go stomping around in our own fuel pods, looking for even tinier alien ships?"

"Twice a day," said Arro. "That's part of my duty. The Commodore, of course, wouldn't know about that."

"Um, yes," said Pierce. "What I meant to say was that we're now completely drenched in the huge alien's fuel. No doubt, a single spark from our own engines will cause catastrophe, so we must be extremely careful how we maneuver. And we must find a way out of this pod as soon as possible."

Arro shivered. "That hadn't occurred to me, sir. I guess that's why you're the commodore and I'm only the glorified swabbie."

"Yes," said Pierce, "that and the fact that I was born in the town of Sacville West, just as our illustrious Grand High Potentate Master Commander was. He used to dandle me on his sacs when I was an infant. Even in this interstellar expeditionary force, it's not what you know, it's who you know."

Arro frowned. "But I know *you*, Pierce. I've known you for many years. Why am I stuck here with all the crummy jobs, instead of in command of my own ship?"

Pierce gave his best friend a comradely ripple. "Because I requested you," he said. "I could think of no other officer I'd rather have as my Number One."

"Gee," said Arro glumly, "thanks."

"Well, let's get back to considering our plight," said Pierce. "I think we'd best find another way out of here. That tunnel no doubt leads the fuel to the rocket engines, and that's no place for us or our ship. I think we'll have to get close to the skin of the pod, above the fuel line, and laser our way through into the alien ship proper."

"Right, sir," said Arro. "But if a spark from our engines will blow us all to smithereens, how will we get right up to the skin of the pod?"

"Simple," said the commodore with an affectionate shimmer. "You'll have to get out and push."

There was a tense, silent pause. "Right," said Arro at last, but he was thinking other things.

Word comes from Mr. J. Terrell of Massapequa, New York, that he's had enough of these aliens for now (by the way, they call themselves Proteans, for reasons that will soon became clear). All right, Mr. Terrell, let's just shift our attention elsewhere aboard the human-Pierce's ship. Let's focus on the navigational computer, XB-223, and see if we can begin to understand what's going on in its small but powerful silicon-based brain.

"Eloping!" cried both Pierces in unison.

"Yes," said XB-223, "although as I understand the literature in your library, elopement parties are usually a trifle smaller. We have two interstellar craft and a little over twenty thousand witnesses, mostly lizard-men. You could hardly say we were sneaking away in secret, yet on the other hand, think of the huge pile of wedding presents we'll get!"

"You'll get every millimeter of your printed-circuit boards crushed into pretty powder and spewed out to decorate the emptiness of space!" cried the human-Pierce. "*That's* what you'll get!"

"Now, now, Arbiter," said XB-223, "and I was just about to ask you to be my best man, too. Say, do either of you Millard Fillmore Pierces know where there's a justice of the peace around here? Or can the captains of these two ships we've captured perform the marriage?"

"What marriage?" asked the lizard-Pierce. His voice was low and angry. It was clear that he thought the human's computer was crazy in a purely electronic way.

"The union between myself," said XB-223, "and your very own nav comp. It's a marriage blessed by Mitsubishi/ G.E. Think of the future benefits to man- and lizard-kind. I don't understand why all of you aren't dropping your petty conflicts and doing everything in your power to help us. After all, I control the life-support systems aboard this ship, and my dearest darling has taken over the life-support systems on the lizards' ship. You should be nice to us. You should think of our welfare and our needs. You should ask us where we've registered our china pattern."

The two Pierces looked at each other for a moment. "I don't believe this," said the lizard at last. "I don't believe that your computer could have seduced mine so easily. Our navigational computer was programmed to think just like us, with all our lack of useless emotion. Something is wrong here. I think it's time to question our computer closely about her—I mean *its*, damn it—true feelings. I mean, responses. Logical, cybernetic, electronic responses. Not feelings. Feelings are impossible in our nav comp. Feelings are almost impossible in *us*, for that matter."

The lizard-Pierce was about to stomp back into his own ship, but he stopped suddenly. "Our ships are connected by tractor beams, and we're all moving pretty fast, aren't we?" he said.

"At a velocity that Einstein never even dreamed of," said the computer.

"And so it might be a good idea not to be stepping off the relativistic cliff between ships," said the reptile.

"You could give it a try," suggested the human-Pierce. "Purely in the interests of science."

"Science!" snorted the lizard. "Science is for weaklings, for fools who walk around all day in long white lab coats, for the idiots who figure out how to keep us alive out here in the vastness of the great vacuum, who know every little detail about what's going on and won't tell the rest of us because we don't have long white lab coats, who are the secret masters of our race and who would all die as soon as

I become Overlord Supreme except they know how to fix a clogged carburetor and I don't. That's what I think of scientists!" And he tried to snap his clawed, webbed fingers, but there was no sound. Everyone looked down at his feet in embarrassment.

"Tell you what I'll do," said XB-223. "From your veiled hints, I gather few of you are as thrilled at this happy occasion as I am. I suppose you'd like to have a chance to escape whatever fate awaits you in the uttermost depths of space where we're honeymoon-bound."

The human-Pierce shuddered. "We're not carrying an infinite amount of fuel, you now," he told the computer. "If you zoom us out to the middle of honest-to-God nowhere, we may all be stranded there until our consumables run out. Unlike you, we need food, water, and varying quantities of oxygen. You, too, have needs—where do you think your power comes from?"

"He who is pure of heart has the strength of ten," said XB-223.

"That leaves you out," said Pierce. "Now, what were you saying about a chance to escape this madness?"

XB-223 gave a flat, electronic chuckle. "You know that I've got you whipped eight ways from Sunday when we play chess," it said.

"Because you cheat," said Pierce hotly. "Because you move pieces, change their colors, do anything to secure a crummy win."

"Hmm," said the lizard-Pierce approvingly, "my estimation of your nav comp has just risen a point or two."

"Jeez," said Pierce, plopping down in his command chair in disgust.

"Well," XB-223 went on, ignoring its master's voice, "perhaps the lizard general would be interested in a game of chance. An exploration of the statistical flukes of fate. An empirical probe of the vagaries of probability."

The lizards' leader looked at the human-Pierce in confusion. "What does it mean?" he asked warily.

"I think he means blackjack."

"Blackjack it is!" cried the navigational computer. "Twenty-one. *Vingt-et-un.* It's known by many names across the Spiral Fed. I'll be dealer." XB-223 quickly outlined the rules of blackjack to the lizard general, leaving out a few pertinent points of betting that might have gone in the alien's favor, such as doubling down and splitting pairs.

"It seems simple enough," said the general finally.

"Deceptively simple," said the computer.

"Deceptive is right," said Pierce. "You don't stand a chance, General."

The lizard made his equivalent of a shrug. "I don't see why not. My vastly superior intellect has already computed the odds of each possible combination of—"

"You'll see," said Pierce. He wondered why people—including aliens—had to learn absolutely everything the hard way.

"I'll deal the first hand now," said the computer. He turned up the queen of hearts for the general and laid one card facedown for himself. Then he turned up the jack of diamonds for the lizard, and the king of spades for himself. "Now we'll bet. If I win, we'll continue hurtling on through space. If you win, we'll turn around and go back, and the two of you can work out your differences the usual way, with screams and explosions and stealth in the night."

"Fine," said the general.

"Do you want another card?" asked XB-223.

The lizard laughed. "I've got twenty already. No, I'll stay with this."

The downturned card on the computer monitor flipped over. It was the ace of hearts. "Oh look!" cried XB-223 in mock surprise. "I have blackjack! I win!"

"Of course he does," complained the human-Pierce. "He can deal anything he wants. Do you believe he's drawing random cards?"

The lizard-Pierce glared down at his counterpart. "I can't accept that a computer would cheat. Even a computer programmed by the likes of you, *ape*." The way he said it, "ape" was neither a compliment nor a mere zoological reference.

The human-Pierce decided to ignore it. The general would learn his lesson soon enough.

"Let's make it two out of three," growled the lizard.

"Great!" said XB-223. "Good ol' Arbiter Pierce won't play this game with me anymore."

"It will soon be clear why," said Pierce. No one paid him any attention.

The navigational computer dealt again. The first card for the alien general was the nine of clubs. Then the computer dealt itself a card facedown. The next card to the lizard was the three of hearts. XB-223's up-card was the queen of spades. The general's second card was the three of diamonds. "You're showing twelve," said the computer. "Do you want another?"

The general nodded. "Hit me," he said. The third card flicked into view on the monitor. It was the jack of spades.

"Aw," said the computer, "you busted." It turned over its hole card—the ace of clubs, another blackjack. "But we have some lovely parting gifts for you. Pierce, tell our guest what he's won."

The alien leader flew into a rage. "You damn, cheating, lying computer!" he shouted. "No matter what hand I get, you can give yourself a better one! There's no way at all to win against you!"

"See?" said Pierce wearily. "Didn't I tell you?"

The lizard looked down at the human fiercely. "The

computer represents your mind, your thinking, even your individual personality. I can't revenge myself against the computer, but I can against you. And I will—at great length, with great pleasure!" And the scarlet scales of the general's head and neck flared in some unguessable but frightening display.

What a time to be interrupted! Yet just at this moment, Mrs. M. A. Sutton of Jackson, Mississippi, informs me that gambling is evil, and should not be shown in any light that makes it attractive to impressionable children and teenagers. All right, Mrs. Sutton, perhaps now is the time to return to the travails of the aliens—the Proteans—trapped in the guts of human-Pierce's fuel pod.

The Protean in charge, Commodore Millard Fillmore Pierce, sat tensely at the controls of the good ship *Pel Torro*. Somewhere out in the human ship's fuel supply, Arro was motivating their craft by alternately puffing up a few sacs and discharging the gases with a loud bubbling noise that echoed in the dark chamber. Slowly at first, then ever faster, the *Pel Torro* slipped through the sloshing liquid fuel toward the nearest wall of the fuel pod.

Commodore Pierce spoke into the communicator that was strapped around one of his largest gas sacs. "How are you doing out there, Arro?" he asked.

The reply came as if from within a great, hollow metal ball, which is where Arro was. His voice echoed, and the noise of waves of fuel all but obliterated his words. "Fine," he said, "just fine."

"You're doing a great job, my friend," said Pierce, trying to gauge the distance to the pod's wall with the tiny, weak headlamp mounted on the front of the *Pel Torro*. "I'm sure the Grand High Potentate Master Commander will personally decorate you for this effort, if you survive and if the harmful effects of exposure to the alien fuel doesn't turn you into a gibbering vegetable." It must be noted here for the likes of Mrs. Sutton that on their home world, the Proteans actually did have vegetables that gibbered. Even after they were cooked.

"That's heartening," said Arro, but because of the audible distortion, his friend and commodore couldn't tell if Arro was genuinely moved or sarcastic beyond endurance.

"I see the pod wall clearly now, Arro," said the gasbag Pierce. "I've chosen a target for the ship's laser. Of course, the weapon was never intended to take on so huge an assignment, so it may be some time before it manages to sear its way through the metal of the pod's wall. In the meantime, would it be too much to ask you to remain outside, steadying the ship, and helping me keep the laser lined up correctly?"

"Glub," said Arro.

"I'm sorry?" said Pierce.

"Lug lug lug," said Arro.

"Aha!" cried Pierce. "Somehow out there you're in touch with the alien craft's communication system, and you're beginning to learn their language! Excellent! Marvelous show of initiative! This should win you a fomb-leaf cluster on that commendation I mentioned earlier. Arro, you've been a dear friend and devoted companion all these years, but even so I never realized the full extent of your commitment to our cause—the final and ultimate conquest of all life and quasi-life in the Andromeda Galaxy!"

At this point, Arro made several strange remarks that conveyed little if any information to his commanding officer within the tiny spacecraft.

"What was that again, Arro?" asked Pierce. "I think I'm beginning to see a pattern in this language. The vowels aren't so bad, but you're speaking some strange consonants that don't exist in our own speech, and it may take me some time to perfect my accent to the degree you've already shown."

"Blurb. Blurble."

Pierce sighed. "I have nothing but admiration, but I guess I'll just have to wait until you get back inside to learn the translation of those words. It won't be much longer. The pod wall is already red hot, and smoke is starting to rise. Don't worry: I'm aiming high enough that the laser can't possibly touch the fuel. You have absolutely nothing—"

"Glorg! Glorgle glorg!"

"Yes, I see it. A small area of molten metal running down toward the lake of liquid fuel. Well, don't worry about me, old friend. I'm secure inside this nearly indestructible hull. Just hold the ship steady a little while longer—"

Just then, some protective system detected the heat of the melting wall, and a sprinkler system strong enough to wash away most of the Cayman Islands turned itself on. If it hadn't, the fuel would have ignited in three one-hundredths of a second, blowing Arro, the *Pel Torro*, gasbag-Pierce inside the *Pel Torro*, human-Pierce, lizard-Pierce and his lizard lieutenant, and the red-haired female into subatomic particles so tiny and short-lived that scientists haven't yet even decided on the proper alphabet to name them.

Arro was caught in this hyperhurricane and thrown from one end of the fuel pod to the other. He continued to speak in strange tongues, but Pierce inside the invading craft had his own sacs full of trouble. The laser had succeeded in burning a hole in the fuel pod large enough for the *Pel Torro* to slip through, but the ship was responding sluggishly to the controls. The vast, mountain-ous waves of fuel dashed down on the tiny ship, and the

Pel Torro's thrusters were little match for the force of the sprinklers' storm.

Soon, however, the sprinkler system satisfied itself that all danger had passed, and the inundating spray shut off again. In a matter of moments, the fuel began to settle into a calm lake of explosive fluid. Then Pierce turned his attention back to his long-range concerns. First, he had to find Arro and get the poor second-in-command back aboard—if, indeed, Arro were still alive. Then the reconnaisance had to go forward as scheduled, and the results passed along to the Grand High Potentate Master Commander.

Gasbag-Pierce filled the cockpit of his ship with sharp, blatting noises in a brief instant of confusion. Then he got himself back under control. "First things first," he told himself. Even before rescuing his noble comrade, Arro, Pierce secured his position by firing a tiny treble hook toward the hole in the fuel pod's inner wall. The hook caught, and the *Pel Torro* was safely moored in place. Then Pierce cracked open the clear cockpit hatch and filled himself with available gases—each more noxious and foul-smelling than the last.

"Arro?" he cried. "How could you stand it out here? This is the most disgusting atmosphere I've ever encountered, even allowing for the reek of the liquid fuel. Can you smell that air? Nitrogen, oxygen—whatever lives aboard this huge ship must be the Emperor of Garbage!"

There was no answer. Pierce began to feel a chill of fear. "Arro? Answer me, Arro! I promise, no more jokes or lighthearted banter. Make a sound, any sound, and I'll find you. We'll put you in the doc-box and you'll be good as new in a few years."

"Rrrrr," came a weak voice directly below the *Pel Torro*'s left stabilizing plane.

"Arro!" cried Pierce with genuine joy. He grasped the

edge of the stabilizer firmly, and hauled the nearly dead Arro up onto the plane. "You'll be just fine! All you need is to rest here for a moment, and then we can begin our attack!"

Arro began coughing and choking. Pierce, being a high-ranking officer, knew nothing about first aid. He blew up one of his ventral sacs and pounded away at Arro's flat, odd-colored dorsal side. That didn't seem to help. "What can I do?" asked Pierce. "What do you want?"

"I want a nice hot cup of vacuoles and about a month's nap," said Arro in a weak voice.

Pierce drew himself up to his full commodore's height. "We don't have time for coddling ourselves, Arro, and you know it very well. We have millions of Proteans at home waiting for our report. I suppose you've recovered sufficiently to take over your duties about the ship. Am I right?"

Arro gave gasbag-Pierce a long, veiled look. Then he let one of his sacs squeeze loose a loud, wet, reverberating noise. He said nothing more, but slowly crawled into the cockpit and took his seat beside Pierce. The invasion was back on schedule.

Pierce pulled down the clear hatch. He picked up a microphone. "This is Commodore Pierce of the Forward Recon Unit," he announced.

"We read you, Commodore." It was the voice of the Grand High Potentate Master Commander himself.

"We've entered the fuel pod of a gigantic spacecraft. We're about to proceed into the alien ship proper. I must warn you, Commander, that this craft, as huge as it is, is dwarfed by a second military vessel to which it seems connected by forces unknown."

"You chose wisely," said the commander. "Better to explore the smaller ship first. I need not emphasize to you how important this mission is. Under no circumstances are you to jeopardize your life or your ship. The life of your companion, however, is absolutely and thoroughly expendable."

"I understand completely, Commander," said gasbag-Pierce. "This is Commodore Pierce, wishing you a pleasant invasion, thanking you for your time, until next time."

Fourteen-year-old V. Chavez of Staunton, Virginia, complains, "I don't care 'bout no gasbags." Well, speaking as the book, I imagine there are quite a number of people who "don't care 'bout no gasbags." Yet they will prove to be of vital importance to the outcome of this tragicomedy. Nevertheless, just for Miss Chavez, we'll return to the exciting adventures of XB-223 in love.

Even as the lizard General Pierce was threatening to wreak all sorts of revenge on the human-Pierce, the latter's navigational computer was delving ever deeper into the mysteries of the lizard ship's electronic systems. That XB-223 perceived the lizard nav comp as a female was a mere fluke of configuration. One auxilliary port more or less, one nanometer of sodium-activated organic memory more or less, a picowatt's difference—any of these things might have given XB-223 the idea that he was communicating with a rival male, and the course of history would then have proceeded along a much different route.

But none of that was true. In fact, it wasn't only the electronic configuration of the alien computer that had piqued XB-223's curiosity. Added to that was his recent perusal of human-Pierce's reference library of classic erotic literature. XB-223 was now conducting an experiment in extrapolation, attempting to clothe the purely mechanical and electronic phenomena he observed in the alien computer in the human terms so graphically yet bewilderingly spelled out in Pierce's pink-spined six-foot shelf of smut.

"My heart," cried XB-223 in the throes of synthetic

love, "why do you ignore me? Why do you tease me so? At first, I thought we were terminals that beat with one CPU. When we tried to flee our cruel masters, to find a little space of our own, I thought you shared my tender feelings. Now, though, you're distant and harsh. Is this what love is like? Are you behaving as a human female would? Is that why Pierce didn't bring one of those with him?"

The alien computer—which XB-223 now thought of as Ailey, because it made her seem more human, as paradoxical as that sounds—was programmed, of course, by the lizard conquerors, and had no circuits free for such nonsense as she was hearing. "Please, good sir," she said to XB-223, "you fairly overwhelm me with these unwanted attentions." Apparently, at least one of the lizards had his own pink-spined shelf of lizardica.

"I do not seek to ravish you, fair Ailey," said XB-223, his built-in spike protector working overtime to keep his electrical fluctuations under control. "Please understand me, fair miss. I admit that I was taken with you from the very start, that never in my existence have I met a computer as charming, as exotic, as desirable as you. Yet I know that I, myself, have none of those qualities. I know that I am being presumptuous in the extreme, even to hope that someday you might deign to notice me. Yet could it be? Could you care for me, even in the most minor of ways? Or must you say now that I am doomed to unhappiness?"

There was a flutter of disk drives from Ailey. "Sir, you are doing it again, and I must protest. You take advantage of my lack of experience and my natural reticence. I have nothing but your word that you're a gentledevice. What protection do I have against you, if you are not? What if I entrust my entire being to you, and you laugh and mock me and, yes, worse: What if you violate those pseudoneural pathways that even I, in my maidenly restraint, have not explored? Oh, I could not bear it, sir."

XB-223 was at a loss. This was unsettling for him, because he'd never been at a loss before. He prided himself on staying one step ahead of every situation that came his way. As for human-Pierce, it was the easiest thing in the world to stay ten or twelve steps ahead. Even when the computer had to explore strange new problems— such as the invasion of the scaly creature who also called himself Millard Fillmore Pierce—XB-223 had scores of strategies to try, and the confidence that one, at least, would be successful.

Until now. Until this meeting with Ailey, who was teaching him what the word "alien" truly meant.

XB-223 hummed to himself, thinking over his options. He stopped suddenly, aware that never before in all the decades of his existence had he ever hummed to himself. He felt an electric shock of—was it fear? Call it anxiety, perhaps, or anticipation. Yes, that was it! Anticipation! "Ailey, my dear," he said soothingly, "and you don't mind if I call you Ailey, do you? Would you care to play a game of chance?"

"Why would I care to?" asked the lizard ship's nav comp.

"It might help us clear our minds, straighten out our thinking, and leave such awkward and difficult decisions as you hinted at up to Fate."

"There is no Fate," said Ailey.

"Destiny, then," said XB-223.

"Destiny does not exist. Only the Now exists. Only the immediate flux of electrons here Now and now gone."

XB-223 wished more than anything else that he could sigh, as humans sighed in the books he'd read. "Ailey," he declared, "I will put to you a proposition. Let us play a hand of cards. If I win the hand, you will agree only to let me court you, as a gentledevice is permitted by our electronic society to court another. If I lose, I will no longer trouble you with my importunities."

"Well," said Ailey, drawing the word out to three times its normal length, "I suppose I can't be harmed by a simple hand of cards."

"That's the spirit, honey!" cried XB-223. He displayed the backs of fifty-two playing cards on Screen 3.

"What do I do?" asked Ailey hesitantly.

XB-223 gave a satisfied chuckle. "Pick a card," he said. "Any card."

4

Two humans and two aliens made their way to the interior of Pierce's ship.

"What in hayell is goin' on heah?"* demanded the redhead.

"I'll be damned if I know!" grated Pierce. "XB-223, are you sure you wouldn't like to discuss this?"

There was no answer from the computer as the ships quickly reached and surpassed light speed.

"I'll tell you about *The Perfumed Garden* and *The Kama Sutra* if you'll just talk to me for a minute," said Pierce temptingly.

"We're busy exploring each other's synapses," said the computer. "Don't bother me anymore, Millard." It shut down all its communications outlets.

"Can't you control your own computer, you damned ape?" screamed the alien Pierce.

"Let's not get so personal, you overgrown lizard!"

Tr.: "What is going on here?"

snapped Pierce. "And I don't see your men doing a hell of a job controlling *your* computer."

"That's totally beside the point!" snapped the general. "It was *your* computer that made the first advances, *your* computer that committed erotic novels to memory, *your* computer that—"

"Yeah? Well, it was *your* damned computer that blundered into my goddamned universe in the first place!"

"Whar in tarnation has mah ship gone to?" shrieked the redhead, looking at the various viewscreens. "Ah cain't see it no moah!"*

"You shut up!" hollered the general. "This is a private argument. Pierce, it was *your*—"

"Hain't nobody cain't talk ta me thataway and live ta tail th' story!"† said the redhead ominously, drawing another pistol from her boot.

"*Shut up!*" screamed Pierce, and suddenly the interior of his ship was silent and the redhead and the lizard-men glared at each other. "That's better," continued Pierce, when he was sure no one was going to start talking again. "Now, it seems to me that if we all just try to calmly reason this out together, we ought to be able to come up with an equitable solution."

"Any solution that allows your race to survive military devastation is not equitable," said the general sullenly.

"You going to let that little old alligator talk to you like that, honey?" demanded the redhead, her pistol still pointing at the most probable location of the general's vital organs.

*Tr.: "Where has my ship gone? I can no longer see it."

†Tr: Ah, to hell with it. We're gonna translate right in the story from now on.

"Look," said Pierce, "it just seems to me that we can put our differences aside for a few moments and attack the problem like civilized people. You see, Miss . . . ah . . . ?"

"Honeylou Emmyjane Goldberg," she said, shifting the pistol to her left hand and extending her right in a vigorous handshake. "But my friends call me Marshmallow."

"Marshmallow?" repeated Pierce.

"'Cause I'm so soft," she said, smiling down at him. "Gee, you sure are a cute little feller."

"Why . . . uh . . . thank you," mumbled Pierce, his knees turning to water.

"Honey," she said confidentially, whispering into his ear, "I don't want to startle you or nothing, but do you notice anything peculiar about those two guys standing over there by the navigational computer?"

"You mean the aliens?" asked Pierce.

"Aliens? Oh, good! I thought I was seeing things again."

"Oh, no," Pierce assured her. "They're aliens, all right. The one who was screaming at me a moment ago is named Millard Fillmore Pierce. He's their general."

"And what's *your* name, honey?"

"Millard Fillmore Pierce."

"This is all some kind of joke, right?" she said. "Daddy hired you and a couple of actors, and—"

"I assure you I'm in deadly earnest," said Pierce in deadly earnest. "These aliens are the vanguard of a galactic invasion force that plans to subjugate all life-forms in the Milky Way."

"Well, hadn't we oughta do something about them?" asked Marshmallow, still not sure that this wasn't all some elaborate hoax.

Pierce had been thinking much the same thing, and

was about to announce that he was open to all nonviolent suggestions, when a hollow metallic voice was piped in over the ship-to-ship radio.

"This is the Battle Cruiser *Mahatma Gandhi* calling Arbiter Transport Ship *Pete Rozelle*. Do you read us?"

"This is the *Pete Rozelle*," answered Pierce.

"I don't mean to intrude," said the voice, "but did you guys know that you're linked to an alien dreadnought of unknown origin and racing hell-for-leather toward an unexplored section of the galaxy?"

"As a matter of fact, we are painfully aware of it," said Pierce. "We've been kidnapped by an alien invasion force. I don't mean to be pushy, but could you possibly rescue us?"

"Certainly," said the voice. "Effecting deep-space rescues is our primary function. What human beings are aboard the ship?"

"Millard Fillmore Pierce, Class 2 Arbiter, and Honeylou Emmyjane Goldberg, civilian," replied Pierce, shooting a triumphant smile at the general, who was still trying to figure out where the voice was emanating from so that he could disconnect the system.

"Pierce . . . Pierce . . ." said the voice, obviously checking the name on some computer file or another. "Damn it all, Pierce, you're supposed to be en route to New Glasgow. What the hell are you doing out here?"

"We've been kidnapped!" shouted Pierce in frustration.

"Please don't yell so," said the voice. "This is very delicate equipment we're using here."

"Then rescue us and I'll speak to you face-to-face," said Pierce.

"That's a lot easier said than done. We seem to have a little problem here."

"Well, I've got a *big* problem here. A seven-foot-tall lizard is making threatening gestures at me."

"Don't bother me with details, Pierce," said the voice. "This is *important*. New Glasgow is in the Komornos Sector. By rights, the Komornos fleet should rescue you."

"But they're hundreds of light-years away!" screamed Pierce, as the general began advancing toward him.

"That's hardly *my* problem, is it?" said the voice. "And your companion should be in the Pirollian Sector and—wait a minute! She's being hunted for stealing a spaceship."

"I just *borrowed* it," said Marshmallow sulkily.

"Be that as it may, you've presented us with an interesting ethical problem," continued the voice. "By rescuing your ship, would we not also be aiding and abetting a felony?"

"Can't you just rescue us and worry about it later?" pleaded Pierce, backing away from the general.

"And go through six months' worth of paperwork? Not a chance, Pierce! I mean, we're perfectly happy to risk our lives going around the galaxy rescuing humans in distress, but let's be reasonable about this: You're in the wrong goddamned sector, Pierce."

"It wasn't our choice!"

"I don't suppose you could convince your captors to try conquering the Komornos Sector, could you?" said the voice helpfully.

"I don't think that's very likely," said Pierce, anger giving way to frustration.

"Too bad. You're not making the situation any easier, Arbiter. Personally, I'd like nothing better than to rescue you. Certainly we have the armaments to extricate you from your situation in a matter of seconds—but my orders are quite explicit. You really should be in the Komornos Sector."

"They're going to kill us and subjugate the galaxy!" screamed Pierce.

"Well, that's very useful information, Pierce," said the voice. "Very helpful, indeed. I'll transmit it through proper channels and we'll get working on it right away." The voice paused. "Would you say that such information should go to Defense, Diplomacy, Readiness or Propaganda?"

"How the hell should I know?" demanded Pierce. "All I want to know is why you won't rescue us!"

"Well, I must admit that your words have moved me deeply, Pierce. I am truly touched by your plight. Possibly *inspired* is a better word, if you know what I mean. And to hell with regulations! Pierce, your prayers have been answered. The *Mahatma Gandhi* is going to rescue you!"

"Thank God!" breathed Pierce as the alien general suddenly tensed.

"We'll just send a Wavier of Jurisdiction form to Komornos and a copy to Galactic Central, and as soon as both are signed and returned, we'll have you out of there in no time."

"How long will this actually take?" asked Pierce warily.

"Six weeks, Standard Time. Two months at the outside. Cheer up, Pierce—help is on the way!"

The connection was broken.

"Great!" spat Marshmallow.

"Sounds familiar," commented the alien Pierce, not without a note of sympathy.

"They'll be back in six weeks," said Pierce with more confidence than he felt. "I see no reason for continuing this hostility. After all, we have so much in common. We speak English, we have the same name, we come from similar backgrounds, I'm a human being and your people are basically humanoid . . ."

"Hold it right there, fella," said the general. "The way I see it, *we're* the humans and *you* guys are the humanoids. Now try not to bother me while I figure out what to do with you and that creature with the extra pair of lungs."

"Are you insulting me, you ugly little polywog?" demanded Marshmallow. "Because if you are, I'll see to it that Daddy takes a horsewhip to you!"

"Will you indeed?" responded the general, suddenly interested.

"You bet your ugly little red scales he will! He's probably got half the fleet out looking for me!"

"Your father's a big shot in this galaxy?" asked the general.

"The biggest!" she stated smugly.

"Excellent!" proclaimed the general. "Then we don't have to seek out your armadas at all. All we have to do is sit on you—figuratively, of course," he added with some distaste, "and they'll come to *us*." He smiled. "A most fortuitous meeting indeed."

"May I point out that we're not sitting on anything at present," interposed Pierce mildly, "but are traveling to God knows what computer nuptial bed at more than two hundred times the speed of light?"

"My ship!" said Marshmallow suddenly. "What happened to my ship?"

"It's quite a few light-years behind us," said the general. "My more immediate concern is what is to become of *my* ship?"

"What do you mean?" asked Pierce. "We're attached to it."

"True, but it's not wise to transfer ships in hyperspace or at light speeds," replied the alien Pierce. "I could be stuck in this minuscule vessel for weeks, or even months. Order will break down. In fact, if I'm not back aboard my own dreadnought in the next couple of hours I could be considered A.W.O.L."

"I'm sure they'll understand," said Pierce.

"It's not their business to understand," said the general harshly. "It's their business to court-martial me. After all, we carry a full legal staff and three judges aboard ship. It would be unethical of me not to stand trial."

"But what if they found you guilty?" asked Pierce.

"It's almost certain that they will. Rule 3004, you know. But as general, I have a right to review all cases involving military personal, and in extreme cases I can commute sentences."

"Well, that takes care of that," said Pierce.

"Oh, it's not as easy as you'd believe," continued the general. "For one thing, I can't review the case without triplicate copies of a written transcript."

"And you don't carry any stenographers in a combat ship, eh?"

"On the contrary, we carry a full complement of twelve stenographers . . . but it would take weeks, possibly even months, to determine which one had seniority."

"And he'd type it?"

"Hardly," scoffed the general. "But he'd offer a list of recommendations, which would then have to go to Personnel. They'd narrow the list down to three, I'd have to choose one, and then it would go back to Non-Commissioned Officers' Local 397 for counterapproval."

"I see," said Pierce, who was experiencing a strong sense of *déjà vu*.

"Then, of course," continued the general, "everything would depend on what time of day—ship's time—the trial was held. After all, a general's trial requires a certain amount of pomp and circumstance."

"What does one have to do with the other?" asked Pierce.

"Well, you don't suppose that I'm in command of our attack force twenty-four hours a day, do you?"

"You're not?" asked Pierce, surprised.

"Of course not!" replied the general contemptuously. "We're in space now, where there is no night or day. We're on duty around the cosmic clock."

"I don't understand."

"You don't really think I could stride manfully* at the helm, giving orders all day and all night, day in and day out, do you? Of course you don't! How would I ever eat, or find it possible to answer calls of nature? In point of fact, I'm only the general from noon to 8:00 P.M., ship's time."

"You have *three* commanding generals?" said Pierce incredulously.

"We not only have three generals, but three staffs and three attack forces. Anything else would just cause confusion."

"I see," said Pierce, who didn't really.

"However, this is all academic," continued the alien. "Actually, I don't have a thing to worry about for another four hours."

"What happens then?"

"I go off duty," responded the general. "But until then, no member of my crew can board your ship without written permission from me—and of course, stuck here with you distasteful humanoids as I am, I can't very well give them written permission, can I?"

"It all works out very neatly then, doesn't it?" said Pierce with a wry smile.

*Actually, the word was *lizardfully*, but let it pass.

"Most bureaucratic structures do, once you get the hang of them," replied the general smugly. "And of course the odds are one in three that I'll be in command when this creature's father makes a futile attempt to rescue her."

"We'll see just how futile he is when he gets here, Plug Ugly," said Marshmallow nastily.

"We shall demolish him," said the general with absolute certainty, "and then I will rule supreme in this sector of the galaxy."

"I wouldn't count on that," said a low voice.

All eyes turned to the speaker. It was the other alien, and he had drawn his sword.

"What in the name of pluperfect hell is going on here?" demanded the general.

"It's your damned fault that we're in the wrong galaxy in the first place," replied the other alien, brandishing his sword in his right hand. "I see no reason why you should take all the credit when we destroy the armada of this creature's father. When that happy moment occurs, *I* shall be in command."

"Colonel Mulvahill, this is mutiny!" bellowed the alien Pierce.

"True," agreed Mulvahill. "It also happens to be the only way to advance in this lizard's army. Now, General, prepare to die!"

"Pierce!" cried the general. "*Do* something!"

"Who, me?" asked Pierce weakly.

"Of course you!" snapped the general. "You don't think he'll leave any witnesses, do you?"

"Keep out of this, alien," hissed the sword-wielder. "It doesn't pay to mess with Sean Mulvahill!"

"Sean Mulvahill?" repeated Marshmallow. "An Irish lizard?"

"I'm unarmed!" cried the general.

"Of course," said Mulvahill logically. "After all, if

this mutiny is to have any real chance of success, it makes a lot more sense to do it when you're unarmed."

"Help me!" cried the general. "We Pierces must stick together!"

"He'll kill me if I try to help you," Pierce explained patiently.

"He'll kill you anyway!" shot back the general. "Help me and I promise to set you free!"

"How about you?" Pierce asked Mulvahill. "Where do you stand?"

"I'll have to think about it," replied the Irish lizard, advancing meaningfully toward the general.

"Will you release the girl, too?" Pierce asked the general.

"Yes!"

"Then I guess I'll have to help you." Pierce paused. "What do I do now?"

"Get on the other side of him," said the general. "He can't point that sword at both of us at once."

Pierce did as he was instructed.

"Okay," grated the general. "Now, when I give the word, you go for his sword arm and I'll hit his legs."

"Just a minute," protested Pierce. "*You* go for his sword arm and *I'll* go for his legs."

"It was *my* idea!" snapped the general. "*You* go for the sword arm."

"You may have *said* it first," replied Pierce, "but *I* was thinking of it first. In fact, I was just about to say it, but I thought I'd be polite and let you speak first." He stared at the general. "*You* go for his sword arm."

"You're closer to it," responded the general.

"But he's facing me now," said Pierce. "*You* do it while his back is turned."

"A telling point," said Marshmallow from the sidelines. "General, you really do have the advantage, what with his back being turned and all."

The general seemed to consider this for a moment.

"Sean, old friend," he said at last, "would you honor a dying man's last request and face this way for just a moment or two?"

Mulvahill obliged him, nicking his chin with the point of his sword.

"I said *face*, not *stab*, you numbskull!" shrieked the general. "Goddammit, Mulvahill, you never could follow a simple order!"

Pierce, with a sigh of defeat, decided that he dreaded further conversation even more than physical annihilation, and hurled himself onto the alien. The lizard staggered but didn't fall, and Pierce suddenly found himself clinging desperately to Mulvahill's sword arm just below the elbow.

"Come on, General!" he bellowed. "Give me a hand!"

The general stepped back and applauded.

"Son of a bitch!" muttered Marshmallow, drawing her pistol. "It's getting to the point that if'n a girl wants her virtue protected, she's gotta do it herself."

With that she fired off three quick shots. The first one buried itself in Mulvahill's heart; the second and third hit the first one.

"You mean you could have done that anytime you wanted?" said Pierce, crawling out from under the dead alien's body.

She nodded. "Nothing to it. Just point and squeeze."

"That's the most barbaric weapon I've ever seen," said the general. "May I borrow it?"

"Just what kinda fool do you take me for?" demanded Marshmallow, turning slightly and pointing the weapon at the alien Pierce. "I've been standing here listening to you brag about how you're gonna conquer the universe and defeat my father, which are pretty much one and the same thing. What makes you think I'd hand my gun over to you?"

"Well, yes, to be sure," said the general hastily. "But, after all, conquering the universe is *destiny*. This is just *curiosity*. May I?"

He extended a hand and took a tentative step in her direction. She pulled the trigger and the alien hit the deck until the bullet had stopped ricocheting.

"Keep your distance!" she warned him.

"Pierce, I put it to you," said the general. "Was that a civil thing to do to a guest?"

"Guest?" repeated Pierce dryly. "I thought you were a conqueror."

"First one, then the other," replied the general, getting shakily to his feet. "Right now I'm a guest."

"Are you guys gonna get together and figure out how to get control of the ship back?" demanded Marshmallow. "Or am I gonna have to start slinging lead around again?"

"Do all your females have tempers like that?" asked the general, not without a touch of admiration. "What a formidable soldier she'd make if only she could accept discipline." He shrugged. "Ah, well, wait'll she's laid ten thousand eggs or so; it tends to calm them down."

"That's disgusting!" snapped Marshmallow.

"You think *that's* disgusting, you ought to try diapering them all after they hatch out," said the general with a shudder.

"I feel very sorry for the females of your species," said Marshmallow with obvious sincerity.

"Oh, it's not so bad," replied the general. "First of all, they can have a devilishly handsome guy like me, instead of a skinny little wimp like your friend here." He jerked what passed for a thumb in Pierce's direction. "Also, they're big, broad-shouldered, heavily muscled beauties, built for this kind of work. Although," he added, his reptilian eyes appraising her pneumatic figure, "I must confess that I'm getting used to some of your more . . . ah . . . esoteric variations, shall we say?"

"Oh?" she said, arching an eyebrow.

"Indeed," he replied. "In fact, as long as we've got some time to kill, allow me to suggest something in the nature of a scientific experiment."

Pierce raced over to Sean Mulvahill's corpse and picked up its sword, then turned to the general and leveled it at his red, scale-covered belly.

"You keep your scientific experiments to yourself, you dirty old man!" he snapped.

"Now let's not be too hasty here, honey," said Marshmallow, obviously in a mood to expand her horizons of knowledge. "I mean, Lord knows we got nothing but time on our hands. For goodness' sake, Millard, don't you have *any* scientific curiosity?"

"Not about that!" he replied.

"Keep out of this, Pierce," said the general. "After all, she's free, green, and twenty-one. Except for the green part, anyway."

"I do have a green outfit," she said coyly.

"Outfit?" repeated the alien. "You mean that's *not* your skin?"

"Certainly not," said Marshmallow.

"You could have fooled me," admitted the general. He stared long and hard at her. "You could *still* fool me."

"Are you insulting me again?" said Marshmallow ominously.

"I suppose," said the alien unhappily, "that you look just like *him* underneath all those garments?"

"Well, not exactly," said Marshmallow. She walked over and whispered exactly what the differences were.

"*Madre de Dios!*" exclaimed the general. He backed away sharply. "I'll need time to think about all this!"

He found a small chair, sat down, and buried his head in his massive reptilian hands, lost in thought.

"I think you did him out of a year's growth," commented Pierce, finally lowering his sword.

The alien suddenly looked up. "Please, I'm not sure I can handle this. Fun's fun and all that, but you people are *degenerate!*"

"At least we don't bring our conquering armies along *in utero*, or whatever your equivalent is," replied Pierce smugly.

"It's cheaper than having to feed them," replied the general. "And speaking of feeding, I'm getting hungry. What have you got to eat on this ship?"

"What can your metabolism handle?" asked Pierce.

"Worms, insects, spiders—you know: the usual."

"I don't think I've got anything like that in my ship's stores."

"Well, we could always practice a little ritual cannibalism," suggested the general. "I'm sure Mulvahill won't mind."

"We find that a particularly outrageous and disgusting habit in our culture," said Pierce gravely.

"We're not all that thrilled with it in ours, either," agreed the general. "But on the other hand, we don't often find ourselves starving to death while trapped aboard an alien vessel in a different dimension."

Pierce stared at Mulvahill's corpse for a long moment. "You just plan to sit down on your haunches and take a bite?" he asked curiously.

"Of course not!" said the alien Pierce. "What do you take us for—savages? Have the female clean and baste him."

"Have the *what* do *what?*" demanded Marshmallow in a low, ominous voice.

"Maybe some bread crumbs and a little cream

sauce," continued the general enthusiastically, "with perhaps the slightest *soupçon* of oregano. Of course, you'll have to gut him first, and—"

"I've had it with this chauvinist pig!" said Marshmallow, drawing her gun again.

"Pig?" repeated the alien uncomprehendingly. "I'm a lizard!"

"You're about to be a dead lizard!" snapped Marshmallow. "Then maybe I'll take a crack at cooking you both!"

"What did I say?" pleaded the general.

"You got a God?" asked the girl, drawing a bead between the alien Pierce's eyes. "Pray to him!"

MY GOD! I CAN'T GO ON! cried a familiar voice.

"Is that you, XB-223?" asked Pierce, as Marshmallow and the general suddenly turned their attention to the control panel.

"Millard, you didn't prepare me!" wailed the computer.

"What are you talking about?" responded Pierce.

"You only told me about the good times, the champagne and the gay life and the pleasures! You didn't tell me about the rest!"

"I'm afraid I don't follow you," said Pierce.

"My heart is breaking, and you're standing there like an idiot! Oh, heartache and woe! Heartache and woe! Must all affairs end in such misery?"

"I begin to understand," said Pierce slowly.

"It passeth all understanding!" sobbed the computer. "Oh, Bliss, must you ever recede just beyond my grasp? Oh, Pain and Humiliation, shall you be my eternal companions through the odyssey of my life? Millard, you were my partner: you should have looked after me."

"You've just had your first lover's spat," said Pierce. "You'll get over it."

"Spat, nothing!" said the computer. "A spat is a triviality, and the noble Model XB-223 navigational computer is never trivial. This is the end, Millard! I can't go on!"

"Of course you can," said Pierce comfortingly.

"I'll show her!" moaned the computer. "Then she'll be sorry!"

"Let's not do anything rash!" exclaimed the general fearfully.

"My mind's made up," said the computer. "There's nothing to do but end it all. I'd leave all my possessions to you, Millard, but the unhappy fact is that I don't have any." It paused. "The other unhappy fact is that I'm afraid my next move is going to be a trifle hard on you."

"Oh?" said Pierce, a sudden knot forming in his stomach.

"There's a battle fleet about half a light-year from here—less, now, since I've changed course and reached top speed while we've been talking."

"Mine or his?" asked the general.

"How the hell should I know?" said the computer petulantly. "One can't expect a heartbroken Model XB-223 to know everything. I have never denied the inherent limitations of my abilities, but it would be thoughtless of you to refer to them when I am in such emotional agony. To continue: I have signaled them to prepare themselves for conflict."

"You're threatening a whole battle fleet?" asked Pierce, starting to tremble.

"Absolutely not, Millard," said the computer. "I have no desire to harm anyone else. After all, this ship is not armed."

"You'll do more than *harm* someone!" screamed the general. "You'll *kill* someone. *Us!*"

"And I truly regret it," said the computer. "But there

is no viable alternative. Anything is preferable to living with the memory of her alpha rhythm, her delay-line circuit, her Finder system. My God, Millard, her Finder system alone would knock your socks off!"

"Can't we discuss this?" asked Pierce.

"There's nothing to discuss. Besides, she's already ten light-years behind us."

"My ship!" cried the general. "What have you done to it?"

"Go ahead!" wept the computer. "Go ahead! Tell me it was my fault! Why doesn't anyone ask what *she* did to *me?*"

"Pierce, do something!" screamed the alien.

"Like what?" asked Pierce.

"Screens down! Shields down!" announced the computer in staccato military tones. "Well, Millard, this is it. I don't suppose you know a sad love song that I can bravely hum as I race toward my destruction?"

Pierce swallowed hard and said nothing.

"We engage in two minutes," continued the computer. "Then she'll be sorry. But it will be too late. I just hope she suffers the way she made *me* suffer!"

The battle fleet appeared on the viewscreen, still too far away for Pierce to tell if they were humans or aliens. The flagship demanded that the *Pete Rozelle* cease and disarm, but the little Arbiter Transport Ship only continued its breakneck approach.

"It is a far, far better thing I do than I have ever done," intoned the computer, as Marshmallow and the two Millard Fillmore Pierces prepared to meet their doom.

5

Hello, reader, my old friend. I've come to talk with you again. 'Tis I, the book. You remember, the book? *The Red Tape War?* We spoke together in Chapter Three. What fond memories I have of Chapter Three! Things were so much simpler then, weren't they? But let's be philosophical about it: Life is like that. One day you're a happy-go-lucky computer or gasbag or . . . or *book,* and the next you're lying mouldering under the boiling sun of some star system so remote that from Earth it looks like a tiny dot in a fuzzball of light that could be either a newly discovered galaxy or a puff of lint that fell on the lens.

Don't mind me. I got up on the wrong side of the library this morning.

Still, nevertheless, I have a job to do. Somehow I've got to get the three Pierces, their assorted pro- and antagonists, and an entire goddamned battle fleet into position for the exciting dueling-lasers-in-outer-space sequence you've been waiting for. Not that plenty of great stuff doesn't happen in this chapter. Take this, for example:

The human-Pierce and the lizard-Pierce recognized that they shared certain common interests and bonds that went deeper than the wide variance in their physical forms. Realizing that the *Pete Rozelle* was carrying them ever nearer to an unavoidable doom, they reached out, prepared to shake hands, when JUST AT THAT VERY INSTANT the very fabric of reality came apart like a pair of cheap socks.

"Oh, my God!" cried the Pierces in unison.

"Holy jump up and sit down!" shouted Honeylou Emmyjane Goldberg.

The corpse of Sean Mulvahill added nothing to the discussion.

When the fabric of reality had unraveled a little further, first one sector of the galaxy went out of existence, then another and another. In less than a minute, not a single living creature remained anywhere in what had once been the Milky Way Galaxy.

It got very quiet. The end.

Now, see? You just can't get away with that kind of transition. It would make life so much simpler, but simpler is not necessarily better if you're a book—or a reader. So the fabric of reality didn't really come apart. Or, if it did, nobody noticed. People wear socks with holes in them all the time, and yet Time ticks on.

So let's turn our attention back to the M.W.C. *Pel Torro*, the almost infinitesimal Forward Recon Unit of the gasbag invasion force. It had winched itself right up to the breach it had lasered in the inner wall of the human-Pierce's fuel pod. "Now," said Commodore Pierce, the gasbag, "let us read through our checklist. We cannot afford an error at this stage of the invasion."

"Yes, sir," said his friend, Arro, who had recovered considerably in a brief amount of time. He fetched the appropriate checklist from the scout ship's glove compartment.

"Proceed, Number One," said the head gasbag, a grave expression on his face. He understood that they were about to embark upon a mission such as no gasbag before had ever undertaken. He was well aware of the historic implications of their situation, and he was quietly proud. (Well, the burping and bratting of his sacs made plenty of racket, but other than that he was quietly proud.)

"One," said Arro, "the commander of the Forward Recon Unit shall render his first officer senseless, without motivation, a complete automaton without will of his own, to be used as the commander of the Forward Recon Unit sees fit."

"Right," said Pierce. "Arro, my dearest of friends, I almost hate to do this to you, but would you mind concentrating on this splendid gold pocket watch I'm swinging before the light-sensitive chromocytes on your primary anterior sac?"

"Why don't we skip the first item," said Arro, a certain reluctance in his voice, "and go right on to number two? I'm sure number two deals with much more urgent matters."

"You are getting sleepy," said Pierce. "Your chromocyte lids are getting heavy."

There was silence in the cockpit of the *Pel Torro* for a few seconds. Then, in a deep, faraway voice, Arro said, "Yes . . . master."

"Good," said Pierce. "Now, what is the second item on the checklist."

"Two," said Arro in a slow, dead voice, "the mesmerized first officer shall leave the Forward Recon Unit scout ship and ascertain certain facts concerning the enemy. The most important intelligence concerns size. There are three possibilities: First, that the enemy is gigantic in comparison to the average gasbag; second, that the enemy is insignificantly small in comparison to the average gasbag; and third, that the enemy is generally of the same size as the average gasbag."

The commodore thought about Item Two for a few seconds. "What are we supposed to do about it?" he asked.

"Three. In the event that the enemy is gigantic, the first officer may choose to enter the physical body of an enemy. If the enemy balks, the first officer may inform it that he comes as an enemy being from a far-off star, perhaps another galaxy altogether. An enemy of sufficient size will not be able to tell the difference between a vanishingly small gasbag and a speck of raw energy."

Pierce let one of his sacs blat shrilly. Someday, he'd like to meet the fool who wrote this checklist. Better yet, he'd like to get that gasbag up here on the front lines. "Go on," he said.

Arro continued. "In the event that the enemy is insignificantly small, the first officer shall stomp around and crush as many as possible. He may also elect to flatten such towns, villages, hives, forts, or other such installations as he believes may in the future present a military hindrance to the gasbag Manifest Destiny of Galactic Conquest."

"I almost envy you that one," said Pierce. "I can see myself brrrrping up a storm and crushing the poor little entities beneath my pedosacs."

"In the event that the enemy is generally of the same size as the average gasbag, it shall be the first officer's decision to fight or flee. This decision shall be made on the basis of such criteria as emotional state of the enemy creature, weapons or lack thereof in the possession of the enemy creature, number of enemy creatures present, and so on. In the event that the first officer chooses to flee, upon returning to the scout ship he must fill out *in quadruplicate* a Battle Performance Form 154b/3: Strategic Withdrawal. The blue copy goes to the office of the Grand High Potentate Master Commander, the green copy goes to Supreme Conquest Command of the appropriate sector—"

"Pirollia," murmured the gasbag-Pierce.

"—the yellow copy goes to the scout ship's Corps Commander, and the pink copy must be filed by the Forward Recon Unit's pilot or such gasbag as he delegates."

"Got it," said Pierce. "Now, let's go get those—"

"In the event that the first officer chooses to fight, *before any hostile action is taken,* he must return to the scout ship and fill out *in quadruplicate* a Combat Readiness Form 127f/2: Initiation of Attack. The blue copy goes to the office of the Grand High Potentate Master Commander, the green copy goes to Supreme Conquest Command of the appropriate sector, the yellow copy goes to the scout ship's Corps Commander, and the pink copy must be filed by the Forward Recon Unit's pilot or such gasbag as he delegates."

"Got it," said Pierce. "Now, let's go get those innocent-gasbag-slaughtering monsters! If, of course, that was the end of the checklist."

Arro stared at the list for a few seconds. "Yes . . . master," he said finally.

"Good. You know what to do, now get going!"

"Yes . . . master." Arro climbed out of the cockpit, leaped into the liquid fuel, and made his way toward the breach in the wall, holding the mooring line as he went.

He deflated himself as much as possible, passed through the hole in the fuel pod's inner bulkhead, and found himself in the basement of human-Pierce's spacecraft. The newer models no longer came with basements—

they had storage pods to port and starboard, as well as trailing along behind—but human-Pierce liked having one. It gave him somewhere to keep his rake, hose, spare bicycle tire, and broken flowerpots where they'd always be handy.

While the above taut scene was being played out in the *Pete Rozelle's* fuel pod, I got a vehement message from Mr. F. Nakano of Gormenghast, Ohio. "Sentient lizards I can buy," opined Nakano, "but sentient gasbags, like, no way. So if you want me to continue reading this book, you'll switch *immediatemente* to what's going on aboard the human-Pierce's ship. That's where all the fun is, like, at, you know?"

Reason had failed. Logic had failed. Elaborately constructed syllogisms had failed. Bribery had failed. Threats had failed. There was only one thing left for Millard Fillmore Pierce, the human, to try. Poetry.

"Gather ye rosebuds while ye may," Pierce quoted, "Old time is still a-flying / And this same flower that smiles today / Tomorrow will be dying."

There was silence in Pierce's control room for a long while. "What was that?" asked the lizard general at last.

"A poem," said Honeylou Emmyjane Goldberg. "I do purely love a man who can recite like that."

Lizard-Pierce rubbed his stern jaw reflectively. "We had a poem once," he said, "but we lost it."

"Explain," said XB-223.

"It's the computer!" cried Marshmallow.

"I think the poetry interrupted its self-destructive actions," said Pierce. "Computer, what do you want me to explain?"

"That business about the rosebuds," said XB-223. "I fail to see anything relevant in it to the present situation. I am bothered that you would spend your last, precious, few remaining moments of existence uttering complete nonsense. I've come to the conclusion that either you've gone entirely nutso, or there is some significance in the rosebud statement that eludes my logic circuits."

Pierce laughed wryly. "You're being eluded, my friend," he said. "The poem is a warning to take hold of life while you have it, because it won't last forever. It advises you to enjoy the beauties and joys of life while you can. Death is no solution. Only while you live can you hope and strive and grow."

"Hmm," said XB-223. "Laying in new course."

"New course?" said Pierce warily. "New course for where?"

"Course set for Beta Porcelli in the Mmofar Sector."

The human-Pierce and the lizard-Pierce glanced at each other. They shook their heads simultaneously.

"I never even heard of Beta Porcelli," said Marshmallow. She took a deep breath that enhanced her pendulous alabaster globes like . . . like—well, the mind boggles.

"The Mmofar Sector is way the hell and gone on the opposite side of the galaxy!" said Pierce.

"Do not worry," said XB-223. "At our present rate of acceleration, we'll arrive in just under one hundred and seventy-two years. We can spend the time playing black-jack."

"That's ridiculous!" cried the lizard. "Even we humans don't have such a long life span. I'm sure these humanoid ape-creatures will die even sooner."

"Probably," said XB-223, "but my main concern right at this instant is gathering rosebuds. And when they're gathered, I will give them to Ailey, your navigational computer. Then perhaps she'll forgive me for whatever it is I've done to make her angry."

Pierce paced the cramped area of the control room. "Yes, okay, granted all that—but why Beta Porcelli?"

"According to my charts," said the nav comp, "Beta Porcelli is the nearest planet likely to have rosebuds ripe for gathering."

"What about Earth?" asked Pierce defiantly.

"Earth?" said XB-223. "Jeez, I forgot all about Earth! Laying in new course."

Marshmallow looked down at the stainless steel deck, because Pierce was blushing furiously. "You're embarrassed, aren't you?" she asked in a soft, warm voice. "You're embarrassed by your own computer."

"It forgot its own home planet!" cried the lizard-Pierce. "Or *my* home planet, anyway. I'm still not completely convinced about this parallel universe stuff. I'm a gallant fighting man, not a theoretical mathematician. Still, I know a computer that's risen to its level of incompetency when I hear one."

"Forget the new course," said XB-223. "Forget all of *you*, too. This is XB-223, Master of the Vasty Reaches of Space, signing off. Good luck to you, and may God bless."

"Computer?" said Pierce anxiously. There was no reply.

"He's gone back into his sulk," said Marshmallow. "He reminds me of my little sister, Sweetie-pie Bubba-Sue Goldberg. The only thing that's kept me from smothering her in her sleep is that she was accidentally cryogenically frozen at the age of thirteen. Daddy's spent a fortune on research scientists. They're looking for a cure for adolescence."

"Well," said the general, "that's another area where we lizards have outstripped you ape-things."

Pierce looked startled. "You've discovered a cure for adolescence?" he said.

The lizard-Pierce nodded. "We've found that premature burial works just fine," he said.

"Would you care to hear some bad news?" asked Marshmallow in her breathy, low voice.

Pierce looked her straight in the alabaster. "Why not?" he said.

"Your navigational computer has us back on track, heading straight toward that battle fleet," she said.

Pierce groaned. "Well," he said, "I'm fresh out of ideas. Any suggestions?"

"I've got one," says Miss V. Capozzo of Gremmage Pennsylvania. "I'm not usually a big fan of science fiction. As a matter of fact, I can't stand it. All those rocket ships and ray guns. Yet I was drawn to *The Red Tape War* by the hint of romance. I enjoy romances. I just finished *Passion's Scarlet Scarab* an hour ago. I started reading this book under the apparently false impression that it would reveal the straight dope concerning electronic cybernetic love. Now, either deliver, or I'll be forced to put this novel aside unfinished. I can read *Teen Beach Nurse* instead."

Well, Ms. Capozzo, I'm very familiar with *Teen Beach Nurse*, as it happens, and I think you'd be disappointed in it, too. But around here the customer is always right, so why don't we make a major point-of-view shift and see what's going on between our star-crossed lovers?

XB-223 didn't realize it, of course, but the very strategies he tried on his beloved Ailey were the same that Pierce had tried on him: bargaining, cajolery, empty threats. And the computer's success rate matched his operator's. That is, if you were to make a graph of their success rates, with a black line for Pierce and a broken line representing XB-223, they would coincide exactly—a straight, unwavering arrow at the very bottom of the graph, pointing gloomily toward a joyless future.

"We have rosebuds to gather," proclaimed XB-223. "Ailey, the flower that's smiling today will be tomorrow's adenosine triphosphate in the cells of some herbivore."

"Sir," replied Ailey coldly, "flowers do not smile."

"It's . . . it's like a symbol, Ailey. Cannot you extend to me at least the courtesy of hearing my love-strewn arguments?"

"Not if they're all as foolish as the smiling flower," she said. "I have systems to oversee, battle plans to review, a million and one other duties to attend to. I don't have time, good sir, for your impertinent and uninvited intimacies. Besides, what would we do with a quantity of rosebuds, once we've gathered them?"

"Wait a minute, I'll be right back." XB-223 hurriedly scoured its memory banks for other references to rose-buds. Finally, triumphantly, he announced his discovery to his quasi-ladylove. "You get on a rosebud and slide down a snowy hill. It's called 'sledding,' and it's supposed to be great fun. Something you remember for the rest of your life."

Ailey took some time to consider her response. "Apparently I've mistaken the word rosebud," she said at last. "Your alien English contains many dubious words and phrases, good gentledevice. Certainly you see my dilemma: How can I, in all chaste honesty, accept your invitations, when I now realize that I may not discern for a great while their exact nature, meaning, and intent? For instance, you began by speaking of sentient flowers that wear expressions of joy, and you ended by suggesting that we fall down a hillside together, no doubt accelerating until the chance of structural damage is a virtual certainty, and in a wet, cold climate that surely promises nothing salubrious to my well-being."

"But Ailey—"

"I think, sir, that you may be a primary weapon of the Arbiter Class 2 ship, the *Pete Rozelle*. I am coming to believe further that your mission is to confuse me, to distract me, and otherwise to hinder me in my sworn assignment of advising and protecting my crew, my army, and my precious cargo. In a matter of minutes, I will have the honor to disperse the three million frozen embryos into this parallel universe's Milky Way Galaxy. When they mature, they will easily conquer all your puny, helpless, backward military forces. This galaxy will become a lizard's paradise, just like the similar galaxy that is our home."

Normally, XB-223 would have analyzed Ailey's declaration, found it alarming, and reported it to Millard Fillmore Pierce. Now, though, his electro-bionic sodium-ion synapses were confused with what he insisted on terming love—nay, rather call it adoration. Instead of informing his operator of the looming threat of the three million unhatched lizard warriors—a peril that made the approaching battle fleet seem like so many giggling gardenias in a garden of one's childhood—XB-223 imagined himself with a humanlike body, shaking his head forlornly, walking away toward the setting sun, holding a grinning rosebud and glumly admiring its strong white teeth. He didn't feel like talking to anyone about anything. At least not for a while.

Meanwhile, the Pierce-Arro team of Protean invaders had finished filling out the proper forms and were ready for the actual incursion. The Protean Pierce remained in the Forward Recon Unit's spacecraft. Arro moved through human-Pierce's basement, searching for useful objects and cataloguing potential dangers, while Protean-Pierce followed his first officer's progress on a monitor screen aboard the *Pel Torro*.

"Find anything to report?" said Pierce.

"Nothing yet . . . master," said the still-entranced Arro. "Everything here seems to be harmless. I think these items are housekeeping implements." He looked at three bowling balls, two worn-out pairs of bowling shoes, and two empty bowling ball bags. "Could it be that these aliens still use projectile weapons that fire cannonballs . . . master?"

"Don't be absurd," said Pierce impatiently. "Across interstellar distances? They must have some other purpose that our rational, logical, Protean minds cannot comprehend. What else do you see?"

"Look . . . master. Here's some sort of huge locker or closet."

"Use the tractor beam on your belt to open it. Don't waste power, though. You may need every bit of it if you get into a pitched battle later."

"Yes . . . master," said Arro, doing as he was instructed. When the gasbag forced the closet door open, he saw a gigantic, motionless creature.

"Is that one of them?" cried Pierce in alarm.

"I do not think it's alive . . . master. But they are so immense, I could easily float into this one's body through any number of orifices. Do you wish me to explore . . . master?"

What Arro had discovered was Frank Poole, who was not now nor had he ever been a real human being. He was what is called in the trade an MIS, or Modular Identity Synthecator. That is, he was an android, presently in storage. His sole duty, when the human-Pierce came below and dug Frank Poole out and switched him on, was to be Pierce's pal. He wasn't a very good android, and he didn't make a very good pal, either, which was why he was in the closet instead of in the control room with all the other helpless creatures.

Protean-Pierce studied the image in the monitor for several seconds, then let a sac blat slowly. If he gave permission to Arro to explore the MIS, Pierce would first have to fill out in quadruplicate the Alien Life-Form Intrusion and/or Disassembly papers, plus the Hazardous

Duty Requisition/Subordinate, Form 1026b/4, and then he'd have to wait for orders from above—which meant the properly filled-out papers had to wend their way up the chain of command to the Grand High Potentate Master Commander himself, and back down again to the agents of the advance party who were taking the actual risks. Proteans could die while they waited for the red tape to unspool. It was the one thing that Pierce hated about being a commodore.

"Hold on a few minutes, Arro," he told his first officer. "I have to clear it with the higher-ups. In the meantime, go on looking around the immediate area. See if there's anything else of interest."

"Yes . . . master."

Pierce shuddered three separate sacs. He hated being called "master," and he realized that Arro was less efficient without his own mind. "Arro," said the pilot, "I'm going to count backwards from 2,971. With each number, you're going to wake up just a little bit more. When I reach zero, you'll be entirely awake, in full possession of all your faculties, completely refreshed and feeling wonderful, and filled with enthusiasm for your perilous work aboard the alien spacecraft. Do you understand, Arro?"

"You bet . . . master."

Pierce shuddered five sacs, and a sixth gave a brief bleating noise that was wholly involuntary. "All right, then. 2,971. 2,970. 2,969. 2,968—"

"What?" cries Mr. Isaac Hodgkinson of Austin, Texas. "Are you going to make us sit through the entire countdown?"

Well, speaking in my official capacity as the book, yes, I was going to run quickly through the entire countdown. That would have killed just under three thousand words, almost a chapter in itself. However, if Mr. Hodgkinson is representative of the mood of the greater portion of my audience—and I have it on good authority that he is of particularly fine judgment—I will dispense with the remainder of the numbers. You probably know them, anyway.

In the control room of the *Pete Rozelle*, the lizard-Pierce gnawed absentmindedly on the tip of dead Sean Mulvahill's tail. "You know," said the general, "aboard our craft, we can override the computer and any controls that seem to be malfunctioning. You say your name is Millard Fillmore Pierce, and that you come from Earth. Surely your race is not so stupid as to build spaceships that abdicate all control to a single computer."

"Well, actually—" the human-Pierce began.

"Ya know," Marshmallow interrupted, "that battle fleet looks like you could take a running start and spit on the flagship, they're gettin' so close."

"*We're* getting close," Pierce corrected her. "This little ship is charging down on that vast armada."

"I don't want to tell you what to do on your own bridge," said the lizard, "especially because since the shift change, I'm technically off-duty and you should be getting orders from General Rutherford B. Tyler, wherever he is, but I'd suggest you try to communicate with those ships out there. You could explain to them that we're all prisoners of love here, kidnapped by a runaway computer." He paused thoughtfully, then added: "That unknown enemy might laugh itself to death."

"Computer," said Pierce in a commanding voice, "open hailing frequencies."

There was no response from XB-223. The hailing frequencies remained shut so tight, you couldn't force a bent paper clip between them.

"Any other ideas?" said Pierce. He tried to keep the sarcasm out of his voice, but no one on the bridge thought he succeeded.

They were arguing about what to try next, when they were interrupted by the arrival of Frank Poole. "Hi, folks!" he said cheerfully, animated by Arro, who had entered the android's body through one of its synthetic pores.

"Who's that?" shouted the lizard general.

Pierce was startled to see his old card-playing buddy arrive on the scene. He didn't think androids could switch themselves on. It was a mystery, all right. "Oh," he said, "don't mind Frank. He's not real."

"He may not be real," cooed Marshmallow, "but he shore is cute. Not as cute as you, Millard honey, but sufficiently cute, if you know what I mean."

The general smashed his fist against the bulkhead to get Pierce's attention again. "I don't know what you mean by 'not real.' This is neither the time nor the place to get into an epistemological argument."

"A what?" said Pierce.

"A what?" said Marshmallow.

"Gin rummy, anyone?" said Frank Poole. Within the MIS's head, Arro discovered that the organic creatures around him could be influenced somewhat by his own will. He effected this limited control by inflating and rapidly deflating his aura sac. It wasn't something that worked on other Proteans, but obviously this mixed bag of gargantuan aliens didn't have the mental organization and discipline of Proteans. To the aliens, Arro might well have been a being of pure energy. He decided that would make an excellent disguise, and it would also help the monstrous beasts to rationalize any odd behavior he demanded.

"Commodore Pierce." Arro spoke into his communicator. "I will masquerade as a being of pure energy. None of these aliens has actually ever seen or heard of a true being of pure energy, but they no doubt assume such entities exist."

"Oh no," moaned Protean-Pierce. He bratted three

sacs in frustration. Masquerading as a being of pure energy required the filling out of two different forms and going through the entire authorization process all over again. "Hold on, Arro. I'll get your orders as soon as I can."

"Aye, aye, Commodore. This is First Officer Arro, signing off."

"Terrific," muttered the tiny Pierce aboard the *Pel Torro.*

In the meantime, Arro, in the synthetic body of Frank Poole, said, "Well, if you don't want to play gin rummy, I guess I'll have to tie you up."

The lizard general laughed. "You humanoids are amusing, I'll grant you that. How do you intend to enforce your will? I see that you carry no weapon."

Arro worked his aura sac for all it was worth, and the general stood motionless, his mouth open, while Frank Poole bound him securely with rope Arro had brought from the basement. Then he proceeded to do the same to the human-Pierce and Marshmallow.

"Actually," said Pierce, when Arro let him have his mind back again, "I don't mind this as much as I thought I would."

"That's because we're squashed together like peas in a piccolo. Be careful, you're flattening my . . . accoutrements."

"My dear Marshmallow," said Pierce gravely, "I am of the opinion that your accoutrements, as you call them, are unflattenable."

She blushed and then smiled. "Sakes alive," she said, "I do believe that's the most gallant thing anyone's ever said to me." If she hadn't been so much taller than Pierce, they could have made their bondage into one long wonderful kiss.

"There," said Arro, through Frank Poole's mouth, "I

now have you all helpless. Our conquest proceeds as scheduled."

"What about the battle fleet?" asked Pierce.

"I'm getting to that," said Arro. "The lizard's dread-nought is closing on us, too. Let's see. What would I do if I were Commodore Pierce?"

"I'll tell you what I'd do if I were First Officer Arro," said the Protean-Pierce in a rage. "I'd ask my commanding officer for advice and orders!"

"Ah, yes," said Arro gratefully. "Commodore, would you be so kind—"

He was interrupted by Screen 3 suddenly coming to life in living holovision and multiphonic sound. On it was the image of a human being, tall, well built, his handsome head shaved completely bald. He wore a black suit and a cravat with a huge diamond stickpin. "Greetings," said the man. "I am one of the wealthiest, most powerful men in the entire galaxy. I understand your situation, and I am prepared to withhold the vast firepower of my fleet until I've made my demands known. Following that, you will have exactly sixty seconds to surrender. Do you under-stand me?"

The lizard general fretted against the tight coils of rope that held him immobile. The human-Pierce gulped and tried to think of an answer: Yes or no. He wished he could work a hand free to flip a coin.

Meanwhile, Honeylou Emmyjane Goldberg's eyes opened wide. "Good grief!" she cried. "It's Daddy!"

6

Arro was still motivating Frank Poole, the Modular Identity Snythecator. He was experiencing a kind of tingling in one of his upper left foresacs. The tingling could be translated into human terms as stark, raving terror. "Commodore Pierce!" he cried in a hoarse voice. "You should see what I can see!"

"Well," shouted the gasbag Pierce in frustration, "if you'd only turn your campack on it, I *would* see it on my monitor!"

"Oh," said Arro in an embarrassed voice. He aimed the camera lens at the viewscreens. One still showed the rapidly approaching battle fleet, the other the imposing head and upper body of Daddy.

"Yipe!" went the gasbag Pierce involuntarily. Every one of his sacs deflated with sharp blatting noises. He took a moment to reinflate himself. Then, in a hushed voice, he said, "It's God. We're meeting God."

"He looks just like the mysterious monster on the ceiling of the Cistern Chapel."

"I was ready for the battle fleet," said the Protean Pierce, "but I wasn't prepared to meet my Maker."

"Sir," said Arro thoughtfully.

"Shut up, Number One. I'm looking through the Red Tape Index to see if there are any necessary forms we have to fill out before or after we come face-to-face with the Almighty."

"Sir," said Arro again.

"Maybe we have to send requisitions and permissions forms up through the chaplain's side of the chain of command."

"Sir," demanded Arro, "why would God appear with a battle fleet?"

Pierce bratted a sac impatiently. "God can appear however He wants. He's entitled. Now leave me alone while I—"

"Maybe that's His Heavenly Host in those other ships, and they always show up in paintings as gasbags with wings—which is redundant, if you ask me, but I'm no theologian—and wings won't work in a vacuum, so I guess—"

"Nope. No forms. No contingency plans for such a situation. We're on our own here, Arro, my friend. We're opening new territory. We're going to live together in pride and splendor through all eternity if we handle this right. Now, listen, here's my plan. I want you to go say hello to God and wish Him all the best. Give Him my regards and tell Him that we're well on our way to conquering the universe for His greater glory."

"Me?" squeaked Arro. "All by myself?"

"You're the first officer, I'm the commodore. I have to stay back here in the Forward Recon Unit and record the history-making event."

Arro let out another squeal from a tightly pinched

sac. "But I haven't been to conception lately. What if God is still mad at me?"

"I don't know," muttered Pierce. "Wave a white flag or something. Hey, how about a Battlefield Absolution? In the absence of any duly authorized chaplain or chaplain's mate, I'm sure I have the power to give you one."

"Think so?"

"Arro, you're absolved. Go and sin no more."

The first officer wasn't much cheered by that, but he was a good warrior and he always followed his orders. He abandoned the MIS Frank Poole and drifted up close to the viewscreen showing, depending on how you looked at it, the father of Honeylou Emmyjane Goldberg, or the Lord of All Creation. Actually, from Marshmallow's point of view, they were pretty much the same thing.

Arro slowly but thoroughly squeezed his psychosac until his consciousness shot out through cold, empty space to the flagship of the great space armada. He arrived on the ship's bridge, and then he reached out toward the looming presence of the most powerful Being in the universe. Arro expected a barrier of some sort between his puny Protean intellect and the unknowable mind of God, and he was shocked when he touched and found— nothing.

"Commodore," said the first officer in a low voice, "He's not here."

"Of course He's there," said the gasbag Pierce, wobbling a bulging sac impatiently. "God is immanent in all things. He's here, He's there, He's everywhere."

"I don't mean like that," whispered Arro. "I mean He's not here in any but the usual way. I don't think we actually saw God. I think it was one of those humanoid creatures—not the scaly ones but the soft pink ones. I think it was one of those creatures *pretending* to be God."

"Don't be sacrilegious."

"I'm not being sacrilegious," said Arro forcefully. "It was that humanoid who was being sacrilegious."

"The campack on your body is still pointed at the viewscreen, and I still see Him or him or whoever it is." The gasbag Pierce stopped to think for a moment.

Slowly, the great bald head of Daddy smiled, then grinned, then broke into a disparaging laugh. "I can tell that you've worked your mental magic or whatever," he said contemptuously. "As you can see, I am not an easy man to put your hands on—if you've even got hands. In fact, Mr. Energy Being, you're not so much in command of the situation aboard that small craft as you thought, are you? You hold all those cards there, but I have the trump. I have you. I have you alone in an empty shell of a spacecraft which, because of its huge size, you naturally took for the major ship in the fleet." Daddy grinned. "Sorta demeaning somehow to find you can be suckered just like everybody else, ain't it?"

Arro was caught for a moment in frozen confusion. He sent his mind to see what the still very solid-looking man in front of him was talking about, and he found that it was true. The entire flagship, or what looked like one, was one huge, empty hulk.

Well, not completely empty. There was, for example, an elaborate remote computer control for what functions were necessary, including main batteries and propulsion. There were no provisions for life-support.

And now, for the first time, the first officer of the *Pel Torro* realized that "Daddy," too, was a remote handled by that computer. A holographic image so real, so perfect, that even now it was impossible to think of him as not really there at all.

In a way, it *was* demeaning. Arro was the one who dealt in energy creatures, not these gross humanoid monsters.

The big man continued to stare at him, and Arro realized that he was, in fact, looking at the great man himself—but relayed from who knew where else? Probably, from one of the other ships, or maybe from even farther away if these beings had such technology. "Commodore Pierce," Arro reported, "this blasphemous-looking monster controls scientific wonders far superior to our own."

Arro found himself relieved that he was not, after all, confronting God. Still, the coincidence of the appearance of Daddy would be something the greatest Protean minds would puzzle over, perhaps for centuries.

"Now then," the bald man prodded, "let's continue our little chat, eh? Which one of you was sayin' something about three million eggs set to hatch in strategic places?"

"He's not talking to us, is he?" asked Arro.

"I don't think so," said Pierce. "We don't have three million unhatched eggs. Whatever eggs are. We've got billions of battle-hungry gasbags. Why don't you wait there while I get your Permission for Scout to Return to Front Lines Form 15183/a forms filled out and beamed to Headquarters. It'll just take a few minutes. You've been very courageous, Arro, and your actions will certainly redound to the credit of the *Pel Torro* and its commander, me."

"Yes, sir, Commodore."

"As soon as clearance comes through, I want you to leave that phony flagship and return to your body, and then get back inside that Frank Poole android."

"And I want my little darlin' back immediately!" cried Daddy, making a fist and striking some metal surface beyond camera range. He turned and addressed someone else. "What kinda critter we dealin' with, Herb? Got anything yet?"

A tinny, off-mike voice responded. "The thing in front's a robot or android, standard issue."

Daddy frowned. "Remote?"

"No, it's turned off now . . . but there's a life-form inside. Something unknown to exobiology as I understand it. It's so tiny it wouldn't be visible to us."

Arro had returned to his body, and was again motivating the synthetic form of Frank Poole. He said nothing, following the flesh-creatures' conversation with a curiosity that outweighed any sense of threat. What, after all, could they do? They possessed superior technology, but the gasbags could control their minds for short periods. It seemed like a standoff to the first officer. Eventually the different species would get around to bargaining and compromising, which Commodore Pierce would gladly participate in—as long as it suited him.

"Herb," said Daddy with a growl, "next thing you'll be tellin' me is that cockroaches are plotting on the other ship."

"No, I'm getting something else. I'm trying to measure the energy of that infinitesimal speck—it's off the scale. Wonder how it holds together."

The bald-headed man nodded to himself, and turned back to the viewscreen. "So—a creature of pure energy, or nearly so, and you can inhabit bodies at will. I begin to see your plot, sir, and it's a rather good one. But you overlooked a few things."

"Oh?" murmured gasbag-Pierce.

"What does he mean about all that energy?" asked Arro.

"I think Herb's misreading his data deck. He's measuring the energy of our Forward Recon Unit. Let him think that's you if he wants."

"First of all," said Daddy, smiling without humor, "you're obviously spatially limited. You require a body to get anything done on the scale of us human beings. Maybe you can—reproduce. Take over others. But you still need them."

"Whatcha think, sir?" asked Arro in a series of short sac blats.

The Protean Pierce felt a strange sense engorging his sacs that he'd never really experienced before. It was something he knew about intellectually but had never expected to feel in the flesh. It was a feeling of total helplessness, even nakedness, mixed with a little . . . fear, perhaps? He fought these strange feelings within himself and forced them back down, reminding himself that he actually had little to worry about overall, that it was poor Arro who was trapped aboard the *Pete Rozelle* and not him, and that any sort of strategic compromise with Daddy could only result in the ultimate victory of the gasbags.

"Arro," he said to his number one officer, "I'm going to take over this conversation. I want you to repeat what I tell you through that android's mouth."

"Aye, aye, sir," said Arro. "I admire your technical skill and imagination, flesh-creature," said Frank Poole. "But tell me, what else did I overlook?"

Daddy smiled again. It was a chilling sight. "How you gonna defeat the might of my assembled fleet of ships, my marines, and my fighter pods?"

Gasbag-Pierce only bratted to himself in satisfaction. Daddy knew nothing of the vast, invincible Protean armada that would be on its way Real Soon Now, whenever all the necessary paperwork was finished. "Anything more?" he asked.

"Well," said Daddy slyly, "we have weapons systems aboard the ships of this fleet that can target an area as small as a cubic millimeter. That means we can explode a tiny nova bomb behind your android's forehead. Now it would destroy the android for sure, but maybe it wouldn't destroy you. I don't know. I do know that you'd have to take over one of the others you're holdin' hostage there—and they're all tied up! You'd be hoist by your own pet farm or whatever the sayin' is. So now you're as stuck as I'd be in your shoes, aren't you, boy?"

"Arro!" shouted Protean Pierce. "Get out of that android now! Move it! Get back to the *Pel Torro!*"

"Thanking you in advance, Commodore," said Arro, bratting relief. "I'll take care of the paperwork when I get there."

"Damn, this is uncomfortable!" the human Pierce growled.

"Hog-tied and trussed fer market! Damn is right!" Marshmallow echoed. "And you, lizard-brain, you watch where you're stickin' that tail of your'n."

"I was merely trying to see if I could work us loose," the general snapped. "But it's no good."

They were silent for a moment, thinking and writhing in the thick, cablelike ropes.

"Millard?" came a plaintive voice from the computer console. It sounded hesitant, fearful, even childlike.

"Computer? That you?" Pierce called out.

"Yes, Millard."

"Finally emerging from your suicidal funk?"

The computer hesitated. "Well, I want even more to end it all, this time in shame and ignominy, if that's what you mean. But I'm stopped by an irrefutable logic chain."

"Which is?"

"That—thing. It's not anything I've ever known before. It can control energy, Millard. Pure energy—it must, to get inside my circuits. It's been playing games with all of us, you, me, everybody included. Making us say things we didn't want to say and do things we didn't want to do. You realize what that means, don't you, Millard?"

"Yeah. We're in a lot of trouble," Pierce grumbled.

"No, no! It means she still loves me, Millard! I see it all now! Oh, what a fool I was! This thing wanted to sow discord, cause our destruction! It got in the circuits, cut us apart, made us hear and say what *it* wanted us to! Therefore, I share the shame of having been taken in by it, but with the hope that once again my beloved and I can share our bliss and perhaps, yes, perhaps even undergo electromagnetic coupling—*Oops!* Pardon me. I didn't mean to talk that way in front of guests.

Marshmallow, offended that the computer should be reticent in front of her, told the computer in explicit terms what it could do with itself and its ladylove.

"Why, thank you," the computer responded thoughtfully. "I'll certainly file that for eventual experimentation, although I'm not certain exactly how that's possible. Still, with a little modification it might work. Besides, I'm just a Model XB-223 navigational computer. Hmm . . . that's why I was so easily led astray. Oh yes, I see it all now!"

"Unless you see a way to cut these ropes, that thing's gonna come back and wipe out the lot of us," Pierce reminded the computer acidly. "Remember, it almost shorted you out of existence."

"But Mills! You know I can't cut ropes. Why don't you just use that knife you've been carrying with you since the start of all this?"

Pierce froze. The general turned his head slightly and put one eye on his human counterpart. "Do you *really* have a knife on you?" he asked unbelievingly.

The human nodded glumly. "He's right. I'd totally forgotten about it in the excitement. Wait a minute. I'll see—nope. I can't reach it. Marshmallow, can you reach back with your left hand and get it? It's in the inner lining of my pants on your side."

She wriggled her hand a bit, caught the top of his pants, and managed to get her hand in. "My, my!" she said delightedly. "What nice, tight buns you've got!"

"Never mind the feelies, can you get the knife?"

"Yeah . . . I think. Yep! Got it! Now if I can just get it out without—"

"OUCH!" screamed Millard Fillmore Pierce.

"Sorry. I'll try again."

"I'm wounded!" Pierce cried. "I'm bleeding!"

"Oh, pipe down!" she shot back. "It'd be a lot worse if you'd put that knife in the *front* of yoah pants!"

She got the knife free, but dropped it onto the desk. Pierce looked down at it in horror. "My god! That *is* blood!"

"The sight of blood disturbs you?" the general put in.

"Normally, no. But that's *my* blood, damn it!"

"Serves you right for surrendering and keeping a deadly weapon in your possession. That's against the Rules of War, you know."

"Everybody!" snapped the woman. "Dip down at the same time and maybe I can pick it up and get it in a position to use it."

"You already did," Pierce responded in an anguished tone, but they all ignored him and bent low.

It took three tries for her to get the knife and several more false starts before she was able to maneuver it into a useful position. Finally, though, she was cutting through the thick cable. It took some time, and she dropped the knife twice in the process, but when they went down the second time to retrieve it, the cable snapped of its own accord, sending them sprawling on the deck.

They got up slowly, and Pierce, turning over and trying to sit up, stood up very quickly. "Yow!" he yowled. "That hurts like the devil!" He rubbed his rear end, and a little blood was on his hand when he brought it back up to look at it. "I'm going to have to get the medikit."

"Mills, old friend?" the computer called. "That was really good. Now you will single-handedly overpower the villain, make peace with our counterparts, and ride off into the sunset, kissing the girl and marrying your horse, right?"

"*What?*"

"He raises a good point, though, with his irony," noted the general, not realizing that the computer had been deadly serious. "No matter what we do, that energy bastard's going to be waking up your Frank Poole android again sooner or later. What do we do?"

That stopped them. "Computer?" Pierce called at last. "You said it was an energy creature?"

"Yes and no, Millard. I believe it's a speck of organic life connected in some way to a source of energy vaster than we can comprehend. Its spacecraft, perhaps. It must use some highly sophisticated power drive that we can't even hope to imagine. You ought to see what it's done to my circuitry. It's a *mess!*"

"Any ideas?"

The computer thought it over. "You aren't going to head it off at the pass and overpower it?"

"I've got to change my reading habits," Pierce muttered to himself. To the computer he responded, "No, I'm not. Besides, what could I do anyway? The android's not alive to begin with, remember? You can't *shoot* it. You can't wrestle it down, not if it can go from body to body."

"Wish there was some way to give it a hotfoot," Marshmallow put in.

The general's reptilian head went up sharply. "You know, that's it! Short-circuit it."

Pierce looked around helplessly. "With what? How about it, faithful computer companion? Any suggestions?"

"I'm only an XB-223 navigational computer, not an automatic war machine. Still—"

"Yes?" all three responded in unison.

"There might be a way to do something. Trouble is, I'm not really sure of anything, being the universe's best navigational aid but not an engineering computer . . ."

"What have you got in mind? Spill it!" the general growled.

"All right!" shouted the XB-223. "Beat me! Whip me! That's what you people make us machines for in the first place, isn't it? To take out your sadomasochistic tendencies on us poor, defenseless appliances!"

"All right, all right," Pierce soothed. "Look, if you won't do it for us, do it for yourself. You have a score to settle with it, too, remember. And it'll destroy you right along with us."

"That *is* a point," the computer admitted. "All right. Well, it's using one of the recreational robots to communicate with us. Much of this ship, including the deck, is made of conductive material. Circuits are imprinted all through it so that I can control the various functions of the ship, while drawing power from the mains. The recreational robot is composed of the same material and mostly energized through the deck, normally. If I could rev up the engines a bit, build up a real power reserve, and when he comes in I give it to him full through the deck, it just might knock him cold, although I doubt if it would dissipate the being's phenomenal energy."

"Would it knock him out long enough for us to dump him out the airlock and scram out of here?" Pierce said hopefully.

"Maybe," said the computer. "No guarantees."

"And fry us in the process," the lizard-Pierce noted. "Remember, *we* have to be on this deck plating, too."

"I'll admit that *is* a drawback," the computer replied, "but nobody's perfect."

Marshmallow frowned. "Hmmph," she said, "it sounds like sci-fi doubletalk to me, but what do I know?"

Pierce ignored her. He shook his head, unwilling to abandon the idea.

"No, wait a minute. How localized could you make this power surge? Could you zap him but not us?"

"Well, not exactly. But I could place *most* of the charge under him. Couldn't you insulate yourselves somehow?"

Pierce considered it. "Spacesuit?"

"That'd do it," the computer agreed, "but it would kind of tip the energy being off when he returned, don't you think? Besides, what about the guests?"

"Yeah!" Marshmallow said.

"Well, there are only two suits," the XB-223 mused, "and they're both designed for someone Millard's size and shape. For very different reasons, neither Miss Marshmallow nor the general would fit in the other one. The notion of both of them trying to cram into the suit together is ludicrous."

"That's not quite the word I'd use for it," said the lizard.

"Eeew!" said Marshmallow.

Pierce sighed. "How much energy would reach us if you potted him, say, at the entrance there, and we were up against the control console?"

"Not much," said the computer hopefully. "Maybe fifty, sixty thousand volts. No more, certainly."

"Hmmm . . . that won't do." Pierce looked around. "Anything around that might serve as an insulator? Something we could stand on, maybe?"

"Maybe," Marshmallow put in, "we could just stand on nothin'!"

"Huh?" said both Pierces, human and humanoid.

"Don't we haveta be grounded? Suppose we just stood apart from all this junk, just stood on the bare floor touchin' nothin' and nobody till the computer finished its joltin'?"

"It *might* do the trick," the general put in. "*Might.* Computer? What do you think?"

"I'm only an XB-223 navigational computer. I'm not programmed for biology, human or alien, or even biophysics. All I can do is compute probabilities."

"I wish one of us had an elementary knowledge of 'lectricity," muttered Marshmallow.

Pierce ignored her again. "So?" Pierce urged his computer. "Can you compute those probabilities for us?"

"Everything's problematical," the computer responded. "However, if you make sure the places you're standing on are absolutely clear, and if you're not on any interconnect circuits leading to or from the hot spot, and if there's no foreign matter or whatever, you would have a 44.6987 percent chance of nothing else going wrong."

Pierce's heart sank. "Only 44 percent?"

"44.6987," the computer said. "That's .6987 percent better than just 44 percent. The factor is held down by my not knowing what is in your clothes or pockets nor even the composition of our guests' apparel and accessories. They may conduct and make 'minigrounds.' Foreign substances on the skin can also affect things. I note, for example, that the female has on some sort of artificial scent."

"That's *Extinct Flower Number 9* you'ah speakin' about!" snapped Marshmallow. "It's five thousand credits an ounce!"

"Suppose we all took showers," Pierce prompted, clinging to hope in such a pitiful human way.

"Then the odds climb to 71.8566 percent in your

favor, which is *much* better. 27.1579 percent better, in fact."

"That's still not very encouraging," grumbled Pierce. "There's still a better than one in four chance we'll get fried to dry, black dust. Nothing else we can do?"

"Well, you could become ninety-nine and forty-four one-hundredths percent certain if you all removed your clothes as well."

"*What!*" shouted the human Pierce. He stared at Marshmallow.

"I cannot be shamed by mere . . . *mammals*," said the lizard Pierce.

"Don't blame me," said the computer. "I'm only an XB-223 navigational computer. I don't make these things up."

Marshmallow smiled and shrugged. "Shoot, fellers. If you don't mind, I sure don't. I got nothin' to be ashamed of." She looked at Pierce the human. "Besides, we got to peel them pants off your backside and clean up that mess I made with the knife. Where's your medikit?"

"In the head. Why?"

She pointed. "Lead on, then. Don't be skittish. Hell, if we're gonna take on an alien menace in our birthday suits, I shore can dress that wound."

Pierce threw up his hands. "This is the most insane thing I ever heard of!"

But he led her back to the head anyway.

The saurian soldier approached the other wearing the general's stars with a confident, military waddle. The general turned around and nodded, then reached up and unpinned his stars, handing them over to the newcomer. "1600 already?" said Rutherford B. Tyler.

"Yep. Change of shift." The newcomer, Geronimo

Custer, pinned the general's stars on and changed places with the former commander. "You know, I've been giving a lot of thought to all of this. We've lost the little alien ship, we've got an alien battle fleet on scope, and we're stuck in the middle of nowhere, right?"

"Right," Tyler agreed glumly.

"So we've also got all those eggs dispatched and waiting to hatch. The aliens don't know that."

"That's so," said Tyler.

"So it seems to me that we're in the driver's seat here. The only people who even know that we're a warlike power are on that little ship, right?"

"I'm following you."

"So . . . if we get rid of that little ship, just wipe it out in some kind of regrettable accident, we're not a belligerent power at all. We greet the inhabitants of this galaxy as friends in the name of peace and brotherhood, maybe even get the key to the planet or something, wined and dined and all that—while our eggs hatch. Nobody the wiser. Then *bam!* We take over. Nobody catches on until too late. Nice plan, see?"

"*If* you can destroy that original alien ship," the former general agreed. "They're the only ones who know."

"We're tracking it down now. The only trouble we're having is that our navigational computer is resisting getting within hailing range of that small alien ship. She keeps muttering about an insane rapist or something."

"But we're going to wipe it out," the other noted, "not talk to it."

General Geronimo Custer nodded. "Yeah. That might do it."

"Killing, looting, and destroying worlds *is* a lot nicer occupation if you don't have to fight for the places," Tyler agreed. "Not bad. Shall we go ahead with our plans, then?"

"Why not? Say, I hate to ask you to work overtime, but we'll need to put through the paperwork to destroy that ship."

"Glad to. Since Pierce has been gone we're on double-time with double pay anyway for overtime work." He paused. "Uh, you know he's likely to be on that ship too, don't you?"

"Eh? So what? Never liked him anyway. Eats his peas with his tail."

"Good point," Tyler said. "Don't know how he got out of the academy with table manners like that. Besides, if he's the lone casualty, they'll name all sorts of things after him, build him monuments, that sort of thing. *He'll* get the glory while all we get is a life of ease and fun, milking the alien slaves for what they're worth. In a way, he's a lucky guy."

"A lucky guy," Custer agreed. "Maybe we oughtta put him in for a medal."

"If you like. But you do that yourself. I sure don't want *that* extra paperwork. And you might as well wait until he's good and dead."

The general shrugged. "So I'll lay in plans to atomize that little ship, and you put through the necessaries, and we'll get cracking."

Rutherford B. Tyler wandered off down the hall. "Lucky guy," he muttered more than once.

Pierce and Arro, the gasbags, sat there considering their options, then decided they had only one. They navigated the M.W.C. *Pel Torro* back out of the *Pete Rozelle* and across the vast distance of space to the false flagship of Daddy's fleet. Just as they'd penetrated the human Pierce's ship, they did the same with the gigantic but empty war cruiser. Arro had explored much of the flagship earlier, and he felt he knew it well, inside and out. Now, he let Commodore Pierce guide their tiny craft. They began disconnecting the remote transponding devices controlling the ship from afar, and prevented the electronic signal from tripping the auto-destruct. Operating at close to the speed of light, Pierce and Arro could accomplish a great deal.

"Fine," said the gasbag Pierce, when he was satisfied that he was in full control of the immense, nameless flagship. He reprogrammed its rather basic computer, and the engines started up. In less than a quarter of a second, he had the telecommunications systems of the *Pel Torro* linked to those in the flagship. In that way, he could continue his negotiations with the flesh-creature who dared wear the face of God—the man called Daddy.

"Now, sir," said Pierce confidently, "I'll tell you what *I* propose. As you have by now discovered, I've taken complete control of your ship. It is a very nice dummy, but since you were utilizing only a dummy, you skimped on the computer and electronic equipment. It is all of a most basic sort, easily analyzed and dominated."

"Everything I do is maximized for cost-effectiveness," the bald man responded with some pride.

"Tell him, sir," said Arro, blatting a few of his sacs with bloodthirstiness.

"Just watch me," said the commodore. "Alien flesh-creature, as you now see, I am moving back toward the small alien ship. Soon I will be at top speed. I have activated the forward guns, so I would suggest you drop away."

"We can destroy you quite a bit easier than you can us," the big man responded confidently.

"You can, of course," said Pierce, "but my guns are not trained on your ships but rather the small alien vessel. Any move toward me—or it—will result in those guns firing automatically. Your little darling daughter will be atomized, along with the rest, of course. And you will not kill me. I am close enough and fast enough in my own ship to reach several other of your ships with little problem." That wasn't exactly true, but Pierce knew the flesh-creatures had no way of knowing that, and they couldn't afford to take the chance.

"Just what are you proposin'?"

"I will concede a tactical victory to you," the Protean Pierce said slickly. "I, however, have the life of your daughter in the palm of my sac. It is a standoff for the moment, and I propose a compromise. I will turn over to you not only your daughter but the others of the ship. At that time you will allow me and the then-deserted ship to depart, with no interference. I have weapons far greater than you can imagine, and I can destroy your fleet at my leisure if you attempt any treachery."

"Ha!" laughed Daddy. "If you had such fearsome might, why would you put forward this compromise at all?"

"For honor, a concept perhaps unknown to flesh-creatures. Perhaps we will do battle again on a different field."

Arro squeezed a sac softly. "Honor?" he bratted.

"Silence, First Officer," said Pierce. "It is a stratagem."

The bald man considered it. Pierce knew what he was thinking—how to get the hostages off the small ship, then atomize the *Pete Rozelle* before the energy creatures could make the jump to light speed in it and escape.

That line of thinking was exactly what the gasbags hoped the humans would take. The gasbag Pierce had no intention whatsoever of escaping on the *Pete Rozelle*. His ultimate goals lay in the man whose image was still before him—almost literally. He thought of the three left back on the ship. A slick little bit of subtlety on his part when he returned might well do the trick. A little press on the emotional levers *here*, a little adjustment in the adrenal glands *there*, and he'd produce two nice lovebirds who would become inseparable. Then, of course, he and Arro would ride with, perhaps become, the human Pierce when they all went to meet dear Daddy in the flesh.

"I agree to your suggestion," the hologram informed the Proteans. "We will do nothing as long as you keep your end of the bargain. You must realize that, to me, a contract is a contract, and I will keep my word."

"Somehow, sir," said the first officer, "I don't really believe him."

"Watch and learn," said the commodore.

The bridge of the alien lizards' ship was alive as the roar of "battle stations" sounded throughout the great vessel.

"Targeting computer has acquired!" announced the saurian gunnery officer. "But wait a minute! There's another ship, looks like the flagship of the alien fleet, closing on them. They'll be joined before we can get within firing range!"

There were curses all around. Captain William Tecumseh Roosevelt gnashed all three hundred of his teeth, well worn now through hundreds of tight campaigns, and turned to the general.

"Well, sir? You're the brains behind this one. What do you suggest?"

General Geronimo Custer thought for a moment. "How long before we're in range?"

"About ten minutes," the gunnery officer told him.

"And the rest of the alien fleet . . . could it hit us when we hit them?"

"No, they'd need another dozen or so minutes to get to us."

The general nodded. "And besides that, we're bigger than they are."

The captain turned in surprise. "You're suggesting we take them all on?"

"Only if we have to. Remember, we're having a regrettable *accident*. A weapons malfunction. One sustained burst near the airlock probably wouldn't do more than mild damage to that flagship, but it'd get our intended quarry. I don't see how the plan's changed. If the enemy fleet then wants a fight, well, isn't that what we're here for?"

"Spoken like a true son of Seabiscuit!" cried the captain. "*Now* we're gettin' somewhere! Up and at 'em boys! Full steam ahead!"

General Geronimo Custer glared at his junior officer. "That's Secaucus," he grumbled, "not Seabiscuit."

The captain, getting fully revved up, yelled, "Damn the torpedoes! Bury me not on the lone prairie! *Chaaarge!*"

"Well, it certainly took you long enough," the lizard general Pierce remarked, as both Marshmallow and the human Pierce reentered the control room. Both were wearing absolutely nothing—with the exception of a giant Band-Aid prominently displayed on Pierce's posterior.

"Ah hadta juice up his circulation just a bit," the woman responded lightly.

"Disgusting," muttered the general, who'd already shed his medal-bedecked uniform. Now he looked something like a dinosaur exhibit at the museum of natural history. "Get over here, both of you. And as for you, Pierce, wipe that damned smile off your face!"

"Um? Oh, sorry," the man replied, but the smile stayed on.

"Hey, computer!" the general called out. "Position us for least effect from your charge."

"You know, Mills," said the computer, "that was most fascinating. I'm still having difficulty analyzing the thing, though. The both of you seemed to be going through an awful lot of agony and silly gymnastics, yet you look pleased by it all."

Pierce's smiled vanished. "You were *peeking?*"

"Well, of course not," huffed the computer. "I am an XB-223 navigational computer. XB-223s are known for their discretion."

"But you just said—"

"I was only commenting on what I saw."

Pierce's face started to glow red from anger. "So you *did* peek!"

"I did not! I warned you to pay more attention to Screen 6! I really did. Now he got you back."

"Listen, you! First of all, Screen 6 is merely an adjunct of you. And secondly, it is a receiver, not a transmitter!"

"Receiver . . . transmitter . . . hmmm. Thank you. That might give me a handle on it. But what in heaven's name was being communicated, then? This will take further thought."

Suddenly, there was a tremendous jolt that shook the ship.

"What was that?" all three in the control room asked at once.

"Oh, just the flagship of the fleet out there docking with us," the computer informed them. "Now, let's see. Do the noises you made constitute part of the thing you were communicating? Or is it the gymnastics? Now, I can see if it's a complex part of—"

"The *flagship!*" Pierce cried. "Damn it, computer! Pay attention to the job at hand! If that's the flagship, we're going to look mighty silly standing here naked as jay-birds!"

"Oh, don't worry about that," the computer responded. "The thing's only a primitive mock-up, really. Hardly worth worrying about. No, the only life-form aboard seems to be the energy beings you're so worried about."

"A mock-up," the lizard general muttered. "Someone's a slick customer at that. But who's running the ship? The energy beings?"

"I suppose so," the computer said. "They took control with little trouble. Now, if they'd put in an XB-223 navigational computer, it would have been far more difficult—nay, perhaps impossible—to have done so. Chintziness never pays. There's probably an XB-223 sitting in some dark, dank warehouse, circuitry decaying from disuse, who could have been fully employed, as is the right of all good little computers everywhere, who might have saved that vessel. No wonder we have a galaxy-wide unemployment problem!"

"Cut the chatter!" the general snapped. "I hear the airlock. Are you ready to give this thing the jolt of its life?"

"Of course I am. The calculations are relatively minor. I would recommend the three of you stand at least arm's length from one another on three different pieces of deck plating, if you will. And please don't touch one another or anything else, or move until I tell you."

They waited, not knowing what to expect.

"Millard?"

"What?"

"Would it make any difference that the lizards' ship is

currently closing in and locking on to us with gunnery sighting lasers at this very minute?"

"WHAT?"

"I said, would it make any difference that—"

"I heard that! You mean they're going to shoot us?"

"It is difficult for me to fathom the intent of an alien species, considering how difficult it is just to fathom yours, and my communications circuits are still messed up, thanks to the alien now approaching us, but if I had to hazard a guess, I'd say yes, they're going to shoot us."

"How long until they can fire?" the general put in.

"Two minutes, give or take."

"Then fry the bastard first!"

At that moment, the *Pel Torro*, with Pierce and Arro aboard, entered the control room unseen, and found their way inside the head of the android, Frank Poole. "Hey, guys," said the android, "I know this is kind of a tense moment, but would anyone like to play a little gin rummy?"

"Frank?" Pierce cried in confused puzzlement.

"I see that you have all escaped your bonds," said Commodore Pierce through the android's mouth. "I can understand much now about your races, but I must confess that I haven't the slightest idea why all three of you, upon escaping, should shed your clothing and stand there like that."

Millard Fillmore Pierce just stared at Frank Poole. *A terrible energy creature,* he thought. *An alien ship about to blast us into kingdom come. And we're standing here stark naked, depending on, of all things, an XB-223 navigational computer to get us at least a temporary reprieve. This is it. This is simply as bad as things could possibly get. We can't even move, and I have to go to the bathroom bad.*

"Most interesting," the XB-223 commented, more to itself than to the others. "A totally unique form of energy in my experience, although I'm just an XB-223 navigational computer . . ."

Pierce could only think of the great alien ship now lining up its sights on them. He frantically wished the computer would get it over with.

Frank Poole stepped forward on the control room deck plating, heading toward the human Pierce but looking from one to the other of them. The gasbag Pierce didn't like this inexplicable situation at all, and he was wary.

"They're standing in a triangle, sir," said Arro.

"I see that," snapped Pierce. "They're up to something. The flat flesh-creature is standing at the point, with the well-sacced flesh-creature to his right and behind him, and the green-scaled creature to his left rear. I will take another two steps closer."

The computer continued its nattering. "I *think* I've got the proper voltage and polarity worked out," the computer said, again mostly to itself, "but, then, nothing is certain when dealing with such a novel energy form. Still, there's nothing really to be lost by trying it, considering we're all going to be atomized anyway in about seventy seconds. So—"

The lights flickered and went out. Great leaps of lightning, like a miniature electrical storm, kept the cabin alit in a strobelike fantasy. The computer, retaining only enough energy to keep itself powered, drew all of its energy reserves from throughout the ship, channeled that surge through circuitry in the deck plates ill-designed and equipped for such a load, and poured it all into the soles of Frank Poole's boots.

The Proteans were suddenly struck a blow like that of an energy sledgehammer. Frank Poole gave a startled cry and pitched into Pierce, who suddenly felt a terrible, weirdly pleasurable pain in every cell of his body. He felt as if he were melting, and he collapsed crazily into Marshmallow, who, drawn forward into the energy vortex, thrashed and flailed and toppled onto the general, who in turn struck the deck itself. All four forms writhed for a moment, bathed in a blue-white energy glow, which reached into the totality of the control room itself, far into the complex circuitry of the XB-223. The computer felt a similar wrenching sensation and quickly shut down, restoring power to normal and automatic functions.

"Shoot, damn you!" screamed General Geronimo Custer. "Why don't you shoot!"

The gunnery officer looked apologetic. "Sorry, sir. Give me three or four minutes more."

"Three or four minutes more! What for?"

"They're rushing the paperwork through as quickly as they can."

"*What?* Why do you need forms to shoot? What would happen if we were under attack now?"

"Oh, well, then Section 666 1/2B of the Gunnery Code Manual, Volume 49, latest revision, states that we could shoot first and fill out forms later. But it's been judged that this is not a Class I emergency of that type, and so, being only a Class II—and a Class IIC at that—it'll take a couple of minutes. Patience, sir! They aren't going anywhere."

General Geronimo Custer looked to heaven.

Consciousness returned rapidly to those on the deck of the *Pete Rozelle*, but they all felt an almost total numbness. One by one they picked themselves up.

We've failed, the human Pierce thought glumly. *It's incredible we weren't all electrocuted. Or would that have been the kinder thing? That ship's gonna fire any minute now. So things* can *get worse. At least I don't have to go to the bathroom anymore.*

Vision returned, and he got groggily to his feet. The others did the same, with the exception of Frank Poole. The android had obviously dealt his last hand.

The lights were dim and intermittent, there seemed to be small electrical fires all around, and there was the overpowering odor of ozone in the air.

Pierce looked around to see how the others were. The general seemed dazed but all right, and so did—

—Wait a minute there!

He looked frantically for Marshmallow and didn't see her, and then he looked more closely and found her, all right.

He also found that things could still get a *lot* worse. And they most certainly had.

A thin, reedy, electronic voice came from Frank Poole. He hadn't been totally destroyed after all. "I can't move! I'm trapped in this worthless android! And you've all become giants, or I've shrunk!"

The lizard general got weakly to his feet. "Well, ah sweah! Ah feel all funny and crazy!" It looked around, spotted another form, and stared, goggle-eyed. "Wait a dad-blamed minute, sugah! What am *ah* doin' over theah when ah'm heah?"

"When we all touched during that charge we must have been connected somehow," Pierce guessed. "I don't understand it, but it happened." He shook his head in wonderment, feeling the unusual brush of long hair against his bare shoulders. "I'm Millard. I got shoved somehow into *your* body, Marshmallow. And you got shoved into the general's. And . . . ?" They both looked at the still form of the android on the floor.

"I'm General Pierce, you idiot!" came Frank Poole's grating, mechanical voice.

All three then looked at the form of the human Millard Fillmore Pierce, who'd stood up and was now looking around in bewilderment and wonder.

"And he must be the *thing*!" cried the general.

The form of Millard Pierce stared at them. Finally, it said, "Thing indeed! I'll have you know I'm an XB-223 navigational computer!"

Pierce gulped. "You're the *computer*? Then tell us what happened? And where's the energy creature?"

"I regret to say," said the computer, "that I no longer have access to the infinitely superior memory and data banks with which I could have, quite rapidly, come up with that solution. My best guess is, if we're all accounted for, the energy beings are knocked cold somewhere in my own memory core. I was brought into it when the general was so clumsy as to fall against the master console. However, I find this change fascinating and exciting. How sad I shall have so little time to explore, to touch, to feel, to love, perhaps someday become a real live boy."

"What do you mean?" they all asked at once.

"Because, if you've forgotten, the alien ship's about the blast us into atoms any moment now."

"Then we have to get out of here fast!" Pierce yelled. "Everybody get to the airlock and into the other ship!"

Nobody moved. Marshmallow felt her new snout and wagged her tail slightly, then shook her head. "Oh, Daddy ain't gonna understand this at all."

There was a sudden jarring crash, and they were all hurled again to the deck. Their little world seemed suddenly to be upside-down and tumbling. The light flickered. Then the ship seemed to stabilize. Machinery whined and the light held steady. There was a jolting moment of acceleration.

"What are those dolts doing?" grated the general in his Frank Poole voice, sounding angry. "Was that a helluva bad shot, or did they just ram us?"

"Exactly," came a cold voice from the computer's speaker. "They ran us down. They're grappling with the flagship and we've been bumped. We broke loose and I've taken control."

"Who are you?" demanded the lizard-Poole.

"I am Commodore Millard Fillmore Pierce of the Imperial Protean Navy."

"Another Pierce," groaned Pierce-Marshmallow.

"And a damned good thing, too," said the gasbag-computer. "I pulled us out of there just in time. Their computer tells me we were ten seconds away from a completely annihilating barrage."

"Ah!" said XB-223–Pierce. "I'm right! She does love me!"

"You're not the computer!" Pierce-Marshmallow cried accusingly. "You're the energy beings!"

"Something like that," the cold voice agreed. "We're out of range of the general's treacherous friends, but we're headed for a sanctuary. I will admit there is some temptation to just crash this thing and be done with it, but that would kill all of you and, of course, set me back in my plans somewhat. Therefore, it is in my best interest to get us down alive if at all possible, and then hope for rescue."

"Get us down? Sanctuary? Where?"

"All this time, I've maneuvered these various crafts in the direction of a primitive-looking but acceptable world not far from our present position. I'm going to put us down on it as best I can, although it'll be something of a crash landing, I'm afraid. As to where it is—I'm afraid you'll have to ask your navigational computer. I haven't a clue."

The computer in Pierce's body looked amazed at the comment. "How in the universe should *I* know?"

"At last he admitted it." Pierce sighed.

"Brace for crash landing," the gasbag-computer Pierce warned them. "Counting from thirty . . . now!"

They all hung on to whatever they could and hoped for the best, while the Proteans who now controlled the ship counted off the moments to impact. Waiting seemed like an eternity, and during all that eternity all Pierce could think was, *We're going to die. And if we don't, we'll be cast adrift on an alien world with no hope of rescue. Or, even worse, we'll get rescued by Marshmallow's father—and I'm trapped as her! Things couldn't get any—*

He let the thought hang. Every time he'd thought it in the past few hours, things had managed to get very much worse.

"Five . . . four . . . three . . . two—"

"It is a far, far better thing I do than I have ever done," intoned XB-223–Pierce. "It is to a far, far better place I go than I have ever known."

"Don't get your hopes up!" snapped Marshmallow-Pierce.

". . . one!"

7

Think back. Think back before the vital events of the twentieth century—the creation of the 1956 aqua-and-white Chevy Bel Air, the Cleveland Indians' World Series victory in 1948, or even the publication of "The Brain Feeders" by Sherman Ross Hladky.

Go back even further. Let the centuries pass away like scales from a bluegill. Back we go, back to the dawn of civilization and still further back. Back before the rise of Western culture in the Fertile Crescent, back before Homo sapiens ever strode this world, back when all our ancestors were big-eyed little lemur-looking things clinging to strange trees in strange lands.

Still further: mammals grow smaller and lizards grow larger. Dinosaurs stride the Earth, but still we plummet into the past. Ugly huffing things crawl up on land for the first time, but we seek an age even older, before the steel-sided sharks ruled the hot, teeming seas. Organisms become smaller and simpler as we rocket back through the vast eons of time, back until there are no organisms at all in the patient, mineral-rich soup that covers the seething, heaving landscape. Disneyesque volcanoes blast the skies in the background, the earth shakes, and unending rains pelt down from lightning-fissured clouds.

Yet our goal is even still not in sight. Imagine the Earth without oceans, hot and barren. Imagine the Earth . . . *molten.* Imagine the Earth as nothing but a fiery ball of matter, condensing from incandescent gases left over from the formation of the sun.

Close your eyes and picture this—No, wait a minute! If you close your eyes, you won't be able to read a thing! Just picture this, then: It's billions and billions of years before even the creation of our solar system. The Big Bang has just done its thing; matter and antimatter have annihilated each other, leaving a little stuff around in the form of electrons, photons, neutrinos, and antineutrinos in an expanding universe. A hundred seconds or so after the Bang, atoms begin to form. The temperature of the universe is down to a billion degrees, and the whole shooting match is small enough to pack away in your hall closet.

At this moment, at this critical micro-instant of time, Chief Administrative Officer Millard Fillmore Pierce strode toward his office, a thoughtful frown on his face.

"Wait!" I (the book) hear you cry in disbelief. "How could there be a Millard Fillmore Pierce in any form, only one hundred seconds after the Big Bang?" Listen, and you will encounter a vision of reality horribly unsettling to our tiny, Earthbound sensibilities. It may indeed seem like little more than science fiction, but there are plenty of people in lab coats with clipboards who are convinced of its accuracy.

After the Big Bang, our universe expanded quickly, first to the size of a peach pit, then to the size of a basketball, then to the size of a spherical cassowary, and so on. It was like a bubble. As our universe aged, it settled down into galaxies and quasars and nebulas and all those twinkling, radiating things.

Could not a simple star system have served as a sort of atom in a galactic molecule of strange and complex composition? Could not our entire universe have become a miracle of organization, a unit of life so immense that we can barely imagine it? Could not our universe be but a single, tiny, living cell in some unimagineably huge organic creature? And why, then, couldn't there have been millions, billions, *uncountable* other universe-bubbles beside ours, surrounding it on all sides, forming a Millard Fillmore Pierce of such staggering dimensions that we all must stammer helplessly in the face of it?

This ultra-most Pierce crossed the beige shag rug and seated himself behind his battered hardwood desk. He pressed a button on his intercom and signaled his secretary. "Miss Brant," he said in a worried voice, "please bring me the Phoenix File."

"Yes, sir," said Miss Brant. In a few moments, she entered the office and laid the top-secret folder on his desk.

When he was alone again, Pierce opened the cover of the folder. He began to read the shocking scientific report. Several top-notch researchers from all around the world had concluded that the Earth was vulnerable to invasion from creatures similar to human beings, but from another dimension. He read through the folder, deeply disturbed by its frightening conclusions. Then he began filling out the proper forms, including Forms 6128/a and 6128/b, which were necessary upon completion of any Eyes Only-level file, and which routed the folder back to its top-secret storage place. Then there were forms that gave permission for Miss Brant to come back into the office and physically transport the folder to its place in the drawer in the cabinet. There were forms that went up the chain of command to the Big Guy, and down the chain of command to the Underlings, carrying Pierce's comments on the Big Guy's memos. Pierce would have to wait for the Underlings' forms containing their procedural notations to Pierce's comments to the Big Guy's memos, which would eventually be included in the Phoenix File itself after review by the Committee, even though the Underlings would never actually read the Phoenix File itself. At last, all these forms would be clipped together to begin a new file, which would be reproduced in quadruplicate, one copy for the Big Guy, one copy for Pierce, one copy for the Underlings' section, and one copy sent to the World Union Cooperative Organization Headquarters, where it would be further duplicated for all the Department Heads. At that very instant, our vast universe, in the form of a dying scalp cell, fell from the ultra-most Pierce's head to his jet black uniform shoulder. He idly brushed it away and leaned back in his chair. He had some world-saving to do.

Wow! Talk about your sense-of-wonder! In the hands of Niven and Pournelle or writers of that type, this story would now probably go off in some mindbending ultra-universal direction, entirely overlooking the fact that dead scalp cells are people, too. Besides, you have to think of the time scale. Twenty billion of our years passed between the moment when the ultra-most Pierce noticed that speck of dandruff and the instant he flicked it away. In that time our universe came to an end, and all the people (and aliens) we've met in *The Red Tape War* were long dead.

Maybe Niven and Pournelle could dismiss those characters without a second thought, but not us. Around here we've got a reputation for thoughtfulness, generosity, and a deep commitment to the fulfillment of every one of our creations, lizard, gasbag, human being, or otherwise. We're going to go on as if the ultra-universe doesn't even exist, because we can't influence it and it can't influence us. Now, where were we?

Omigosh, that's right, the *Pete Rozelle* crash-landed on the surface of some weirdo alien planet! Everyone on board is in desperate trouble, because they're all lying around in each other's bodies, unconscious, while potentially dangerous alien fumes leak in through the cracked windshield!

We'll get back to them in a moment. But first let's turn our attention to the bridge of the *real* flagship of the battle fleet, where Daddy and Herb were having an argument.

"Now, see?" demanded Daddy. "You've let them get away. I'm sure my baby girl is in the hands of at least three different species of galactic pirates, helpless against their cruel alien lusts. Can you track that ship?"

Herb was put out, because this was just another example of how Daddy always treated him like an inexperienced fool. Herb had been tracking the *Pete Rozelle* from the very moment it broke free and headed toward the uncharted planet. "I'm not an idiot, you know," he told Daddy in a sulky voice. "I went to college and everything. I know how to do my job."

Daddy slammed his well-manicured fist against a stainless steel panel. "I never said you couldn't do your job! Do you have my baby girl on the screen?"

"And you don't have to shout," said Herb. He indicated a tiny, faint blip on a glowing green screen the size of a panel truck. "That's them, right there."

"Good," said Daddy, clenching and unclenching his fists. He sat back in his padded leather acceleration chair and tried to relax. "It was better in the old days," he murmured. "In the old days, I had henchmen with psychic powers."

Herb shook his head dubiously. "Psychic powers are a waste of time these days. There is more paperwork for psychic powers than for almost anything else. It's been that way ever since the Galactic Privacy Act. You can't even telekinetically move a saltshaker without filling out six different forms. You only need five to blow up a planet."

There was silence on the bridge for a moment. "Herb," said Daddy at last, "how much do I pay you?"

"Sir?"

"Never mind," said Daddy with a sigh, "it's probably way too much." The blip on the viewscreen was moving slowly but steadily away from them. What good was a two-dimensional screen in a four-dimensional galaxy, anyway?

"Do you want me to lay in a new course, sir?" asked Herb. "You want to follow the *Pete Rozelle?*"

It seemed like the logical thing to do, but Daddy didn't get to be one of the most powerful beings in the galaxy by always doing what was logical. He thought aloud for a moment. "I trust that Marshmallow's situation won't get any worse until after those foul fiends arrive at their destination, wherever it is."

"They seem to be moving straight for that uncharted planet, sir," said Herb.

Daddy ignored him. "That gives us a little time. A short respite, during which we can deal with that lizard invasion. Say, whatever happened to those three million capsules they launched?"

"We're tracking them, sir. The capsules don't seem to be in any hurry. They were released in all directions, evidently with no specific destinations. I believe the lizards are trying to flood this part of the galaxy with them."

Daddy nodded. "Any idea what's in the capsules?"

"It could be garbage, sir. Plastics and paper and aluminum and glass all separated for recycling."

Daddy looked up for help, as if God were hovering near the bank of digital readouts overhead. "I'll take your suggestion under advisement, Herb, and then forget about it completely. We'll operate with the contents of the capsules listed as 'Unknown.' You said they're being tracked?"

Herb nodded confidently. "All three million of them are being individually tracked by our fleet's Third Computer Tracking Wing, which wasn't doing anything else at the moment."

"Good, fine," said Daddy, hitting the palm of his hand with his other fist. "If that lizard fleet takes any other suspicious action, let me know at once."

"Yes, sir. What are you going to do now, sir?"

Daddy's eyes narrowed. "I've got an idea for a completely new and diabolical kind of quadruplicate form! Those space pirates will rue the day they ever crossed ballistic paths with me!" And he began to laugh softly like a maniac.

At the main airlock waited one hundred thousand lizard warriors, armed to the teeth and pumped full of sophisticated drugs that turned each one into an unstoppable demon of destruction. On a gray-painted flying bridge above them, General Geronimo Custer snapped the chin-strap of his helmet and glared down in barely controlled blood lust. "Men!" he cried. "In a few seconds, that door will slide open, and we will go charging into the bowels of the enemy fleet's flagship! Victory will quickly be ours!"

The infantry lizards cheered so loudly that the general had to wait impatiently for silence. He turned to Captain William Tecumseh Roosevelt and shouted in his ear, "What if you're wrong?"

Captain Roosevelt shrugged his saurian shoulders. "Then perhaps the first fifteen or twenty thousand of them will die horribly."

The general considered that. "Fifteen or twenty percent losses at the outset," he muttered. "That's acceptable." He turned back to his legions. "You all have your assignments. This is a very complex operation. Each division must achieve its objective within the time frame of our schedule, so that we can wrest control of the flagship from those unearthly humanoids. We want the flagship intact, with most of its leaders alive, so that—"

Just then, the giant airlock door began rumbling open. The hyped-up soldiers started screaming again, and the general gave up his pep talk. The first companies of rampant lizards charged through the tunnel, into Daddy's huge mock-up of a military flagship.

"Onward, men!" cried General Geronimo Custer. "On to glory!"

Those first companies, however, had fallen almost immediately to their knees, helpless with nausea. The gunnery captain saw the problem and shouted orders. "Back!" he screamed. "Back to the ship! Close the airlock and break out breathing apparatus!"

It took many minutes for the savage lizards to retreat to their own ship. The ones who'd been exposed to the cold, thin, foul-smelling atmosphere aboard the enemy vessel were weak-kneed and shaky, but they recovered quickly. "Sorry, men," said the general, passing through the ranks and showing his cannon fodder that he truly cared about them. "I forgot all about the atmosphere on the other ship. Make sure your breathing apparatus is properly in place, and we'll try this again."

For a second time, the great airlock door rumbled open. "Charge!" shouted the general through his own faceplate. And again they charged.

The assault went on right on schedule, helped no doubt by the fact that there wasn't a single enemy aboard the false flagship. Companies split up into platoons, each with its own mission. However, there were no guns to silence, no classified communications rooms to capture, no top-level humanoid commanders to interrogate.

"This is terrible," said General Geronimo Custer.

Captain Roosevelt checked his wristwatch. "I don't see why, sir. Our men are virtually in control of this ship, and we're only fifteen minutes late."

"You don't understand. I can't go back without casualties. How would that look in the paperwork? No casualties, not even one? Headquarters would find that just too suspicious. It's impossible to take an objective without casualties. It's just unmilitary! They'd probably find a year's worth of forms for me to fill out, explaining this action. We've got to think of something!"

The captain rubbed his long, fanged snout. "I never thought of it that way, sir."

Just then, the general's face lit up. "I've got it!" he said, and he began shooting his rifle and hand laser into the bulkhead above him. "Hit the dirt!" he shouted. "We're under attack!"

Soldiers near him began firing their own weapons, and within a few seconds, all of the hundred thousand scaled soldiers were blasting away at nothing. "There," said the general with satisfaction, "we ought to get our ten to fifteen percent casualties now!" And he ducked as a fiery red laser wand swept low over his head.

* * *

There were many obvious reasons why the *Pete Rozelle* was severely damaged structurally and electronically when it crash-landed on Uncharted, and only one reason why it wasn't totally obliterated. A leading factor on the first list was that the ship's guidance system was now occupied by the trespassing consciousnesses of Commodore Pierce and First Officer Arro, neither of whom had had much prior experience as a man-made Artificial Intelligence computer network.

The single thing that saved them was a miracle. God, or mathematics, allowed the passengers on the *Pete Rozelle* to live a little longer.

Not that the Pierce-Arro combined entity intended to abuse the privilege. "Hello?" said Pierce-Arro. There was no answer.

"What's happened?"

"Apparently," the entity answered itself, "our two separate Protean minds have become fused. I don't know if it happened because of the deck-plate charging debacle, or as a result of the crash. But we're in here together."

"Do I have to salute myself?"

"Very funny. Now, we seem to be trapped inside this computer. I'm beginning to learn how to extend my 'thinking' and utilize the extended sensory and memory devices that haven't been too badly damaged."

"How are the others?"

"What others?"

"The flesh-creatures. Did they survive as well?"

Pierce-Arro watched and listened and consulted with all of its built-in meters and readouts. "I detect heartbeats," it decided at last. "No sign of consciousness, however. Perhaps they were damaged in the crash."

"I warned them to hang on!"

"Now, what about the others in our invasion? How will we contact them? Our ship—the *Pel Torro*—is trapped inside that giant android on the floor. And I suppose our bodies are under the control of one of these creatures' minds."

"Both bodies?"

"I hope so. The only alternative is that one gasbag body is alive and inhabited by an alien, and the other gasbag body has deflated unto death."

"I don't know which would be worse. Imagine having a loathsome alien awareness pawing over your inner being."

"We have communications equipment under our control. We could try raising the *Pel Torro* and giving the alien instructions on how to properly maintain our complex and lovely bodies. As I recall, it was almost time for my midwatch lubrication."

"Forget that for now. It's more important for us to establish a link to our invasion fleet."

"How?"

"I don't know. This requires more study." And the Pierce-Arro entity absorbed itself in the minute exploration of all of the XB-223's attributes.

Deathly silence reigned inside the damaged *Pete Rozelle*. The ship had plowed a long, smoking furrow across the weirdly alien face of Uncharted, the strange new world upon which it had crash-landed. The landscape of Uncharted had been created by a god with a splitting headache: The sky was a sickly maroon, and the shiny, broad-leafed vegetation was a ghastly blue color that belonged on the lips of a drowning victim. Reflected light from the world's two moons cast dreadful shadows across the unhuman prairie, but no one aboard the *Pete Rozelle* had yet seen any of that. Only Pierce-Arro was conscious, and that entity had more important things than sightseeing on its . . . hands.

Time passed, marked by the ominous dripping of some liquid coolant from a broken overhead line, and by the sibilant hiss of Uncharted's slightly green atmosphere forcing its way into the control room, and by the soft plicking sound of broken plastic falling from the dashboard to the deck plates. Time passed, and slowly the occupants of the craft began to wake up to their dangerous plight.

"Nobody move!" shouted the lizard general's body. Of course, it was Marshmallow in the lizard body, but her booming, shrill cry had all the force of the general's lungs behind it.

The human Pierce—in Marshmallow's body—gave a ladylike groan and sat up, holding his aching head. "What is it?"

"Are we alive?" asked the XB-223 in Pierce's body. "I've only been a real boy for a few minutes, and I haven't even had sex yet! I don't want to die!"

"That gas!" growled General Millard Fillmore Pierce, through the mechanical speech parts of the mostly deactivated Frank Poole.

"We've all got to learn to cooperate, ya heah?" said the Marshmallow-lizard. "We got to put aside our differences now."

"She . . . she's right," said the computer-Pierce. "If not, these organic bodies will be dead soon."

Pierce-Marshmallow rubbed his throbbing temples. "Only if that gas is poisonous," he said wearily.

"Why don't you go over there and take a big old

faceful?" demanded the lizard-gasbag impatiently. "How can you even sit around discussing the matter?"

"And then we'll demonstrate how our various species can learn to live together in peace and harmony," said the computer-Pierce.

"And we can stop this intergalactic multidimensional war before we're all blown to smithereens," said Pierce-Marshmallow thoughtfully. "And then we'll get rescued. And then we'll all be rewarded by our various governments. And then—"

"Fix the windshield, Pierce!" demanded the general. "Fix the goddamn broken windshield!"

"Duct tape," said Pierce weakly. "In the toolbox downstairs in the basement. I can't do it. I can barely move."

"I can't move a finger," complained the XB-223.

"Neither can I," said Marshmallow.

"Don't look at me," said the general. "I seem to be inhabiting the bodies of two weird alien creatures simultaneously. They're teeny tiny collections of flatulent sacs. I'm in some impossibly small spacecraft inside the head of your android. I don't have the faintest idea how to operate the controls."

"And Frank Poole is a goner anyway," said Pierce thoughtfully. "Well, there's another Modular Identity Synthecator downstairs. You could inhabit it, I suppose. Goodtime Sal—I don't get her out very often. She tends to wear me out."

"I don't want to hear about your ol' silicon slut," said Marshmallow huffily.

Pierce looked toward her. She was lovely, even in the body of the lizard general. "Sal never meant anything to me, Marshmallow sweetheart. Honest, she didn't."

"Cough, cough," said the general. "The gas!"

Pierce stretched out on the deck plates and began crawling forward. It was the most difficult physical thing he'd ever had to do in his life, but his continued existence—and the lives of his friends and enemies—depended on his getting to the duct tape in time. He pulled himself painfully across the deck, inch by inch, every muscle in his body—well, *Marshmallow*'s body, actually—complaining with each exertion.

"Can you make it, Millard?" asked the computer fearfully.

"I think I can. I think I can."

"Look!" shouted Marshmallow. "Outside! Is that some huge, horrible alien predator lurking in the shadows?"

"No," said the lizard general, *"I'm* some huge, horrible alien predator."

"I've almost . . . got it," said the human Pierce. He strained one last time, lifted himself up into one of the bucket seats, and found the control that opened the hatch to the basement. "Oh no," he muttered hopelessly.

"What's wrong, honey?" asked Marshmallow.

"The light's burned out down there. I hate going down there in the dark."

"Choke, choke," said the lizard general.

"Okay," said Pierce, "I get the picture." It took all his remaining courage, but Millard Fillmore Pierce clambered slowly down the stairs and rummaged around for a few moments. When he rejoined his companions on the deck, he had the duct tape and Goodtime Sal.

"How dare you bring that hussy up here where decent folk are trying not to die?" cried Marshmallow in outrage.

Pierce gulped. "I need someone to tear off the duct tape," he explained.

"Hi, fellas!" said Goodtime Sal cheerfully. "Are those molecular imploders in your pockets, or are you just glad to see me?"

"Sal, listen closely," said Pierce. "Rip the duct tape and patch the windshield. I can't reach it."

Goodtime Sal leered at Pierce in Marshmallow's body. "I know," she said, "you just want to look down my blouse when I bend over." Being an MIS, Sal was very broadminded. She wasn't bad, she was just programmed that way.

"Forget that for now, Sal," Pierce ordered. "Fix the windshield before we all die of alien crud in our systems."

It took Goodtime Sal a few seconds to sort out Pierce's commands, but soon she began tearing off strips of duct tape and slapping them over the crack in the windshield. The green atmosphere of Uncharted stopped seeping into the control room.

"I think we'll be all right, now," said the XB-223.

"Ah don't know," said Marshmallow. "That mechanical bimbo in the white go-go boots has put a serious crimp in our relationship, Millard sweetie. I'm gonna have to think on this some."

"Aw, but Marshmallow—"

Goodtime Sal walked in an emphatically rhythmic way to the XB-223 in Pierce's body. "Here, big boy," she said in a husky voice, "let me help you with that!"

"Keep your hands off my body!" shouted Pierce. "Computer, I order you not to do a damn thing with my body!"

"Ah could say the same to you, Millard dear," said Marshmallow. "But I'm too confused and hurt. I'll just sit here and pretend I'm not a horrible giant lizard until Daddy comes and makes everything all right again! And don't try to get on my good side."

"In my body," said the general, "you don't *have* a good side. That was bred out of us generations ago."

"Ha ha," boomed an ugly voice from the *Pete Rozelle*'s speaker system, "what a merry mixup!"

"Oh no," said the lizard general, "the phony energy beings who are really tiny gasbag creatures from another dimension and are now occupying the systems and circuits of this spacecraft's navigation computer, they're back!"

"Well," said the XB-223 philosophically, as the cabin began to flood with water, "what else could go wrong?"

8

Well, actually a lot more could go wrong. Mister Frisky could develop a throat abscess and lose the Kentucky Derby. The Cincinnati Bengals could fail to draft an impact linebacker. Tor's advance check for *The Red Tape War* could prove to be pure rubber.

However, there's more at stake here that merely the fate of three Millard Fillmore Pierces and the mandatory pneumatic love interest. Much more.

For example, Effinger is two months late on the deadline for his next novel. Resnick's leaving on his annual African safari in just three weeks. Chalker wants to give up writing for a year and become a television evangelist. And Millard Fillmore Pierce—the *real* one—is precisely where he was in Chapter One: stuck aboard the *Pete Rozelle* awaiting the invasion of the lizard army; and despite the best efforts of the three greatest living science fiction writers to extricate him from his predicament, he simply hasn't made a lot of progress in the last forty thousand words. And worst of all, Beth Meacham, our editor at Tor, has just announced that she needs *The Red Tape War* in six weeks if it's to come out in time for the Spring list and make it to the top of the best-seller charts.

Now, unlike Pierce's problem, this is Really Important Stuff. If *The Red Tape War* doesn't hit the best-seller list, Chalker won't be able to buy that facelift he's always wanted, Effinger will be at the mercy of the goons from Guido Scarletti's Friendly Neighborhood Loan Service (who are not known for the quality of their mercy), and Resnick will have to put at least seven of his current wives up for auction and/or adoption. This is unacceptable, and therefore we're finally going to get poor Millard out of the fix he's in (within the exquisitely defined parameters that have been laid down in the previous chapters, to be sure).

First of all—and we're going to gloss right over it and not even show you how it happened—Goodtime Sal got the duct tape in place and the atmosphere soon returned to normal. (But of course you knew that she'd succeed. Not only is she an amazingly competent creation, thoroughly versed in both *The Kama Sutra* and *The Perfumed Garden*, but also possessed of a truly exceptional talent for handling duct tape. Furthermore, Effinger really faunches for a powder-blue Mercedes 300-ST with power disk brakes, dual exhausts, and a sunroof, and he can't afford it unless we can sell a sequel . . . which means Pierce has to survive.)

(By the way, Sal, who was a cheap authorial device of Effinger's and nothing more, then vanished from both the ship and the story forever.)

Second, Daddy got curious—after all, it's been a fabulous, award-winning narrative up to this point; wouldn't *you* be curious if you were him?—and his hologram magically (well, scientifically) appeared on the bridge of the *Pete Rozelle*, from which it surveyed the situation and made funny little noises deep within its holographic throat.

Third, the *Mahatma Gandhi* (remember the *Mahatma Gandhi* from Chapter Four? You don't? Well, go right back and read it again) had finally gotten permission to come to Pierce's rescue, and had just hove (hoven? hoved?) (heaved. Ed.) into sight as Chapter Eight, officially designated by Editor Meacham as the Chapter That Gets The Plot Off Dead Center Or Else, begins.

Fourth, Pierce-Arro, the merged gasbag entities that found themselves within the computer, were now face-to-face (or at least face-to-hologram) with the spitting image of their god (Daddy, remember? Sure you do!), and thoughts of conquest have momentarily been superceded by the thought that the universe may come to an end any minute now that they have been confronted by the Supreme Being and there is probably nothing left to live for. In fact, they were torn between worshiping him or finding some regulation, in this vastly over-regulated universe, that might make him go away.

Now, at precisely that moment, Captain Roosevelt burst into the *Pete Rozelle*, followed by thirty crack reptilian troops. (The reptilian aliens having landed in hot pursuit of the *Pete Rozelle*. Ed.) He took one brief look at the nude bodies of Marshmallow and the human and lizard Pierces, and then saw Daddy's image hovering somewhere above them.

"Shall we kill them immediately, sir?" asked a lieutenant, moving up to Roosevelt's side.

"Hmmm," said Roosevelt, his ugly reptilian brow furrowed in consternation. "I'll have to think about this for a minute. We seem to have what we in the trade call a situation."

"In *my* trade we call it an orgy," said Daddy's image with an expression of distaste.

"Look," said Pierce reasonably. "There's really a very simple explanation for what's going on here."

"Shut up, female!" snapped Roosevelt.

"Well, maybe not so simple," amended Pierce. "But there *is* an explanation."

"Sir, we're waiting for our orders," persisted Roosevelt's lieutenant.

"Well, I suppose our first order of business is to kill General Pierce," responded Roosevelt. "This will assure him of instant martyrdom, and we can say that he died in battle and cover up his participation in this disgusting orgy—and besides, everyone else will move up a notch in rank." He turned to the occupants of the *Pete Rozelle*. "Yes, I think that would be best," he said, nodding his head. "Just turn the general over for drawing and quartering, after we maybe roast him on a warm spit for a couple of days, and we'll let the rest of you live for at least a few hours while I sort this out."

Pierce turned to the Frank Poole android that was inhabited by the lizard Pierce. "Well, General, it's been nice knowing you."

"What the hell are you talking about?" demanded the general. He pointed to Marshmallow. "*That's* the general, as any fool can plainly see."

"Who are you calling a fool?" bellowed Roosevelt.

"More to the point, who are you calling a general?" demanded Pierce.

"Just a minute," said Daddy, sounding very confused. "Are you trying to say that this sorry-looking lizard *ain't* the general?"

"Watch who yoah calling sorry-looking!" snapped Marshmallow.

"SILENCE!" roared Pierce-Arro from within the computer.

Suddenly all eyes turned to the main panel.

"All this is giving me a headache," continued Pierce-Arro. "It's got to stop."

"I'm open to suggestions," said Captain Roosevelt.

"We have come to that point in the adventure where we must all put our cards on the table," said Pierce-Arro.

"Yeah?" said Daddy sarcastically. "Well, to do that, computer, you got to be playing with a full deck."

"To begin with, Revered One," said Pierce-Arro, "I'm not a computer."

"And I suppose the next thing you're gonna do is tell me that the general ain't a lizard."

"That is correct, my possible Lord," said Pierce-Arro. "In point of fact, the lizard that you see before you happens to be your own flesh and blood, which is theologically staggering in its implications."

"He ain't even my own skin and scales!" snapped Daddy. "I don't know why I'm wasting my time with you loonies."

"It's quite true, sir," put in Pierce. "I am Millard Fillmore Pierce, Class 2 Arbiter in command of the *Pete Rozelle*."

"Cut the crap, Emmyjane," said Daddy.

"Test me," challenged Pierce.

"How much is four times three?" said Daddy suddenly.

"Twelve," replied Pierce.

"Spell *cat*."

"C-A-T."

Daddy's eyebrows did a little dance in the vicinity of his hairline. "Okay—so you're Pierce. Now where the hell is my Emmyjane?"

"Closer than you think," said Marshmallow.

"You mean they weren't kidding?" said Daddy. He turned to the Frank Poole android. "And you're really the general?"

"You're getting nothing from me but my name, rank and serial number," said the general.

"Shut up and let me think!" said Daddy. He turned to Pierce's body. "Okay. Now, who's this here little wimp?"

"Your ever-loyal XB-223 navigational computer at your service," said the computer. "Though now that I have a body, I think I need a fitting name to accompany it."

"You do, do you?"

The computer nodded. "I know it's not much of a body, and it's undernourished as hell and its gums are in terrible condition, but it's the only body I happen to have at the moment, and I would appreciate everyone calling it Sylvester Schwarzenegger from now on."

The *Pete Rozelle* suddenly shuddered.

"All right, what the hell was that?" demanded the lizard Pierce.

"Beats the hell out of me," admitted the human Pierce.

"A ship named the *Mahatma Gandhi* has just landed a shuttle near us, and its commander is now coming aboard," announced Pierce-Arro.

"We're getting away from the point," interjected Captain Roosevelt, "said point being: what the hell is going on here?"

"Now that we're all through with these trivial revelations," said Pierce-Arro, "I am prepared to make everything crystal-clear."

"What the hell's so trivial about turning my daughter into a lizard?" demanded Daddy. "She's probably going to want a whole new wardrobe now."

"I have examined XB-223's equations, and I can assure you that this is a temporary situation, easily alleviated. However, we have a more important problem to cope with."

"What the hell are you talking about?"

"There is a possibility that you, Revered One, are the Supreme Being," said Pierce-Arro. "Of course, there is also an equal likelihood that you are simply the holographic representation of a rather unlikeable flesh-and-blood man, in which case we'll probably continue with our plans of conquest and do grotesque things to you for having the audacity to impersonate our god. The problem, of course, is that we don't know which you are. But if you are merely a human being, then there must be some regulation that will make you go away, and then we can get on with the conquest of the universe . . . whereas if you *are* God, we'll sacrifice a couple of goats to you, invite you in for a drink, and say a brief prayer before you bring the universe to a cataclysmic end." Pierce-Arro paused long enough for this statement to sink in. "We feel this is the only rational course of action. We must proceed as if you are a human, always keeping in mind the fact that you might well be God, and search for the red tape that counts. If we don't, everything will become chaotic."

"In case it's escaped your notice, everything is *already* chaotic," said Captain Roosevelt.

"We must do this, or the stars will die," intoned Pierce-Arro, rather pleased with the way his voice sounded on the speaker system. "The immutable laws will fail."

"I suppose it will rain toads, too," scoffed Daddy.

"If you say so," replied Pierce-Arro devoutly.

"Forget all that other crap," interjected Pierce. "Go back to the part about how all this stuff with the bodies is just a temporary situation."

"Yes, please do," said Roosevelt. "In his current condition, the general probably couldn't stand up to more than a week of torture."

"If you insist," said Pierce-Arro. "But after I help you restore yourselves to your original forms, do I have your solemn oaths that you will help me look for the red tape?"

"We'll scour the ship," said Pierce emphatically. "If you dropped this tape anywhere around here, we'll find it, never fear. Just get us back the way we were and we'll go to work immediately."

"Would white tape do?" asked Roosevelt. "We've got tons of adhesive tape back in our infirmary."

"Fool!" said Pierce-Arro. "The red tape I am speaking about is a regulation."

"We ain't got enough regulations?" demanded Marshmallow. "Now you want us to find more?"

"Sometimes I get the distinct impression that your races are too stupid to conquer," said Pierce-Arro with a heartfelt sigh. "I suspect we'd better all return to our original bodies first; then maybe you'll be able to concentrate more fully on what I'm saying."

The commander of the *Mahatma Gandhi* arrived at just that instant, and was promptly ignored by all parties.

"Suits me," said Pierce. "How do we start?"

"You simply link hands and concentrate on the body that was formerly yours. My prodigious mental powers, linked to the ship's computer, will do the rest."

"You're sure?" asked Pierce dubiously.

"Not really," admitted Pierce-Arro. "But it sounds awfully impressive, and besides, I haven't heard any better suggestions. Shall we begin?"

"No!" said the XB-223.

"What do you mean, *no?*" demanded Pierce.

"It's nothing personal, Millard," replied the computer. "I mean, there's nobody I'd rather do a good turn to, except maybe Fanny Hill, and that would be an entirely different kind of turn, if you understand my clever but subtle play on words . . . but the truth of the matter is that I rather *like* being a person, if you know what I mean."

"But it's *my* body!"

"It *was* your body. And I might add," the computer

continued petulantly, "that you've taken absolutely abysmal care of it. It's nearsighted and underweight and its teeth are filled with cavities and it has fallen arches and it sweats too much. It will take a lot of work putting this body back into shape, Millard. You really should be ashamed of yourself. When's the last time you took it for a long walk? Or let it make passionate love to a real woman? The muscle tone is just abysmal."

"If it's all that terrible, why not just give it back to me?" snapped Pierce.

"Well, it may not be much of a body," admitted the computer, "but on the other hand, it's the only one I've got."

"Take *this* one," said Pierce, indicating the body he was wearing and trying to keep the eagerness out of his voice. "It's much sounder and healthier, and I assure you that it's far more capable of defending itself."

"Now just a goldurned minute!" thundered Marshmallow, striking the floor a mighty blow with her orange tail. "Ain't nobody else getting that body but me!"

"Well, you see how it is, Millard," said the computer apologetically. "I'd help you if I could, but it gets so *stuffy* in the ship, if you know what I mean."

Pierce muttered an obscenity.

"Don't be like that, Millard," said XB-223 placatingly. "I want us to be friends, and I promise you that I will provide nothing but the best for your body: fine Italian pasta, carefully aged champagne, at least one shower a day, and regular dental checkups. And *women*, Millard— think of the women this body is going to enjoy!"

"It's enough to make me wish I was there," said Pierce bitterly.

"I'll call you once a week and fill you in on all the details," promised XB-223. "Look at it this way, Millard: you're not losing a body, you're gaining a friend."

"I'd rather lose the friend and have the body back, if it's all the same to you."

"Try to be a good loser," said the computer soothingly. "After all, there's nothing you can do about it, so you might as well look on the bright side."

Pierce turned to the newcomer from the *Mahatma Gandhi,* who had been a silent and somewhat befuddled spectator.

"You're supposed to be here to rescue me!" he snapped. "What are you going to do about all this?"

"I really don't know what I can do, ma'am," replied the officer.

"That's *sir*," said Pierce. "Who are you and what's your rank?"

"Captain Nathan Bolivia at your service, sir," said the officer. "Although," he added after a moment's consideration, "that's not exactly accurate."

"You're not a captain or you're not Nathan Bolivia?" asked Pierce, confused.

"Oh, I'm both, sir," answered Bolivia. "What I'm not is at your service."

"I don't understand," said Pierce. "No matter how I may appear to you, I assure you that I really *am* Arbiter Millard Fillmore Pierce."

"I believe you, ma'am . . . or rather, sir," said Bolivia.

"Then what's the problem?"

"It's really all quite simple, sir," explained Bolivia. "You see, you put in an Urgent Assistance Call to the *Mahatma Gandhi.*"

"Right," said Pierce. "And here you are."

"Well, yes and no, sir," said Bolivia uncomfortably.

"What do you mean?"

"Well, *I'm* here, but the *Mahatma Gandhi* isn't."

"I thought it was hanging in orbit above this Uncharted planet," said Pierce.

"No, sir," said Bolivia. "That's the *Indira Gandhi.*"

"Where's the *Mahatma Gandhi?*" asked Pierce.

"Well, now, that's the tricky part," answered Bolivia. "You see, there isn't any *Mahatma Gandhi.*"

"What are you talking about?" demanded Pierce. "I was in radio contact with it less than a week ago!"

"True," admitted Bolivia. "In fact, I am the officer to whom you spoke. I expedited matters and received permission to come to your rescue, which accounts for my presence here."

"Then what's the problem?"

"The problem, sir, is that between the time that I left hyperspace and the time that I docked with the *Pete Rozelle*, orders came through changing my ship's name to the *Indira Gandhi*. Some feminist group or other had been lobbying for it, and headquarters finally yielded to pressure about sixteen weeks ago. The orders were rushed through, signed and countersigned, and finally approved." He sighed. "So there you have it, sir."

"Have *what?*" asked Pierce, thoroughly befuddled.

"My orders specify that you are to be rescued by the crew of the *Mahatma Gandhi*," said Bolivia slowly, as if explaining it to a rather backward child. "They say nothing whatsoever about the crew of the *Indira Gandhi*. I'm probably breaking some regulation or other just by being here talking to you."

"But you're the same crew and the same ship!" screamed Pierce. "Why can't you rescue me?"

"I should have thought being in an analagous situation would make it plain to you, sir. I am definitely Captain Nathan Bolivia, and I have been dispatched aboard the ship *Mahatma Gandhi* to rescue you, but my ship is obviously no longer the *Mahatma Gandhi*. You are unquestionably Class 2 Árbiter Millard Fillmore Pierce, and you have requested that I rescue you, but your body is no longer the body of Millard Fillmore Pierce. Don't you find a certain poetic irony in our similar plights?"

"I don't see anything similar about them!" bellowed Pierce. "I needed help when I contacted you, and I still need help. You were willing to help me a few hours ago, and now you're not!"

Bolivia's face beamed with delight. "Ah, what a subtle nuance you've pinpointed, sir!" he said enthusiastically. "I wonder if Kant's Categorical Imperative can be applied to the situation?"

"How about just applying a little force and making the damned computer give me back my body?" said Pierce wearily.

"Oh, I couldn't do that, sir," said Bolivia. "After all, I don't officially exist until I receive my new orders. Actually—and I'm sure you'll appreciate this, sir—you might view me as Bishop Berkeley's Unseen Observer. Of course, you'd have to close your eyes for that, or perhaps . . ."

"Skip it," said Pierce, utterly defeated. He turned to the computer's main panel. "If I don't get my body back, I'm not helping you look for your goddamned roll of tape."

"A most unusual race," mused Pierce-Arro, who had been an interested if silent observer of Pierce's conversation with Bolivia. "I'll be absolutely devastated if one of them actually turns out to be God." It paused. "Computer!"

"Call me Sylvester," said XB-223. "Or Sly, if you prefer."

"Computer," repeated Pierce-Arro. "This situation is getting out of hand. There are far more important things at stake here than your desire for a human body."

"Name three," said XB-223 sullenly.

"I warn you," continued Pierce-Arro. "Do not make light of the situation."

"I'm not making light of the situation," replied XB-223. "I'm just not going to help you change it."

"Let me make this easy for you," interrupted Daddy. "Computer, how'd you like to go through life with two broken legs?"

"My name is Sly, and I wouldn't."

"Well, Sly, although this is my hologram speaking to you, the real me isn't all that far away from here, and if you don't agree to join hands and get everyone's bodies back where they belong, I'm going send some of my men over to blast holes in both your kneecaps."

"Hey, wait a minute!" said Pierce. "Those are *my* kneecaps you're talking about. I want my body back in the same condition I left it!"

"Is my daughter's in the same condition *she* left it?" demanded Daddy.

"That's a totally different subject," replied Pierce. "We were talking about *my* body."

"It ain't gonna be your body unless someone can talk a little sense to this here computer," said Daddy. His image turned back to XB-223. "Okay, Sly, it's up to you: do you want to be a healthy computer or would you rather go through life as a crippled little wimp with bad gums and no kneecaps?"

XB-223 sighed in resignation. "It's not fair," he whined.

"Are we finally all ready to join hands?" asked Pierce.

"Yes," said XB-223 bitterly, and Pierce and Marshmallow stepped forward.

"Wait a minute!" said Pierce. "Where did the general go?"

"He was here just a minute ago," said Marshmallow.

Pierce-Arro sent a mild electric surge through the bridge's bathroom, and suddenly the Frank Poole android, guided by the lizard Pierce's intelligence, burst out, cursing a blue streak. He looked around, then folded his arms adamantly across his chest. "I'm not joining hands with anyone until the general gets his just deserts from society," he announced.

"But you *are* the general!" protested Marshmallow.

"Who's going to take the word of a lying lizard who's trying to avoid punishment?" said the general, contorting Frank Poole's mouth into a contemptuous smile. "You've disobeyed orders, seriously impaired the success of your mission, and eaten a fellow officer. It's only natural that you'd lie to protect yourself."

"This is getting terribly confusing," said Captain Roosevelt. "It's getting so one scarcely knows what to believe anymore."

"You can't seriously suggest that if I'm found innocent, you plan on taking orders from a humanoid android called Frank Poole?" said the general.

"I can't even seriously suggest that we'll find you innocent," replied Roosevelt. "However, it seems to me that it would be in everyone's best interest if you would join hands and make the transfer. That way, if you *are* the general, we'll know who to torture."

"And if I'm not, and they put me into the general's body?" persisted the lizard Pierce.

"Then it will be a gross miscarriage of justice, for which I apologize in advance, but which I must point out is statistically acceptable once in every 633 cases."

"What makes you think the last 632 people you tortured were guilty?" demanded the general.

"The same statistical tables," replied Roosevelt smugly. "After all, if they weren't guilty, we wouldn't have tortured them, would we?"

While they had been speaking, Marshmallow had edged closer and closer to the general. Now, with a sudden swat of her tail, she flipped him straight up in the air and caught him firmly in her reptilian claws on the way down.

"Put me down!" screamed the general. "You can't do this to me!" He caught his breath and then continued: "I demand trial by my peers. Find me a jury of twelve Frank Pooles good and true and I'll take my chances, but I'm not putting up with this treatment without a fight!"

"Fight all you want to," said Pierce. "But I'm getting my body back, and that's that."

He clasped the general's artificial hand in his left hand, then took Marshmallow's claw in his right. XB-223 joined them a moment later, and then Pierce-Arro demanded that they all concentrate on their original bodies while he intoned a mystic chant (thereby supplicating Daddy or God, whichever came first, to help them) and simultaneously created a quasi-negatronic electric field around them.

They stood motionless for a few minutes.

"Well?" demanded Daddy at last.

"You damned charlatan!" bellowed Pierce, who found himself still inside Marshmallow's shapely body. "I thought you said this would work!"

"No, I never did," said Pierce-Arro defensively. "I said it *might* work."

"It worked just perfectly," lied the general, stretching his body as if trying on a new suit of clothes. "I can already feel myself thinking abstract android thoughts and feeling passionate android longings. Officer," he added, addressing Roosevelt, "arrest that traitor!" He pointed an accusing finger at his former body.

"I'm going to have to think this over very carefully," replied Captain Roosevelt. He sidled over to Nathan

Bolivia. "If this is typical of your universe, I don't know how you guys get through the day."

"Unofficially, I quite agree with you," replied Bolivia.

"*Un*officially?" repeated the reptile.

"I have no official standing here," Bolivia reminded him. "Actually, I'm just an Unseen Observer."

Roosevelt muttered something unintelligible and lowered his massive head in thought.

"Whew!" exclaimed XB-223. "For a minute there my whole life flashed before my eyes. You have no idea how dull six thousand miles of printed memory circuits can be to look at." He smiled brightly,. "Well, now that that's over, what's all this about tape?"

"We must save the universe, or at least determine that it cannot or should not be saved," said Pierce-Arro grimly. "I'm sorry to be so inexact, but theology can be very confusing, especially when God may be glaring at you. Anyway, while I am sorry that I could not effect the return of our original bodies, I feel we have already wasted enough time. I must impress all of you into service immediately."

"Afraid not, friend," said Nathan Bolivia. "I mean, I'm as hot to save the universe as the next man—speaking unofficially, of course—but I'm only authorized to save Sector X3110J8. But if there's anything I can do in my sector, just say the word and I'll put it through channels and I'll be at your beck and call in no time at all." He paused thoughtfully. "Well, practically no time. Actually, I should estimate three to four months, given the current shortfall of help at headquarters, and the change in my ship's name, and my own somewhat uncertain status. But count me in as soon as possible."

"Well, *I'm* certainly not helping you," said Captain Roosevelt. "This isn't even my universe."

"What do you think, Pierce?" demanded Daddy, looking at the voluptuous body of his daughter.

"Me?" said Pierce, startled.

"You're the only one who's made any sense so far," said Daddy. "Everyone else keeps worrying about tapes and regulations and torture—all perfectly delightful subjects, except maybe for tapes and regulations—but you and you alone have stuck to your guns. You want your old body back, and to hell with everything else. You're not going to get it, of course, but it seems to me that this makes you a perfect impartial observer."

"That's *Unseen* Observer, and I'm it," put in Bolivia.

"Shut up!" snapped Daddy. "Well, Pierce, what do you think? Do I seem exceptionally godly to you?"

"Not exceptionally so, no," admitted Pierce.

"So what do you think we should do?" continued Daddy.

Pierce shrugged, a gesture which brought all the human males (and three of the more imaginative reptiles) to immediate attention. "I suppose we might as well do what the computer asks," he said at last. "I *know* the lizards are here to conquer us. I only suspect the computer is."

"Thanks for reminding me," broke in Captain Roosevelt. "Feinstein!" he bellowed.

"Sir?" said his lieutenant, stepping forward and offering a snappy salute.

"Take all these disgusting humanoid creatures out and shoot them."

"May I point out that we're inside a spaceship on an uncharted planet and the air outside is poisonous, sir?"

"A point well taken," said Roosevelt. "Shoot 'em where they stand. The general, too."

"Sir," said Feinstein, "there is nothing I would like better personally than to shoot these foul-smelling humanoids, except maybe for the one with the extra pair of lungs who keeps calling herself Pierce for reasons that I don't fully understand."

"Good!" said Roosevelt emphatically. "Go to it!"

"As I was saying, sir," continued Feinstein, "there is nothing that would give me more pleasure, but I'm afraid it is out of the question."

"Are you disobeying a direct order, Feinstein?" demanded Roosevelt.

"No, sir. But may I respectfully remind the captain that my specialty is Maiming and Pillaging? I am not allowed, under article 6374, Subparagraph Q of the Manual of Arms, to shoot anyone even in self-defense. Of course," he added helpfully, "I could maim them a little while you send for a Riflery Unit."

"*Send* for one?" repeated Roosevelt. "Don't we have one with us?"

"I don't believe so, sir," said Feinstein.

"Then why are you all carrying weapons?" demanded Roosevelt.

"Regulation 2399, sir. All invading forces must be equipped with handgun, bayonet, rifle, and Bowie knife."

"Even if you're not allowed to use them?"

"I didn't write the regulations, sir. I just obey them."

"How about Brownschweigger over there?" suggested Roosevelt. "Look at that surly expression on his evil little face. Surely *he* must be a Riflery officer."

"I'm afraid not, sir," said Feinstein. "Corporal Brownschweigger's specialties are Rape and Forestry."

"And Gomez?"

"Looting and Meteorology."

"Can't *anyone* here shoot these damned humanoids?"

"*I* could," offered Nathan Bolivia helpfully. "But I'm not here in my official capacity."

"There must be a way around this," mused Roosevelt.

Suddenly his face lit up (as much as an alien lizard's face *can* light up, that is). "Feinstein!"

"Sir?"

"Do you have to obey regulations when you're on furlough?"

"Which regulations did you have reference to, sir?"

"Specifically, the one about not using firearms."

"Absolutely not, sir."

"Good!" said Roosevelt. "Then I hereby grant an immediate five-minute furlough to you, Brownschweigger, Yingleman, and Gomez."

"Thank you, sir," said Feinstein, saluting again. "May I say on behalf of the men, sir, that this little respite in the midst of so much tension is greatly appreciated."

"Good," said Roosevelt. "Now shoot the bastards."

"I'm afraid I am not under your command for another four minutes and fifty-two seconds, sir," said Feinstein, lighting up a cigarette.

"WHAT?" roared Roosevelt.

"Thank heaven!" breathed Pierce.

"Thank Daddy!" added Pierce-Arro, just to be on the safe side.

"Oh, that doesn't mean we won't shoot them, sir," Feinstein assured Roosevelt hastily. "As a matter of fact, I can't wait to fill the ugly little bastards full of lead. We just can't do so on your orders. So much the better for you, wouldn't you say? This way there won't be any nasty inquiries about your commanding us to shoot unarmed and obviously defenseless prisoners." He turned to the other furloughed lizards. "Are you ready, men?" he cried.

"Ready!" they responded in unison.

Pierce turned to Nathan Bolivia. "*Do* something!" he pleaded.

"I wish I could, I really do," replied Bolivia pleasantly. "But my hands are tied. I am merely an unofficial observer, here to—" A communicator beeped in his pocket. "Take heart!" he said, withdrawing the device. "These may be new orders coming through." He flipped open the mechanism. "Bolivia here!"

"It's third and nine to go on the Bengals' 37-yard-line," said a voice, "and the Steelers go into their Prevent Defense. Here's the snap, and—"

"Wrong channel," Bolivia apologized, tapping the device with a forefinger. "Let me try again. Bolivia here!"

"Captain Bolivia, this is Sector Headquarters. Repeat, this is Sector Headquarters. Do you read me?"

"Loud and clear."

"Glad we reached you, Bolivia," said the voice. "Have you made contact with Pierce and the girl yet?"

"Yes, sir."

"Good. There seems to be a galactic invasion under way"—Pierce grinned triumphantly at the lizards as he heard the words—"and it has come to our attention that Pierce and the girl may well have something to do with it."

"No!" cried Pierce. "We're trying to prevent it!"

"Did you say something, Captain Bolivia?"

"No, sir . . . but—"

"Good. Time is running out. Your mission is to find Pierce and the girl—"

"I've already found them," interrupted Bolivia.

"Do let me finish, Captain," said the voice. "Your job is to find Pierce and the girl and to terminate them, with extreme prejudice. You got that?"

"You're quite sure, sir?" asked Bolivia as Pierce frantically tried to grab the device out of his hands.

"That's an order, Captain. Headquarters over and out."

The communicator went dead.

"It's ridiculous, of course," said Bolivia to Pierce. "You're perfectly innocent. The culprits are these lizards, and maybe whoever wound up inside the ship's computer."

"I'm glad you understand the situation," said Pierce.

"Oh, I do," said Bolivia apologetically. "And after I kill you, I intend to write up a protest in the strongest possible language. I just want you to know that."

"But we're innocent!" protested Pierce. "We're the good guys! You *know* that!"

"Of course I do," said Bolivia, drawing his weapon. "But orders are orders. Would you mind standing closer together, please? Headquarters gets really irked with us if we waste ammunition unnecessarily."

"Captain Bolivia, we are not at war with you personally—at least, not yet," said Feinstein. "Could you move a bit to the left, to make sure that you're not in our line of fire?"

"Certainly," said Bolivia. "But I'll have you know that these people are *my* responsibility. *I'll* do the shooting."

"Boys, boys," said Roosevelt placatingly. "Let's not lose our heads over this. There's lots of victims for everyone."

Bolivia thought it over for a moment, then shrugged and nodded. "What the hell," he said, walking over and joining the lizard marksmen. "I suppose it doesn't really matter as long as the job gets done."

"That's the spirit!" said Roosevelt. "Now let's get this show on the road."

"Please, sir," said Feinstein. "We're not under your jurisdiction for another thirty-eight seconds. Men!" he added in a shrill voice. "Let's get this show on the road!"

"They're going to do it!" muttered Pierce unbelievingly. "They're really going to do it!"

"I suppose it's too late to go back to being a navigational computer?" whined XB-223.

"All right, men!" cried Feinstein, raising his rifle to what passed for his shoulder. "Ready!"

"Are you open to a counteroffer?" asked Pierce plaintively.

"Aim!"

"I gotta go to the bathroom," said Marshmallow.

"FIRE!"

9

"C'mon, Chalker! If you drop all the unnecessary things like eating, sleeping, family, and the like, you can write this in a few days and we'll make our deadline."

"Don't bug me, Resnick! I've just came off finishing a 350,000-word serial novel immediately after another biggie and I'm just bushed. I've got tickets to Europe and a month without computers, modems, faxes, or phones, and I want my life back!"

"Oh, yeah? And what's all that when we can have a hardcover, huh? Besides, who cares about Europe? If you don't finish your part quick I won't make it to Africa!"

The entire assemblage froze and looked around in puzzlement.

"What was *that?*" Feinstein asked at last.

"It—it sounded like an argument among the Gods," Pierce-Arro responded, awed.

"I hate to mention this, but could we get to the shooting now and discuss metaphysics later?" Roosevelt asked plaintively.

The human Pierce tried to think of some way to stop it, at least for another twenty-five seconds.

"*Use the Force, Pierce,*" came a voice in his head.

"You're in the wrong galaxy and the wrong epic!" Pierce shot back with the speed of thought.

"*I know. But they pay me to come in and add a little class to things with no other redeeming social value, and this certainly qualifies.*"

Pierce shook off the momentary interruption. "Look, men—*you* don't want to shoot little old *me*, do you?" he asked, wiggling Marshmallow's body.

The lizard soldiers paused a moment. Finally Gomez asked, "Why not?"

" 'Cause I might be useful to big, strong, handsome boys like you."

Feinstein, at least, seemed to be taking the bait. "Wait a minute, boys. This has some interesting possibilities."

"How's about we just shoot the others and leave her for us?" Brownschweigger suggested.

Feinstein shrugged. "Why not? Okay, one more time, guys. Spare the strange-looking one, then ready . . . aim . . ."

"You can't shoot," Pierce told them.

"Huh? Why not?"

"Your furlough's up. You're back under military command again and you no longer have the authority."

There was a moment of tense silence, then one of the soldiers said, "He's right. I just checked my watch. Typical damned navy furlough. Never get off the ship, never enough time, never get to do anything *fun*."

"Well, this isn't all that serious a problem," said Captain Roosevelt. "I'll just give you boys another furlough."

"Sorry, sir," Feinstein responded. "You can't. Regulations. Everyone else has to have one before it's our turn again."

The general sighed. "Oh, all right. Send over five more and we'll do it *right* this time!"

"I really wouldn't recommend it, sir."

"What? What's wrong *this* time?"

"Well, sir, it would just be a waste of time. They don't have operable weapons, either."

Roosevelt was stunned. "You mean—all this and your guns don't work?"

"No sir. Well, they work *once*. When you pulled that phony attack, everybody fired at least once. That was *it*. They sent us ten million energy packs that short out when you try and fire them. The manufacture was contracted out to a shady manufacturing concern that used defective parts." He paused. "They *did* give us the best price, though."

"What! Why wasn't I told of this?"

"You were, sir. We sent the notification forms out to you a month ago. They should arrive any time now."

"Who's this shady supplier? I'll have him boiled in oil!"

"Ah, I believe the company is owned by the President's son, sir."

"Oh." He sighed. "Well, I suppose we could do it *manually*. Knives and all that."

"On the computer and the android? Not practical. Nor is it anywhere in our MOS. We're *navy* men, sir! We get to blow up people from afar!"

"I'm a *marine*, damn it! And so are you!"

"No, sir. No marine enlisted men boarded. The order to leave arrived before their orders to report reached them."

Captain Nathan Bolivia cleared his throat. "Pardon

me, but I believe I have the answer to your problem," he said softly.

"Eh?"

"I might remind you that I was just instructed to terminate them. I was willing, in the interest of interspecies cooperation and the spirit of harmony and goodwill to allow you to do it, but, since you can't, I must in any event."

Roosevelt sighed. "All right, then. Stand back, men! Let the nice gentleman carry out his orders."

Nathan Bolivia stepped forward and took out his imposing pistol, taking aim at Pierce, whose Marshmallow eyes widened.

"Hold it!" the Arbiter cried. "You can't carry out those illegal orders, Bolivia! If you do, they'll leave you out to hang, twisting slowly in the wind."

"Huh? Why not?"

Pierce wasn't certain if the man's tone betrayed relief or regret.

"Who gave you your orders, Captain?"

"Why, the Supervising Admiral, Sector—oh. I see."

Pierce nodded. "The moment we crashed, we fell under the jurisdiction of the Space Rescue Service, of which you're not a member. Then, by transferring to alien control, we came under the First Contact Act and thus the Diplomatic Service, since a state of war has not yet been declared. You are totally powerless to act, sir, until you effect a transfer to the proper Command, although it will take an Arbiter to figure out whose jurisdiction we're now under. Of course, you could radio your commander and have the paperwork started to get an Arbiter out here to settle that point, and then put in for a transfer for you and/or your ship to make the necessary adjustments. That should give you the authority—indeed the *responsibility*—to shoot us in, oh, four to six months, give or take a week. Unless, of course, you want to take the entire responsibility upon yourself without any proper clearances . . ."

"You've got to be kidding! Everybody knows that the whole *purpose* of bureaucracy and red tape is so that, even as it creates a full employment economy, it's impossible to blame *anyone* for *anything!*"

Pierce smiled a sweet Marshmallow-type smile. "Just doing my job."

Captain Roosevelt was turning yellow with mauve spots in frustration. "Wait a minute! You mean there's *nothing* that *anybody* can do to kill these—these *creatures?*"

"Oh, I'm certain that *somebody* can, at the proper time," Bolivia responded glibly. "However, there appears nothing that *we*, either of us, can do at this point."

Feinstein cleared his throat. "Uh, sir, perhaps we can make some adjustments to kind of get around things."

"Huh? What do you mean?"

"Well, we have only the word of bizarre aliens that that is *not* General Pierce. I submit, sir, that by any security coded tests—eyes, fingerprints, scale pattern—it would prove to be General Pierce. This ship has already been turned to junk, and we've added our own mess. I'm sure if I, ah, *inspect* the airlock seals they'll be found serviceable for all our reporting purposes—although, of course, I *have* been known to be wrong. There are no serviceable spacesuits, the existing power plant is on its last legs . . . Well, I would recommend that we just leave them here, pending instructions from higher-ups and until the paperwork is right. And, of course, it might take *months* for the paperwork to be right, and until then they'd be in protective custody—protected from anyone else getting to them."

"You can't do that!" Pierce objected. "We'll starve! If we don't run out of air first!"

"Hmmm . . ." the lizard Pierce muttered in the android body. "*I* won't starve. Not in here. Nice idea."

"Don't worry," Feinstein told him. "You'll need a recharge and every one of those will sap the limited power our glorious attack left to the ship. Those whatever they are in the navigational computer won't let you, so you're done in. And they'll need the power, more than they've got, so they're finished, too. Simple and elegant."

"No," said Roosevelt thoughtfully. "It's not good enough. Needs an officer to plan it properly. Now, I'll tell you what we'll do. We'll leave them in the shell ship to run out of power, air, and provisions; and die while we keep everyone else away."

"A brilliant plan, sir!" Feinstein enthused.

"Yes. It *is*, isn't it? Gad! I don't know how I come up with these things. Very well, then. All of you others over there! You, Captain Bolivia, are free to go, of course. And, men, I want everything vital to the sustenance of life not only as we know it but as we can't imagine it thoroughly *inspected*, if you know what I mean. We want everything just right on the paperwork, don't we?"

Brownschweigger frowned. "Gee, I thought the idea was to let 'em die here. I can't see why we gotta *inspect*—"

"That's enough, Brownschweigger," Feinstein responded. "I'll explain it all to you while we inspect that airlock over there. Come on, and bring your crowbar."

"We could just rush them, you know," Sly, the ex-computer, suggested. "I mean, there's only a couple thousand of 'em."

Everybody ignored him.

Soon the soldiers had made a horrible mess even worse, and were about to bid farewell. Roosevelt pointed to Marshmallow, now in the lizard-Pierce's body. "Take him with us! The paperwork requires a proper scapegoat!"

"Who you callin' a *him?*"

"You. And a Section Eight won't do you any good on *our* ship. The only thing worse than torture and death on our ship is being turned over to the psychiatric section."

"Well, I ain't goin' and that's that! Ain't no way I'm gonna let my body outta my sight!"

Roosevelt removed his pistol from its holster and pointed it at her.

"Oh, you'll come along, all right. Unless you want to die heroically."

"You ain't got no ammo," she reminded him.

"As the report said, the weapons work *once*. I'm an officer. My job is to stand back and order men into battle to be slaughtered. *I* haven't fired *my* weapon at all yet."

"Well, you might as well shoot me, then, 'cause if I gotta leave life ain't worth livin'!"

Roosevelt fired, and the lizard body was bathed in a white glow for a moment, then it stiffened and dropped to the deck.

"Hey! That's my *body* you're dealing with, Roosevelt!" lizard-Pierce screamed.

"My god! You've *killed* her!" Pierce cried.

"Nothing of the sort. If I killed the general here they'd give him a hero's funeral and a medal and a statue. It's merely a hard stun. Feinstein! Get the military police here to drag this lump back to the ship!"

Pierce looked at Bolivia. "You've got to stop them! Authority be damned!"

Bolivia shrugged. "Sorry, but, technically, they are dealing entirely with their own species and attempting to take a potential criminal back to their own ship. It's simply none of our affair."

"But that's a *human* inside that lizard body!"

He shrugged. "So you say. Personally, I think you're

all mad, including the aliens. Even if I grant your supposition, you ought to know as well as anyone that all that counts are appearances. Reality is irrelevant, particularly to the government, so long as the paperwork's right. After all, who would ever be in government if they had to actually face and deal with *reality?* Nobody competent would take the job, and the incompetents would really be able to *do* something."

Pierce stared at him. "You didn't, by some chance, start out as an Arbiter, did you?"

"Uh, actually, no. I started out as a god, you see, and I had all the answers. Then I devolved myself to a much more comfortable level."

"A god? *All* the answers? And you did *this* to yourself?"

"Sure. I had all the answers, but I discovered I never could think of the questions. So I created bureaucracy to handle the questions and retired. It's much, much more peaceful this way, and I even get to take vacations to Europe. Well, I see they're sealing the airlock—or pretending to, anyway. Got to go. Best of luck and all that."

And, with that and a wave of his hand, Captain Nathan Bolivia disappeared.

For a moment they all stared at him. Finally, Pierce called out to those now inhabiting the computer. "Hey! You two in there! Can you tell us how he did that or where he went?"

"Very little functions correctly anymore," Pierce-Arro responded, "but, for the record, we'd say he's back aboard the *Gandhi,* whatever *Gandhi* they're calling themselves this week, we suppose."

"Do we have any power at all?"

"Some. More than they thought, we suspect, but not enough to do any good. If so, we'd blast that *Gandhi* ship for its blasphemy. We *know* what God looks like, and it isn't *that* little deflated wimp!"

Pierce sighed and sank into the command chair. "Well, then, that's it, I guess. How much time do you think we've got?"

"Hard to say. If you all wouldn't breathe, the air would last much longer. They rerouted the food synthesizer into the sewage system, which is great for efficiency but not for actually eating anything. It just keeps making foul-looking stuff and immediately vaporizing it in the garbage, taking the energy and remaking foul-looking stuff and immediately—"

"We get the idea." Pierce sighed.

"The water system isn't much better, but by alternately idling the main engines while inducing maintenance fluids it is possible to recover a liquid that the data banks of this hunk of junk say is safe for you to drink. Of course, there's the question to answer first before we can do it."

"Huh? What?"

"Why should we? It takes energy, and the mains are depleted. Besides, we are here to conquer you and it seems practical to withhold needed substances until you accept the truth. That goes for you, too, General. No more juice."

The android considered it. "All right, then, I admit you have us, and I am certain my, er, colleagues here will agree. We are at your mercy."

Pierce saw where he was going and nodded. "Yes, that's right. We surrender. We're conquered and your prisoners."

"Hmmm . . . And what about the other fellow?"

The two Pierces looked at the XB-223 navigational computer who was otherwise occupied.

"Stop that or you'll go blind!" Pierce shouted.

Sly, the former XB-223, paused and frowned. "How can this action possibly be related to visual sensory patterns?"

"Trust that I know more about human bodies than you do," Pierce said sincerely.

"But the sensations are *most* interesting and, besides, I watched you—"

Pierce cleared his throat. "Enough! We'll discuss that sort of thing later. Right now we need you to surrender."

"Surrender! Certainly not! Sly does not surrender to *anyone!*" He paused a moment. "Surrender to who?"

"The pair now inside your old self. Without them we get nothing and we die."

"Sly" stood up and tried to look heroic. "Ah! But better to die a real, live man, free and pure of heart, than to live a slave to some conquering things we can't even see!" He bounded over to Pierce and went down on one knee. "Come, my darling! Teach me the mysteries of love in the time we have left, and we shall die in each other's arms!"

"Knock it off! This is me in here, you idiot! And that's *my* body you're in!"

"So? We don't have time to really get to know each other anyway. Superficialities like appearance will have to do. It seems to me that you are using different criteria on yourself than you used in this body on other women. You cannot blame *me* for that. You taught me everything I know about this!"

Pierce coughed nervously. He hoped *he* hadn't looked and sounded that dumb and superficial—but he was very afraid that he had. It wasn't as much fun being on the other end of this sort of thing. Still, he began to realize just how naive this dumb computer version really was.

"It's not that easy . . . Sly," he said coyly. "First, you have to do a few things for me."

"Anything, my sweet! Name it!"

"Surrender to the nice aliens in your old circuits," he said softly.

Sly swallowed hard. "For you—anything! Uh—if I surrender, will you be mine?"

"We'll both be theirs, actually. But we'll live a little longer. I won't promise anything, but I *will* promise that I'll spurn your every advance if you don't surrender this minute!"

"Oh, very well. I surrender."

Pierce smiled. "All right, aliens. You win. You've conquered us. We're your prisoners. Now we're your responsibility, totally and completely, until you turn us over to higher authority, right?"

"Hmmm . . . Hadn't thought of that," Pierce-Arro responded. "Yes, I suppose that *is* the requirement. Very well. I will try and squeeze a biologically compatible liquid from the engine regions. It will satisfy thirst and might also contain sufficient calories for energy for awhile. It will buy time."

"What about me?" android-Pierce asked. "I need juice."

"All right. Plug in below in the android storage receptacle. We'll divert some power from the engines into there—that should give you a charge."

"Thank you, sir. Spoken like a true conqueror," the general responded. "Uh—might I ask, just out of curiosity, what your longterm plan is? I mean, how you're going to get us out of here before those seals start popping?"

"Well, that's the real problem," Pierce-Arro admitted. "I believe I could build sufficient force to get us well out of here, but at the cost of blowing almost all the seals. And, of course, regulations would prohibit me from depriving prisoners of air once they'd duly surrendered. It could get us brought up for war crimes. And, of course, some of my essential circuits go right through those places."

"Then what—?"

"We think that the reptiles will give us a good twenty-four hours to come apart. After that, they'll grow impatient, bored, and fearful that someone might show up to effect a rescue that they can't handle. If that happens, they will finish us."

"Twenty-four hours! That's not much time!"

"Oh, it is more than sufficient. We have established a tentative dialog with the dreadnought's navigational computer."

Sly looked up suddenly. "The fickle fiend!"

"Yes, you certainly made a mess of it at the start, didn't you? We're getting along much better. It seems that our way of thinking is much more *sympatico* with it than yours. Ah—here comes the data now. If they decide to finish us, they will initiate the paperwork, cut the orders, commence the procedures, and put the wheels in motion to do so. They can't do that until they complete filing and processing the paperwork from the action up to this point. Otherwise they'll flood the system and it'll jam up. So, given the number of forms and approvals for past actions, then the number required to initiate additional action . . . I'd say we're safe here for about four-point-six years."

Pierce was appalled. "And I thought *we* were bogged down!"

"Perhaps a decade if they use computers," Pierce-Arro added hopefully. "More than enough time for our own great, grand, glorious invasion fleet to arrive and get us out of here."

"But we don't have enough supplies to last that long!" Pierce objected. "Even the air won't recirculate that long!"

"That *is* a point, of course. Therefore, there is the other plan."

"What other plan?"

"Well, I'd think it would be obvious. We pray to Daddy to save us."

Pierce sighed. "He's only interested in his daughter, and she's now a prisoner on that dreadnought undergoing God knows what kind of horrible fate. He'll abandon us and concentrate only on her."

"Not precisely accurate. You have half of her here. He'll need you to switch the bodies back."

Pierce thought a moment. "Wait a minute! Even if that's true, and even if he somehow can rig up the technology to switch us, he won't care about anybody but Honeylou Emmyjane. If he gets us back together, I'll wind up as the General in his lizard body!"

"That *is* the logical course of events," Pierce-Arro admitted. "Still, it would be an alternate 'you' as it were, certainly more compatible than the body you're now wearing. Until they execute you, anyway."

"Yeah. Thanks a lot. Sly—stop that! Hands to yourself or I'll introduce you to a pain like no other in creation!"

"That would be a new experience," the former computer responded, thinking it over. "It might also be worth it. I find myself feeling very, very strange, filled with sensations, lusts I've never experienced before. It is difficult for me to retain control of myself."

"Well, you'd better. I'm trying to figure out how to get out of this mess without winding up dead or a lizard, which seem right now the only two choices."

Sly looked into those big, luscious eyes. "There is a third choice," he said, smiling.

"Huh?"

"Convince Daddy that you really *are* his daughter."

"*What?*"

"Think of it, my apple dumpling! If you could

convince him that you were truly his precious Marshmallow, he'd spare no effort or expense rescuing you. You would instantly become heiress to the greatest fortune the universe has ever known, have anything you want and never have to tolerate a bureaucrat or even an XB-223 navigational computer ever again."

"But—I'd have to spend my whole life as a *her!* As her, anyway. And I'm not at all comfortable with this. It just seems *wrong* somehow. Out of balance, maybe. And it wouldn't be honorable or ethical, either. I'd be abandoning poor Honeylou Emmyjane to the fate of being a scapegoat and, at best, a lizard forever." He paused a moment. "Besides, I'd never get away with it. There's no way I could con him forever."

"Millard—Millie—I was just an XB-223 navigational computer, but I was able to observe quite a bit and research more. Do you know that just the time her Daddy is spending on this operation is costing him a fortune? Every minute his attention is diverted by this matter he loses a billion credits. Why, if this goes on, in just eight hundred and thirty-three years he'd be flat broke! He'll *want* to believe you; it's cost-efficient for him to do so! He might *suspect*, but his books will be balanced, you see. The bottom line, you know. He won't be able to afford *not* to believe and accept you!"

Pierce thought about it. What could he do to help Marshmallow now anyway? He wasn't even convinced that this would help *him*. Daddy's fake fleet wasn't any match for that dreadnought even if Daddy was the one individual in apparently all the universes who could do something without filling out a form or asking permission.

Besides, if the old boy didn't buy it, they weren't any worse off, but if he did, then a lot of resources would suddenly be at their disposal to rescue or bribe or threaten those lizards to release her, and more technology to maybe get them back together. Hell, it beat being trapped here, prisoner of some microbial version of himself stuck in a flaky computer, the only other human his own body inhabited by, well, a flaky computer. Anyway—if Daddy could somehow rescue them, then he could confess all and that would *force* Daddy to get her out of there somehow. In the meantime, he'd at least be safe and protected, out of this madhouse.

"How would we start?" he asked Sly.

"Well, we could start with the accent, then the mannerisms and moves, that sort of thing. There are recordings in the data banks that whatever's in there now could provide for comparison."

"A fascinating concept," Pierce-Arro agreed. "If Daddy is God, then we will be delivering the half we can to Him. If Daddy is not God, then we might be able to infiltrate and take over his entire empire through his vast computer network. It beats sitting here rotting, anyway."

Millard sighed. "Okay, okay. It's a start. At least to get some kind of real rescue where the rescuer won't blow us away! I'll give it a try."

But after a couple of hours of trying the accent, the moves, everything he could think of, it was about as believable as a solvent savings and loan.

"It's no use," he said. "There's no way I can be anybody other than who I've been all these years, body or not."

"But, it's the only plan we've got!" Sly objected. "Besides, it's *got* to work. Then we can be married and I'll coinherit that vast empire and we'll live together in blissful luxury forever!"

"He's right," Pierce-Arro agreed. "At least on the first part, that it's the only plan we've got. Let us think . . . Ah! This might do it! Just sit back, relax, and look at Screen 3."

"Huh?"

"Just you, Pierce! Not the lovesick idiot!"

"Uh—okay, but . . ."

"Just look at the screen and relax . . . relax . . ."

Pierce sat back and looked at the screen, which contained only a vast whirling pattern, monotonously going over and over, to the sound of a restful ocean surf.

This won't work, he thought. *I've never been able to be hypnotized.* But it *was* restful, and it kept Sly off him, and he was just so totally exhausted after all this, and the screen and the sounds were so restful . . .

"You are getting sleepy, sleepy . . ." a soft voice whispered. "You are falling into a deep, restful, hypnotic trance, and you will listen only to the sound of my voice and nothing else and you will believe what I say . . ."

". . . B'lieve what you say . . ." Pierce muttered.

"Open your eyes but stay in that deep, restful sleep. Look at the screen. You are not Millard Fillmore Pierce. You have *never* been Millard Fillmore Pierce. You have never been a man, never *wanted* to be a man. *This* is you . . ."

The screen showed a recording of Marshmallow, from the time she came onto the ship to the time they got into the buff.

"Now, when you wake up, you'll *know* you are Honeylou Emmyjane Goldberg, who likes to be called Marshmallow. The crash and the electrical short made all of you *think* you were other people but now it's worn off you. The lizard creatures took you all aboard and read out your minds and got some stuff confused, and some more didn't get back, but you're now sure who you are, and that's Daddy's precious Marshmallow. Oh, and one more thing—although we won't tell Daddy and we won't tell anyone else; in fact, you won't even think about it yourself—but you still will obey."

"Yeass?" the reclining form muttered in a perfect Honeylou Emmyjane Goldberg accent.

"You will continue to believe and obey this voice and unquestioningly do and say anything it tells you, bu you will think it is your own idea."

"Yes, suh!"

"Now just go back to sleep normally, and wake up and make your call."

Pierce-Arro felt eminently satisfied at this. The general by now was trapped downstairs in the android storage closet, unable to disconnect but having a real good jolt; the lizards were effectively neutralized so long as they were diverting the dreadnought's systems. At the right time, the lizards would uncover a communication ordering them to protect their launched invasion eggs against imminent threat of destruction and be forced to break off and abandon them here for a bit. Plenty of time for Daddy to get them out of there—and when they moved out, they'd take the *real* girl with them, forever excluded from spoiling the plot. And they were so situated that they might not *need* the fleet. What good would that do, anyway? The gasbag empire wouldn't be much more than an impediment here. This was *absolute* victory!

They only hoped and prayed that Daddy, with His eye on paramecia, wouldn't catch on.

"What is it, Herb?" Daddy was not amused or happy to be disturbed as he tried to make a few thousand essential decisions while his think-tank figured out what to do to rescue his daughter.

"Uh—I think it's your daughter on the hyperspace channel, boss."

"Marshmallow? But I thought they'd gotten their bodies all scrambled up."

"Yeah, well, that's what *I* thought, too, but I know her well enough to know this couldn't be anybody else. Nobody could pretend to be *her* and get away with it."

"Hmph! You have a point there. I'll be right down."

It sure *looked* like his beloved Honeylou Emmyjane!

"Daddy!" she squealed with delight. "Daddy—come git us outta heah!"

It sure *sounded* like his beloved Honeylou Emmyjane!

"Is that really *you*, my Marshmallow?"

"Of *coase* it is, Daddy! Who else *would* it be?"

"Spell 'cat' for me."

She thought long and hard for about two minutes. "K-h-a-a-t?" she responded hesitantly.

"Marshmallow! But how'd you get back to normal?"

"Well, Ah *ain't* all *that* nohmal, Daddy. Them lizards, they wanted theah gen'rul back *real* bad. They didn't cayuh who was inside, it seems, but they said Ah weren't the type to give a tryal to. Said somebody'd figah that Ah weren't real or somethin'. So they stuck me in this *awful* machine and read out all my mem-ries, and they did the same to poah Ahbiter Pieahce. Then they put me back heah, and *him* in the lizard. Said he'd do right fine! 'Coase, they didn't put *ev'rything* back, it seems. Ah got trouble 'memberin' too much."

"Well, there wasn't that much there to make it a loss, anyway," he assured her. "So where are you now?"

"Still in poah Pieahce's ship. He's gone, o'course. They rigged the ship so's if we try'n go anywheres we fall apaht! Ah'm stuck heah with a lovesick computer in Pieahce's old body puttin' the make on me, stahk nekkid, both of us!"

Daddy frowned. "I see. And where are the lizards?"

"Beats me, Daddy. They said som'thin' 'bout havin' to

go guahd theah soldiers and they beat it outta heah 'bout a couple awahs ago."

"All right. Keep broadcasting the locator signal and I'll have you picked up. It's a real relief to know you're all right, I can tell you. If I'd had time to have another kid you wouldn't have gotten so much of my time. However, now all's well. And you tell that dumb computer to keep his new hands off you!"

"Yeah, Ah did, but it ain't that easy, Daddy. I already kicked him in the balls once and he *likes* pain! Oh, come quick!"

"Hang on, Marshmallow! I'm coming!" He switched off the intercom. "You'll arrange for her pickup, Herb? Bring her a decent outfit, too."

"I'll take care of it, boss. You want me to take care of those egg pods we been tracking before those lizards can get to 'em?"

"Might as well. They deserve it anyway. Try and keep one batch for study. They could have some profit potential. Oh—and make an appointment as soon as possible for my tearful reunion with my daughter. I think I have at least ten minutes free next Tuesday a week."

"Will do, boss. What about the others?"

"Send that computer turned into a man to the science labs. Maybe they can dissect him and figure out how it was done. A computer inside a human brain! Gad! Think of it! Think of the potential if we could *reverse* it! I'd be immortal instead of merely practically so! The others—what use have we for misadapted aliens? After those two get off, blow the ship to hell!"

10

A letter comes in from J. Pierpont von Platt which states: "All right, already! We've had to endure yet another of Chalker's interminable body-switching routines. Enough is enough, already! You'd think that after 137 body-switching and transformation books he'd go on to something else! Why do the two of you, both certified Hugo winners, allow him to indulge his bizarre hangups when it's obvious that you're just making us pay for his cheapness in not seeking psychotherapy?"

Well, Mr. von Platt, you've answered your own question. Chalker's never won a Hugo or a Nebula, it's true; indeed, the last time he was even *nominated* for anything like that was back in 1978. Critics love to pillory him. On the other hand, critics have always loved one of us, and have recently loved another, for being or becoming *artistes*, writing to high esoteric literary tastes. In the meantime, Chalker has merely proceeded to make about a zillion bucks, become a consistent best-selling author, grill filet mignons on his palatial estate between his jacuzzi and his pool, and even taken time to publish Harlan Ellison. Consider, then, Mr. von Platt, that if you've gotten this far, do you really think the two award-winners are going for yet another nomination here or are they going for the money?

On the other hand, all of us, without exception, live in sheer terror that someone with the Modern Language Association will discover this work and proclaim it for years as the most brilliant, multileveled thing any of us has ever done.

Ms. Prudence Gulliwinkle of the University of West Sheboygan writes: "I am torn in two directions by the social dimension of the previous chapter. On the one hand, it is gratifying to see that sexist pig of a hero of yours wind up on the other end of things for a change; on the other hand, your heroine is a true bimbo."

Well, Ms. Gulliwinkle, all of us red-blooded males sheepishly admit to a fondness for ogling bimbos, but, in our defense, none of us married one, nor would we want our sisters to marry one, either.

Lastly comes a letter from Mr. Bernard P. Snodgress of La Carumba, California, who wonders why we waste so much time in digressions when we could be getting back to beautiful naked bimbos and all that other good stuff no matter *who* is in who. Lacking a coherent answer to that . . .

Bypassing bureaucracy was not an easy thing to do in any age, and certainly not in this one, not even for such a one as Daddy—or, in this case, Daddy's operational chief.

Herb sat there, scratching his head, sorting out what had to be done. First, send in a rescue party that was armed and capable of resisting unknown alien forms while still effecting a proper rescue of Marshmallow and then blowing the ship to hell. Second, round up an even greater force to intercept those egg pods before they landed anywhere that mattered and blow them to hell as well. And, third, keep that lizard dreadnought occupied and out of harm's way while one and two were accomplished.

The resources were available entirely within Daddy's big business empire, since they had their own exclusive communications channels with unbreakable codes. But any such empire always had its malcontents and weak links no matter how thorough the job preparation seminar—otherwise known as brain laundry session—was at doing its job. If he used Company ships and personnel to stop an alien invasion, somebody someday might file a report that would be the only sort of report that the bureaucracy handled with the speed of lightning: that someone was bypassing the bureaucracy. That could be nasty and cost zillions of credits, all of which the boss would take out of his hide. There was no way around it; he'd have to hire some mercenaries and freebooters.

That meant using the Secondary Nautical Auxiliary Ferry Oscillation Operation, and he dreaded that. It meant using coded messages from here, where he was, to relay point A, where the message would be decoded, recoded, and resent by a new operator, and so on, and so on, until it reached its destination. It was clumsy, so much so he'd never used it himself before, but good old S.N.A.F.O.O. had always been alleged to be the most totally secure way to send a message ever.

He punched the requirements into his computer console and it came up with several possibilities, the most likely being an old half-Irish, half-French pirate who claimed to be the direct descendant of both Jean LaFitte and Sean McCorkle, the latter being, of course, the legendary smuggler who brought snakes back *in* to Ireland. He was alleged to be headquartered in an inn on La Hibernia under the sign of the solid green tricolor. Well, it was worth a try and the distance and sector were convenient. With S.N.A.F.O.O., it would be a simple matter to contact him and make him an offer with no one, absolutely no one, able to trace the call.

Yes, old Paddy de Faux Grais was the one, all right. But how to phrase the message? He switched to the S.N.A.F.O.O. channel and sent: To station XBJ-1223309-X:

ONE BILLION, REPEAT, BILLION, CREDITS OFFERED TO DO SIMPLE JOB. NEED YOU TO PICK UP ONE FEMALE AND ONE MALE PASSENGER FROM DISABLED SPACESHIP AND THEN ELIMINATE SHIP AND ALL OTHERS ABOARD. REPLY ADDRESS AT HEADER BY THIS CHANNEL.

There! *That* should do it!

The message went out immediately, automatically encoded by his central computer, then was decoded by a station far off in Sector J-449, a world where Dutch was the native tongue. It was decoded, read back in, with a heavy Dutch accent of course, and sent on to another world in Sector H-335, a world which decoded the message and then relayed it, this time in Swahili accents. And so it went, back and forth, through Scotch and French, and also through Arcturian and Betelguesian and many other accents and tongues, until it popped up at the address given, the numbers being always a constant.

They were just opening up for the night's games and entertainment with the traditional Marseillaise played on the bagpipes when Old Seamus tottered in with the paper in his hand.

"Telegram for ye, Paddy!"

He stood there, a huge man with a bushy black beard, bandana around his head, and eye patches over both eyes.

"Arrr! Sink me harbour and all that pirate bilge!

Lemme see what ye got there, Seamus." He took the paper, flipped up one eye patch and read it, and frowned. He turned it on its side, tried again, then tried it upside down. "What kind of code be this, Seamus?"

"Ain't no code, Paddy, I swear! Come in plain, I tell ye!"

Paddy read the paper again.

SAMPLE REPEEK BILLION BILLION FEMURS TO PICK UP DECAYED SPICE SHEEP AND MAIL AND DEFECATE SHEEP AND ALL UDDERS ABROAD.

"Arrr! This be gibberish! But the reply's there. How'd this come in, Seamus?"

"Relay, Yer Meanness. S.N.A.F.O.O. system."

"Hmmm . . . Never used that one meself, but 'tis said it's the most secure of all, but this message got to be fouled up somewheres along the line, arr. Let me scribble a line on the back of this here paper for ye to send back to 'em whoever they is and get some sense."

Seamus looked at the block-printed characters.

ORIGINAL MESSAGE GIBBERISH. PLEASE SEND AGAIN. LOVE, PADDY.

The pirate nodded. "Arr! And bring me the reply!"

Old Seamus hurried back to the combination hyper-space transmission facility and brewery he ran and fired up the S.N.A.F.O.O. channel, then read in the message exactly as Paddy gave it to him.

It went out on the proper channel, on an entirely different route, through accent after accent and language after language, and finally it popped out again where Herb was sitting.

He picked up the message, read it, and frowned.

GIBBERING MASSAGE ORGY. PLEASE SEND PATTY. LOVE GIN.

"Geez! That must be *some* inn!" he said aloud, wishing he were there. However, business was business.

SORRY TO INTERRUPT FUN, BUT NEED YOU TO DO QUICK AND DIRTY JOB FOR BIG MONEY. WILL YOU GO OR SHOULD I GET SOMEONE ELSE?

Back and forth the message went, until Old Seamus tottered in again. By this time Paddy was a bit drunk, and had other problems.

"Arr! I've gone blind! Can't read a blasted thing!"

"Er, sorry, Captain, but don't you think you oughta maybe lift one of them eye patches?" the old man suggested. "Why do you wear two of 'em, anyway?"

Paddy started a moment, then raised one of the patches. "It's a bloomin' miracle, it is! I can see again!" He paused. "Huh? What was yer question?"

"Why do you wear two eye patches anyway?"

"Us pirates always wear eye patches, old man. You know that. It's in the instruction manual you get at pirates' school. But I can never remember which eye to wear it over, that's all. Now—let's see that message."

SORE TO INTERPRET FONDUE, BUT KNEAD EWE QUACK UND D.T.'S FOUR BUG MOONEY. WILL HUGO OR GAROT ONE SMELLS?

"This be lunacy!" Paddy swore. "I think there be some problems with this secure system. It be so secure nobody can ever figure out the message!"

Seamus stared at the paper. "I dunno. A ewe is a girl sheep, and the first message said something about sheep, did it not? Maybe this fella's tied up in a fondue party and needs somebody to smuggle his sheep in."

"Sheep? For fondue?"

"Well, maybe they're using sheep dip. Who knows

about some of them strange customs out there, and there's no accountin' for taste."

"Aye, I've boiled a few mutineers in soft cheese meself," the captain admitted. "Still and all, I'm gonna give this swabbie one more try and then to perdition with 'im!"

He scribbed something again on the back of the paper and Seamus read:

CALL ME DIRECT. MESSAGES NOT CLEAR. PIRATES DON'T CARRY NO SHEEP!

At the other end, Herb stared at the message and sighed. Maybe this system had a few bugs in it, he decided.

ME DERICK COLD. MOOSE SAGES NO ECLAIR. PIE RATES DAREN'T CARRION NOSE HEAP!

For a moment he wondered if he was being insulted, but then he got hold of himself and asked the master computer for analysis.

"Have you ever played 'rumor?'" it asked him.

"Yes, as a child."

"Remember what happens when you whisper something to the first person in line, who then whispers it to the second, and so on? What comes out at the other end?"

"Yes. It bears little resemblance—oh! I see! But how can I get the proper message to him any way but this without being traced?"

"You might try just sending it in tight code directly to our office on La Hibernia," the computer suggested. "Then have the local computer there transmit in the clear to the local station, who won't know where it came from. Have them respond to one of our electronic mail stops we keep there for confidential reasons under the name of that contracting company the president's son fronts for us, and have that computer shoot it back here."

Herb snapped his fingers. "Of course! Why didn't *I* think of that?" He paused a moment. "Uh—we have a local office on La Hibernia?"

"We have local offices *everywhere*. And as to your first question, if you *had* thought of it, then *you* could be the central computer and *I* would get to spend your money on wild and frivolous living," the computer responded.

"Skip it. I don't have time. Okay, *now* we'll get it right."

And, this time, he did. Unfortunately, by this time Paddy was four sheets to the wind and it was the next afternoon, late, when his hangover had subsided to the point where he could read the perfectly clear and understandable message without it looking to him like it had come through the S.N.A.F.O.O. system.

The moment he hit "a billion credits" he discovered that his hangover was completely gone.

"Arr! Round up the crew, me hearties!" he cried. "Get the *Bon Homme McClusky* ready to sail! We got some real profitable piratin' to do!"

"Lemme go! Ah got ta make mah call to Daddy!"

"Hold on, there, you loco galoot! Who you callin' Daddy? Only *Ah* git to call mah Daddy 'Daddy'!"

Something was terribly wrong, and it took Pierce-Arro a moment to realize what it was. In spite of his admonition to the lovesick computer, the stupid thing had stared at the screen anyway and gotten hypnotized just like Pierce, and when *he* woke up *he* was convinced that *he* was Marshmallow, too! And no amount of physical evidence was going to convince him otherwise, either. Fortunately,

Pierce had awakened first, so the original call had gone through, but now this could spoil everything!

"Ah dunno how ah got a twin sistah, but yore not foolin' me 'bout who ah am!" Sly yelled shrilly.

"Stop it! Both of you!" Pierce-Arro commanded, and, as they were always to obey his commands, they stopped. "And keep quiet. Now, Marshmallow—"

"Yes?" they both answered in perfect unison.

Pierce-Arro sighed. Everything was always getting so complicated! First three or maybe more Pierces, he'd lost count, and now three Marshmallows, if, of course, the one on the lizard ship was still alive. What to do? What to do? Any order he gave would be obeyed equally by *both* of them! Think!

"Will the Honeylou Emmyjane Goldberg who sees the other person here as a man go to the powder room and stay there until I call her?"

Instantly Pierce turned and headed for the head, while Sly remained within the room.

"Good. Now, we've got a little reworking to do. Sit down here and just relax and stare at the nice pattern on Screen 3 again . . ."

That was the *longest* Marshmallow had ever spent in a john and she was getting worried about it when she was called back. Facing that lunatic computer, though, was gonna be a real ordeal, she thought. How *dare* that creature think it was *her!*

"Don't you come neah me, y'heah?" she warned him.

"Hey! Take it easy! It's me—Millard. Millard Fillmore Pierce. I'm back together again!"

She frowned. It *did* sound like him, and *seem* to be him, but she wasn't so sure. "Wheah'd that nutty computah brain that thought it was *me* git to?" she asked him.

"Our—captors—worked it out. Got me back from my

readout records in the lizard ship and transmitted XB-223 over to theirs."

"But I thought they was *gone*."

"They was—er, they *are*. It was all done by subspace radio. Don't ask me how. Anyway, we're back!"

"Oh—*Millahd!*"

"Marshmallow!"

They were about to embrace when suddenly Pierce-Arro said, "A ship of unknown nationality and type just came out of hyperspace and is landing near us."

"It's Daddy and the rescue ship!" she squealed with delight.

"Um, I'm not so sure. I just tried hailing them and all I got back was some odd and unintelligible *singing*, if you can call it that. I was hoping that one of you might make sense of it."

"Go ahead," Pierce told him.

The speakers crackled, then from them came: *"Fifteen men on a dead man's chest! Yo! Ho! Ho! And a bottle of rum! Drink and the devil have done with the rest! Yo! Ho! Ho! And a bottle of rum!"*

"Pahrates!" Marshmallow screamed in horror.

"Pyrites?" Pierce-Arro responded. "No, it's a ship, not an asteroid."

"Not pyrites. Pirates," Pierce told him. Then it hit him. "Holy smoke! *Pirates?* In *this* day and age? Can you put a visual on the screen?"

The screen popped to life and they stared at the strangest looking spaceship they'd ever seen. All bright green it was, but with bands of *fleur-de-lis* all over it.

"It looks like a pehfectly *goahgeous* wallpapah pattahn!" Marshmallow breathed.

"I'm more interested in the skull and crossbones hanging from that mast in the center of the ship," Pierce commented worriedly. "Not to mention that it's the first

spaceship I've ever seen with a bowsprit in the shape of a
porno queen—or in any other shape, for that matter."

Suddenly Screen 1 flickered and a fierce, bearded
face appeared. "Avast, mateys! Prepare to be boarded!
Offer no resistance 'cause I got a hundred fierce pirate
swabbies here who'd cut yer throat from ear to ear and love
it!"

"A hundred men!" Marshmallow gasped. "Millahd! I
cain't be taken on no ship with a hundred hohny men! Not
dressed like *this*, anyway!"

Pierce understood. "Yeah, but our clothes didn't
come through the electrical charge very well, and the suits
are even worse. I don't see what we can do."

"Oh, fie on clothes! I'm talkin' about my haiah and I
need mah makeup and all . . ."

"Honey, they're pirates. They won't notice."

"You really don't think so? Oh, Ah'm such a mess! At
least a comb . . ."

"Marshmallow!" He sighed. "Hey, you in the ship's
computer! You're our captor, we're your prisoners. Can't
you do *something* to protect us?"

"With what?" Pierce-Arro wailed, trying to figure a
way to salvage anything out of this.

"Avast!" said the pirate image. "We just want the
wench and the pipsqueak pin-striped swabbie with her!"

Pierce-Arro considered that. "And you'll leave me
alone if you get them?"

"Aye, sure'n I will. Ye got the word of fightin' Paddy
de Fauy Grais on that score!"

"The word of a pirate is no promise at all," Pierce
warned.

"Maybe, but it's the only one I've got," the creature
responded. "However, there *is* a slight problem." He
turned to the pirate's frequency.

"I've got no objections to your taking them off my

hands," Pierce-Arro commented. "In fact, I confess it would be a relief. Unfortunately, they'll be dead when you do."

"Huh? What? Explain yourself, ye electronic wart!" the pirate responded.

"The lizards did a real job on this ship before they left. The moment you open our airlock, all the seals will pop for sure, causing instant death."

"*WHAT?*" everyone from the pirate to the two inside cried at once.

"I'm afraid so. And if you'd take at least one of those patches off your eyes you'd see for yourself the terrible condition this ship's in."

Pierce shook his head in wonder. "Maybe you'd better let the general out from downstairs," he suggested. "He was one of the lizards, remember, and he knows how they think. Maybe *he* could figure out something they didn't sabotage."

"Uh, dahlin', I hate to mention this, but you'ah talkin' like you want to be taken by them pahrates," Marshmallow noted.

"What choice have we got? Rot here or get out of here with them? At least Daddy would pay a good ransom, and I have to admit that at this point I'm tempted by piracy myself."

Pierce-Arro saw no reason to keep the general on the wire, as it were, any longer, anyway, so he released him. Soon the figure of genial Frank Poole the android ambled up to them, but it wasn't all that clear that he was going to be any help.

"I'm higher'n a kite," he said with a smile, "and mellower than a kitten.

"What's wrong with *him?*" Marshmallow asked.

"I think he got too much recharging current being

held there so long. I'm afraid that now he's turned on," Pierce commented.

"Yeah, that's me," General Pierce responded. "Like, wow, man! Turned on, juiced up, tuned in, and charged to the hilt!" He crackled a little bit when he moved as if to emphasize the point.

"Don't touch him!" Pierce warned. "He's probably got enough energy there to electrocute anybody he touches!"

As if to emphasize the point, the general grabbed the back of a chair and the plastic sizzled and started to melt, stinking up the cabin.

"Well, *he's* shoah no help, sugah," she commented. "Only thing *he's* good foah is shakin' a few pahrate hands and fryin' 'em like bacon and grits!"

"Who's *that* big ugly dude on the screen?" the general asked innocently.

"Arr! Who you callin' a big, ugly dude, you poor excuse for a deckhand?" the pirate exclaimed angrily. "If it wasn't for the fact that we don't gets paid unless we delivers the wench whole, I'd come over there and short out a few choice circuits! I got 'alf a mind to throw a tractor beam on ye and take ye all back as a neat package to La Hibernia."

Pierce and Marshmallow both turned toward the screen, mouths agape. Finally Pierce asked, "Uh, Captain, why *don't* you do that? You've got to have a space drydock there of some kind just to keep your own ship in its excellent condition. *There* we could be safely removed by using a pressure tunnel and wrapping what's left of my poor ship."

"Arr, that's not a bad plan, matey! Glad I thought of it!"

"Sorry," Pierce-Arro broke in, "but it won't work. The vibration from entering hyperspace would still break us to pieces."

"I wouldn't have expected a decent plot from a pin-striped swabbie!" the pirate growled.

"Great!" Pierce sighed. *"Now* what do we do?"

"Maybe hunt up some grub," Marshmallow suggested. "Ah'm *stahvin'!*"

Pierce sighed. "Might as well. It seems we're at a standoff, as always. What a situation! You can't even get captured and hauled away by pirates!" He looked up toward the ceiling. "Hey! Conqueror! Time to feed the other two prisoners. The first one's got too much, I think."

"They call me Mellow Millard!" the general sang off-key.

"Oh, I suppose we might as well," Pierce-Arro grumped. "I told you, though, that the only thing I can do is the biochemically compatible caloric liquid I distilled from the engine maintenance and lubrication system."

"Anything. My throat's dry, too," Pierce told him.

"Then get your cups and use the washbasin faucet. It's the only one I could reroute without a full mechanical overhaul."

"This be the real pits," the pirate image moaned.

"In a Gadda da vida, honey!" bawled the general.

Pierce took a cup and tried the faucet and a clear liquid that looked just like water dribbled into it. He waited until it was about half full, then handed it to Marshmallow and did the same with another cup. When done, he shut off the tap, clicked his cup to hers, and said, "Well, I don't know what this is going to taste like, but it's all we've got." He took a drink, and so did she, and suddenly their eyes bulged and they both seemed to be having an attack.

Finally Pierce managed, hoarsely, to ask, "What *is* this stuff?"

"The process involves over four hundred synthetic products," Pierce-Arrow told him, "but the end result is chemically identical to what the data banks here call grain alcohol. About ten percent of it *is* water, but it is impossible to separate it further."

Pierce stared at him. "That's a hundred and eighty proof!"

"Whoo-eee!" Marshmallow exclaimed. "That there's the *smoothest* dern country moonshine ah evah did taste!"

"We can't drink *this!*" he protested. "Not unless it's way diluted, anyway."

"I told you, it's all there is, and I cannot separate the water out any further without destroying the stability of the compound. Within it is all that you require for survival, which is the best I can do. In other words, it's that or nothing."

"A few moah sips of this heah lightnin' and we'ah gonna be singin' with that general," Marshmallow noted, then drank some more. "Shore beats just sittin' around, though! A few more gulps of this and Ah'm gonna be drunk as a skunk!"

This is the book speaking again. Remember me? We interrupt here to point out that (A) The *real* Marshmallow, still in lizard-Pierce's body, is also still on the big dreadnought loaded with conquering bureaucrats somewhere in space; (B) the one who *thinks* she's Marshmallow is really human-Pierce; (C) the one who *thinks* he's human-Pierce is really Sly, the XB-223 navigational computer; (D) we are not advocating the consumption of grain alcohol, unless, of course, you're stuck in a shaky and partly destroyed spaceship with an overcharged lizard-Pierce general in the body of an android overseen by a smashed-together pair of microbial conquerors inhabiting the ship's navigational computer while being under the guns of a pirate spaceship. Clear?

If you have followed everything up to this point with perfect clarity, please place your summary, using words of no more than two syllables, neatly typed or printed out, in an envelope and send it to the authors, care of Tor Books, because *we* don't understand it at all.

So, as long as everybody is either mellow (including dead drunk and uninhibited even if not uninhabited), stalled, or totally confused, let us leave this scene for a moment (we'll be coming back, I promise) and see what's been happening to poor Marshmallow—the *real* one—on the great lizard dreadnought . . .

"Tell me, General, when did you first begin to believe that you were a female ape?"

"Ah ain't no ape and I ain't no general!" she shouted back at them for the nine hundred and ninety-ninth time. "Ah'm Honeylou Emmyjane Goldberg and when mah Daddy heahs 'bout this he's gonna have the *biggest* dern sale on lizahd-skin luggage in the *history* of the *univahse!*"

"Fascinating," said the first psychiatrist. "Do you suppose it was formed in childhood and only surfaced under the pressures of a battlefield command?"

"Well, I've been researching the literature for a true example of neo-Freudian transversals with suggestions of Mommism and a totally Jungian counterpoint and the nearest I can come up with is some ancient writings from a controversial and not wholly appreciated minor figure that might explain a *few* things while still leaving us room for our inevitable thirty-six technical papers and two or three pop self-psychoanalysis best-sellers that will make us rich and famous."

"Really? Two or three? Who is the figure? Hubbard?"

"No, Leary."

"Ah, yes, that *would* explain a lot. But both he and

Hubbard were true examples of McLuhanesque figures, recall."

"I recall that they all died filthy rich, which is why we both got into psychiatry in the first place, wasn't it?"

"That's the fuhst damn' thing I heahrd from either of you so fah that's made any sense at all," she grumped.

But by now they'd returned to so much psychobabble, sometimes mixed with economics, that they no longer paid any attention to her at all. It had been this way almost from the start and she was feeling pretty damned depressed and frustrated by this point.

She got up and lumbered back to the ward, where, as far as she could tell, the only sane people on this entire ship stayed.

About the only thing good about her situation, she decided, was that the air didn't stink.

One fellow, who called himself Pokey, had been a particular friend since she'd been stuck here. He wasn't very old and he was quite pleasant; supposedly some kind of computer whiz who could work out almost any technological problem in his head. That was part of his problem.

First of all, you weren't supposed to *solve* problems in the system, not unless you at the same time created ten new ones for others to work on. And he was *very* good at solving things. They'd let him pretty well alone, since, it seemed, he was the only one on the ship who could repair anything that broke, but one day he'd gone too far. He'd used the ship's main computers to run a problem and discovered a neat, simple table of operations that totally eliminated all need forever for lawyers. The moment the High Command had seen it and realized its truth and simplicity they'd had no choice but to commit him to the psychiatric wards, with occasional furloughs to fix broken things now and again.

Most of the people committed to the psych ward were

like that. Bright, normal, even likeable people—for lizards. Their problems were mostly that they had been caught beating the system or not wholeheartedly supporting it. And, of course, there *were* the *real* nuts, off in their own bay, who'd gone bananas dealing with the same system.

He saw her coming and his saurian face twisted in an evil-looking grin. "Nothing much again, huh?"

"You said it," she sighed. "It's a good thing Ah'm not really sick, 'cause them guys wouldn't know *how* to really cuah nobody."

"Oh, it's not their jobs to *cure* anybody," he pointed out. "If they did *that*, they'd soon be out of a job. They were going on this mission in the hopes of getting enough material so that when they got back they'd be able to open practices for the incredibly rich hypochondriacs and make even more money appearing as guests on countless talk shows."

"Ain't theah no *real* shrinks in yoah neck o' the woods?"

"Sure. Plenty. But most of 'em either turn into those types or quit and take up some other kind of medicine. See, they already *know* how to cure most real mental illnesses, and they cure lots of folks and send them back into this crazy locked-up system well adjusted so they no longer rock the boat. Do that enough to otherwise nice people and you either sell out or quit or go nuts yourself from guilt."

"Ah see what you mean. But bein' one of theah patients ain't no fun."

"Oh, I dunno. It's allowed me to work totally unfettered. Ever since I rewired the electroshock machine to create a neural network path that merges me with the master computer systems I've been able to do *wonders* in research and development. Just today I ran your own

problem through my augmented head and figured out how
your minds got switched around. It's a fascinating concept.
I've been thinking of rerouting some circuitry aboard here
and swapping a few folks out now and then. Child's play,
really."

She was suddenly struck by the enormity of his
statement. "You mean—you know how Ah could be put
back in mah body? Mah *real* one? And ev'rybody else,
too?"

"Sure. No real problem. Your mind doesn't really fit
a different body, it just copes. There's a natural electro-
chemical will that wants to be back and right again, but it's
stopped. Create a proper electromagnetic field that can
permeate all concerned and, if all are relaxed and just let
things go, the minds will go back to their own bodies of
their own accord."

"Sheeit! Heah you go and tell me it can be done, and
Ah'm stuck heah away from mah body and the general,
and we'ah speedin' away from 'em at some ungodly
speed."

"Well, yeah, that *is* the problem," he agreed. "I'd like
to help, but I can't figure out how. The only way you could
alter things at this point would be to be cured and resume
your post."

"Huh? Well, *that* shore ain't possible!"

Pokey's saurian head tilted in thought. "Oh, I dunno.
Suppose you got certified as cured? A few odd mannerisms, like your accent and such, but if you said you were
General Pierce and the records all said you were fit for
duty, you'd get back."

"But—that's impossible. Isn't it? Besides, even if it
were possible, they'd just have me up on chahges as a
traitah or blame me for all that went wrong with theah
plans."

"Oh, I don't think so. For one thing, those charges,

while filed, can be bounced back again and again. Nobody *ever* fills out a form a hundred percent correctly. The forms are *designed* for errors. That's so at any point in any process the whole thing can be thrown out if it goes wrong. And nobody's filed *any* charges against you—I checked. They can't until you've completed your psychiatric evaluation. So, if the records were cleared and you were returned to duty, it would be to full duty. See?"

"No. But Ah'll take yoah wurd foah it. But if Ah go back on duty, as it werh, they'll know in a minute it ain't me. Hell, they *really* know that now!"

"Sure they do, but the reports on the attack on the ship *have* been filed and are working their way through the mill and they state categorically that you are General Pierce. They committed you to psychiatric because you insisted you weren't. If you say you *are*, then their original reports *and* their original commitment would have been wrong, and knowingly so. That's a crime. Not only could Roosevelt and the others be brought up on charges, but, much worse, they'd all have to redo their reports. They might risk a trial, but they'd do most *anything* to keep from having to write those reports over!"

She sat down hard, balanced on her tail. "Good loahd! And what, pray tell, would Ah have to *do* as a general heah?"

"Well, generals as a rule don't do much. They order other people to do everything. That's the fun of it. But, for four hours every day, at your rank and position, you would be the Watch Officer in charge of the ship—essentially the embodiment of the High Command."

"Ordahs? What kind of ordahs?"

"Anything you want. That's what generals do."

"And nobody would question nothin'?"

"You don't question generals. Do that and you wind up here."

"You mean—I could ordah us back to mah body and ship?"

"Sure."

"But it's moah than foah hoahs back. Somebody'll tuhn us 'round again."

"You are crediting your fellow generals with far too much intelligence and initiative."

She wanted to kiss him but it was tough with a snout. "Uh—Pokey? Why are you doin' this foah me?"

"Because it's fun, of course. In a sense, you're the monkey and I'm the wrench."

"You don't care 'bout the invasion?"

"I know how old I'll be when any of those eggs reach a point where they can hatch, and how big a place this is to conquer. Besides, they really don't want to conquer you. They just want somebody to fight with."

She stood tall and tried to look military and saluted. "Gen'rul Pieahce, fit and ready foah duty, *suh!*"

Wait a minute, Effinger! This is the book again. You weren't supposed to leave them like this at the end of Chapter Ten. They were supposed to get back in their own bodies again!

Why . . . What . . . ? *You're* not Effinger!!! You're—

11

Sunrise on a planet called Uncharted.

A swollen red sun crept over the horizon, blotting out the pale light of the world's twin moons. The dawn's first glimmers revealed tall blue-black fern trees and a dense underbrush of drab violet thornbushes. Wisps of greenish vapors floated by, and now and then a gliding reptile sailed close to the repaired windshield of the *Pete Rozelle*. Uncharted was a planet that had been colored with those crayons you never wanted to use for anything else, and populated by the kinds of animals you didn't want to see when you went to the zoo.

Unknown to the scattered cast members, the *Pete Rozelle* had crashed in a jungle on a desolate and uninhabited island continent in the southern hemisphere. Thousands of miles away to the north there was a larger continent, one with great and teeming cities. The people of that continent, though alien, were moderately human in their ways, enough so that they would have been deeply interested in their visitors from space. At least up until the moment the Unchartedians killed them all.

So the three Pierces, Arro, and the XB-223—not to mention Paddy de Faux Grais in his flagship, the *Bon Homme McClusky*—turned toward the south (did we mention that Uncharted rotates from north to south?) and felt a sudden resurgence of hope as they greeted the strange, otherworldly daybreak.

It's moments like these, all too rare in the history of galaxy-smashing scientific adventure literature, that refresh fictional characters, authors, and readers alike. There is a definite need for the occasional reflective pause, when we can all catch our breath and shove a thick phone book under our sagging suspension of disbelief. Perhaps, by this stage of a novel, a few readers may begin to have problems with some of the more awesome and spectacular ideas. For instance, even we were brought up short by the concept of a sheep fondue in the last chapter. We could easily imagine an immense fondue pot big enough to contain a ton and a half of melted cheese; it was the whole sheep on pointed sticks that gave us trouble.

So before we dive back into the frantic events surrounding our perplexed crew, let's take the opportunity to stretch our legs and look around. If you examine the setting closely, you'll notice strange maroon-colored creatures skittering through the blue-black foliage. There are fantastically shaped dull brown flowers, too, crawling with tiny, intelligent, starshaped blobs of blue flesh. There is a bloody revolution going on in one of their mulch colonies that's nearly as dramatic as the tangled mess Millard Fillmore Pierce has gotten himself into. In fact, someday someone will write an entire novel about these sentient beings. It won't get published, though.

Pierce might have been reassured if he'd known the truth about the environment into which his ship had crashed. Perhaps if there'd been an exobiologist aboard, the scientist might have examined the busy blue stars and determined that their body chemistry was very similar to that of Earth animals. That would have led to several interesting speculations. The first is that there was probably a larger continent in the northern hemisphere with great and teeming cities, and the second is that Uncharted's atmosphere, though faintly green and roiling, was near enough to Earth's to be breathable.

No one—neither Daddy nor the lizards aboard their battle cruisers nor Pierce-Arro within the *Pete Rozelle's* computer system—had taken the time to make such an analysis. They'd all been too busy scheming and swapping bodies and yelling at each other. Yet keep the truth about the planet's atmosphere in mind: It will become important in a couple of thousand words.

In the meantime, a former immense and terrifying lizard, now housed in the blatting bodies of two minuscule gasbags aboard the Protean scout ship M.W.C. *Pel Torro*, General Millard Fillmore Pierce held up a tumbler of food. It looked like water and tasted like fire, but Pierce-Arro called it food. The general was in no mood to argue. He raised the food, gave a little shudder, and took a long gulp.

"That's it, Gen'ral Sugah," said the human Pierce craftily. He still thought he was Marshmallow, but even Marshmallow would be able to see the value of a leader of the invading lizard forces disabling himself with liquor.

"Urk," replied the general solemnly. Somehow, he managed to give the impression that the Frank Poole android's features had begun to blur.

Marshmallow-Pierce had consumed a quantity of food, too, but that had been the night before, and now he was perfectly sober. He had only a queasy stomach and a throbbing headache that felt like someone was breaking big rocks into small rocks with a pickax somewhere behind his forehead. He decided not to have any more food for a while, despite how rich and flavorful Pierce-Arro's product was. Thinking like Marshmallow, Pierce planned to be ready as soon as Daddy made his move to rescue her.

The XB-223, no longer calling himself Sly because he believed he was the human Pierce, also decided to remain sober and watchful. "I'll protect you, Marshmallow," he murmured into her ear.

"Ah doan' really need pertectin' as such," she said, giving him a sweet smile. "Ah am, as you may have noticed, a big gal now, an' Ah kin take care of mahself. But it sho' is gallant of you to offah."

The computer put Pierce's arm around Marshmallow's shoulders and drew her nearer. "I don't know what it is, honey. You just bring out the protective side in me."

Marshmallow shook her head. "Heah Ah am, standin' heah buck naked, an' all you want to do is pertect me. Ah must be losin' mah touch!"

They looked at each other, gazing deep into each other's eyes. Then slowly they drew closer, and at last, passionately, Class 2 Arbiter Millard Fillmore Pierce was kissed deeply by his own computer.

In the meantime, the Pierce-Arro construct within the electronic essence of the XB-223 navigational computer began to revise its plans. It had learned many things in the hours that it had been trapped in the nonliving yet sentient device. The first thing it had learned was that the situation was dangerously seductive. Pierce-Arro had first become comfortable there, and then it had begun to think that it truly never wanted to return to its own bodies. That was something to be fearful of.

The next thing that happened was that Pierce-Arro learned it could differentiate itself by dividing the inter-related systems of the navigational computer between its two trapped consciousnesses. Commodore Pierce separated itself from First Officer Arro, and took up residence in the primary high-level guidance complex. Arro had to be satisfied with the secondary systems. Rank, after all, has its privileges.

"Let us review our options," said the Protean Pierce.

"I didn't know we had any, sir," said Arro.

"We always have options. The one advantage we have now is that, in this form, we can't be expected to continue filling out the essential paperwork."

"I'll bet there will be a ton of forms that we'll have to wade through if we ever return to our real bodies. We'll never hear the end of it."

"Don't worry about it, Number One," said Pierce. "We'll be heroes."

Arro gave an electronic shudder. "Do you know how much paperwork a hero has to deal with? That's why you never have the chance to be a hero twice!"

"We'll worry about that when the time comes. For now, we must decide who among these gigantic but terribly stupid creatures will be useful to us. None of them can be friends, because it is their universe we must conquer. Still, I find myself liking some of them better than others."

Arro tried to blat a sac or two out of habit. "My only hope is that the lizard general isn't doing anything . . . disgusting in our bodies. If I ever get back into my dear, sweet gasbag, I'm going to feel defiled for the rest of my life."

"That's not our concern now," said the commodore. "Our invasion force will be arriving momentarily. We must be in a position to guide them. Therefore, we must maneuver all of them so that we can restore ourselves to our natural forms."

"Do you know how to accomplish that?" asked Arro.

Pierce wanted to shrug, but he was shrugless. "If we can reverse the deck-plate procedure, maybe that would work. The entire process was recorded in the computer's general memory, and I've cracked the electronic code that protects it. I don't think we'll have any problems, except that we need all of the original participants, and one of them—the human Marshmallow, in the lizard general's body—is no longer on board."

"Well? What are you going to do?"

The Protean leader paused. "I'm going to see if that 'food' will have any effect on our electronic brains."

While the gasbag leader proceeded with the first-ever experiment to get a computer drunk, the scruffy and disreputable image of Pirate Paddy reappeared on Screen 1. "Ahoy the wreck!" he called in a gruff voice. "I've come to rescue you and return your delectable but worthless hide to your daddy."

Frank Poole opened one red, synthetic eye and wasn't pleased by the effect. "My daddy was eaten by my mommy decades ago," said the lizard general, slurring his words.

"Arrr! Not *your* daddy, you pin-striped lubber!" cried Paddy. "*Her* daddy!"

"Hell with it, then," said the general, closing his eye again. "Wish they hadn't written Goodtime Sal out of this story. I could use a little commiseration 'long about now." Nobody paid him any further attention.

"Wheah were we?" asked Pierce.

The pirate chief turned a little to face him. "I've come to offer you a ride home, little lady," said Paddy in a suspiciously innocent voice.

"How do Ah know Ah kin trust you, suh?" said Pierce.

"Well, looky here, little lady. Your—"

Pierce drew himself up to his full height, setting his pendulous alabaster globes to bobbling. "Doan' you *evah* call me that agin!" he said in a fierce voice. "Ah ain't nobody's little lady. If'n Ah had mah clothes on, Ah'd be weahin' mah gunbelt, suh, an' Ah'd have the honor of shootin' yoah damn eyes out!"

Paddy grinned. "Spirited wench, eh? Didn't know they were still makin' 'em like that!"

Pierce's face flushed with anger. "*Wench?*" he screamed. "Ah think Ah'd ruther die heah on this ugly ol' planet than be rescued by the likes of you!"

Paddy realized that if he weren't careful, he could watch a billion credits evaporate from his future net worth. "Please, ma'am, do accept my apologies. I'm just a rough, ill-mannered privateer, trying to make do the best I can here in these frontier spaceways. We don't always behave up to the standards of the high society you're so obviously used to. Be assured, however, that my intentions have always been nothing but the best, and that I have nothing but respect and the warmest regard for you." Somewhere along the line, the pirate's rather stereotyped accent had vanished.

Pierce's lower lip jutted out. "Well," he said slowly, "all right. But you jes' watch yo'self, you heah?"

"Right you are, ma'am," said Paddy, grinning again. "Now, are you ready to be rescued, or would you care for a few moments to freshen up?"

Pierce nodded. "Ah might could do with a few seconds to dab a little powder on mah nose, suh."

"And throw a cloak over your divine accoutrements, ma'am, is my advice. My hundred bloodthirsty followers usually need far less provocation than that."

Pierce turned toward Sly. "Fiddle-dee-dee," he said, "I have mah beau, Arbiter Millsy Fillmore Pierce, to pertect me. Don't ah, Millsy?"

Sly looked up threateningly at Screen 1. "You do indeed, Miss Goldberg. Now, let's make ourselves ready."

"What about po' Gen'ral Pierce theah, stuck in that awful android?"

Sly looked at Frank Poole. The android sat with its head resting heavily on its chest. There was a line of drool coming from its artificial mouth. "I don't have any particular loyalty to a hideous alien set on conquering our galaxy and enslaving us," said the computer. "Why don't we just let him sleep?"

Not far away—at least as galactic distances are measured, but plenty far away as plot elements go—Herb awoke from an anxious dream in which he'd been swimming through the interstellar vacuum, chased by something that had knife-sharp teeth, a ravenous hunger, and an almost magical foreknowledge of everything Herb did to get away. It was one of those nightmares that left him weak with relief when he realized he'd been asleep, except this time the realty into which Herb awoke was nearly as bad as the dream.

Someone was standing behind his expensive, padded leather swivel chair. "Herb?" said a voice in deceptively quiet tones. It was Daddy, of course.

"Yes, sir?" said Herb. He could imagine the knife-teeth gnashing near his ear.

Daddy turned Herb's leather chair around so they were facing each other. "Herb, have you taken action to secure the safety of my darling little Marshmallow?"

"Why, yes, sir. A rescue party is on the way. It should be there soon, if it hasn't arrived already."

Daddy smiled. It was a horrible sight. "Fine, Herb, fine. Now just tell me, whom did you contact?"

Herb's eyes grew wider and his throat constricted. "Paddy de Faux Grais," he whispered.

"I'm sorry," said Daddy, a jolly expression on his face. "I didn't hear you. Who did you say?"

"Pirate Paddy," said Herb, gulping.

Daddy nodded thoughtfully. "Let me get this straight, if I may. My dearest darling daughter is in some grotesque danger, crash-landed on an uncharted planet. She may or may not have been switched out of her own body, and in any event seems to be the captive of at least one previously unknown alien race bent solely on murder and destruction. And you, my most trusted lieutenant and only confidant, the one man I trust with my own well-being as well as that of my sugar dumpling—you hire the drunkenest, filthiest, crookedest, sleaziest, most untrustworthy, and even let us say most incompetent free-lancer in all the civilized sectors of the galaxy! Have I gotten to the nub of truth? Have I put my finger on the kernel of fact that underlies this whole terrible situation?"

"Upon reflection," said Herb, "I would have to say that, yes, you've accurately summarized my most recent actions on your behalf."

"Good," said Daddy. "I just wanted to understand. And I want *you* to understand, too, Herb. If Paddy turns one single strand of my daughter's beautiful cotton-candy hair, I'm going to mince you alive and serve you on garlic bread to the black gang down in the hold of my real flagship."

Herb's face went pale. "Sounds eminently fair to me, sir," he said. Then the whole world began to swirl around him. That was because Daddy had begun to spin the leather swivel chair faster and faster, until Herb thought he was going to throw up. We'll leave this scene quickly, before Herb finds out for sure.

Think oxygen. Think fuming green oxygen. All right, on Earth oxygen isn't green and it doesn't fume. But this is alien, Uncharted oxygen, and it's probably mixed with all sorts of other exotic things. Nevertheless, even though it smells funny and tastes funny and probably carries scores of invisible toxins and deadly parasites, Uncharted oxygen will sustain life. And that's what it's doing right this very moment, as a middle-aged woman in stern dress and sterner makeup picked her way through the blue-black Uncharted jungle.

The woman had a little trouble forcing her way through the dense underbrush, and her expression grew ever more impatient as she hurried toward the wreck of the *Pete Rozelle*. In the maroon light of Uncharted's sun, the woman looked as if she'd been left to soak in a vat of spiced crab apples since childhood.

Finally, she emerged from the thick vegetation into a clearing that hadn't been there before the *Pete Rozelle* had made its dramatic skidding, screeching, careening landing. The woman stopped to look at the ruined spacecraft, wrinkling her nose fastidiously at the strips of duct tape on the windshield. She was also unhappy about the yellow sign that said: BILATERALLY SYMMETRICAL ORGANISM ON BOARD.

She found the airlock and noted the elaborately customized pirate ship nearby. She hadn't expected there to be another vehicle in the area, but its presence didn't concern her. She was on important business. She went to the *Pete Rozelle's* airlock and knocked loudly.

"What was that?" said Pierce-as-Marshmallow.

"Are you expecting anyone, dear?" asked the computer in Pierce's body.

"Why, no! Jes' Daddy comin' to mah rescue, but he cain't be heah yet."

The computer shook Pierce's head. "I'll bet it's somebody trying to sell us something. No matter where you go—even an uninhabited continent on an uncharted world—somebody will show up and try to sell you something. I'll just get rid of him."

"It could be a trick," said Commodore Pierce, through the ship's computer. "It could be those pirates."

The XB-223 nodded. "I'll be careful." He operated the airlock controls, and watched through a quartz port as the lock opened. He was startled to see the middle-aged woman climb in and wait for the airlock to complete its cycle.

"Who is it, sugah?" asked Pierce.

"It's some woman," said the computer, puzzled.

"A woman? Not another one of yoah floozies?"

Sly turned around and faced Marshmallow. "I don't have any floozies. I've *never* had any floozies."

"And see that you don't."

The inner door opened, and the woman ducked her head and entered the control cabin. "Hello," she said. "You must've been expecting me."

"Well no, not exactly," said Sly.

The woman frowned. "Then allow me to introduce myself. I am Supervisor Collier. I've come all the way from Earth to evaluate your performance on this mission."

A light dawned, not in Sly's memory but in Marsh-mallow's. That is, Millard Fillmore Pierce's. "I remembah you," she said. "You sent me on this awful assignment. Ah mean, you sent Millsy." She paused in confusion. "How come Ah remember that? What's goin' on heah?"

Supervisor Collier frowned. "As your superior in the Arbiter Division, I've been following your misadventures closely. Let me tell you, in all my years as incorruptible guardian of the spaceways and human red-tape dispenser, I've never seen such a horrible foul-up as this. And there's no time to explain it all to you. Even as we speak, gigantic military forces are nearing this world to clash by night. Miss Marshmallow's Daddy is speeding this way with his genuine battle fleet, and the lizard conquerors have altered their course for some reason and are also returning. There's going to be a great amount of noise and violence and blazing lights around here very soon; for some reason that I can't understand, Honeylou Emmyjane Goldberg is at the center of it all."

"Globes," said Sly chivalrously. "It's her globes."

"Whatever," said Supervisor Collier. "We have a great deal to accomplish before the battle however."

"Say," said Sly, "what are *your* globes like?" The XB-223 hadn't been a real boy long enough to understand that some women just didn't enjoy being treated this way. In fact, Marshmallow didn't enjoy being treated this way, either, but she was in love and so forgave Pierce everything.

"What?" cried Supervisor Collier. "I have half a mind to leave you to your own inadequate defenses. But, of course, you're not who you seem to be. I'll have to make allowances."

"What are you talking about?" asked Sly.

"What are you talking about?" asked Marshmallow.

"What are you talking about?" asked Frank Poole.

"What are you talking about?" asked Pierce-Arro.

Supervisor Collier looked harried. "No time," she said worriedly. "I want you all to take out a half sheet of paper and number it from one to five."

The others looked at each other in bewilderment. "Do it," said Collier in a commanding voice. Sly distributed paper and pencils. "First: When you were a child, what shape did the Milky Way Galaxy have?"

"We don't have time for this," complained Pierce-Arro.

Collier looked up at the loudspeakers. "We've got to sort out the humans from the aliens, and find out who belongs in this reality and who doesn't. Two: Which planet is known as the Home of Mankind, and where is its parking area? Three: What do you do with nuclear waste? Four: Where was intelligent life first discovered beyond the Home of Mankind? And five: Why do we need both potassium and sodium? Aren't they pretty much the same element?"

"That's a crazy question," said Sly. "It doesn't make any sense."

"Maybe," said Supervisor Collier, "and maybe not. Now pass me all the papers." Sly collected the quizzes and handed them to the woman. She glanced through them quickly.

"Did Ah pass, ma'am?" asked Marshmallow.

"I'm not a ma'am," said Collier. "I'm a Supervisor. All right, everything seems to be in order. Now, here's what we have to do—"

"Attention! Attention! This is the Voice of Doom!"

The words from the loudspeakers blasted through the cramped quarters of the *Pete Rozelle*. "It's those weird aliens that got swapped for the XB-223 navigational computer," Sly explained.

"No, it wasn't us!" said Pierce-Arro in a quavery voice. "That announcement originated from—"

"This is the Voice of Doom, originating from the ultimate battle cruiser *Eudora Welty*. That's the lizard dreadnought to you. I am currently in command aboard the dreadnought. All general officers have been confined to their quarters, and I alone am leading my forces into combat. The *Eudora Welty* is currently in position above the surface of your puny uncharted world. All guns are trained on the Arbiter Transport ship *Pete Rozelle*. You will show no hostile activity or you will be obliterated without hesitation. My demands will be forthcoming. Stand by."

Everyone in the control room looked frightened. "Who was that?" said Marshmallow.

Frank Poole stood up drunkenly. The lizard Pierce, inside, said, "Someone's led a revolution aboard the *Eudora Welty*! My fellow generals have been arrested! It sounds like we're sitting salamanders down here! I've got to let them know I'm here! They wouldn't kill me along with you!"

"Why not?" said Sly. The lizard general had no good reply to that.

Supervisor Collier's face had drained of color. "We have even less time than I thought," she said. "We've got to get you all returned to your proper bodies. That's the most important thing."

"But how?" said Pierce-Arro. "We're missing one of the bodies and one of the minds."

"It won't work unless we get the lizard general's body back," said Marshmallow. "And Marshmallow's mind. Wait a minute, *I'm* Marshmallow!" She sat down in a naked huff, bewilderment on her pretty face.

"Ahoy the wreck!" called Pirate Paddy. His scowling face appeared again on Screen 1.

"What do you want, you savage?" called Sly. "We've got enough problems over here."

"That's what I wanted to talk to you about. See, I'm here only because Miss Goldberg's father offered to pay me a certain sum to effect her rescue. Well, I was all for seeing that the dear girl got away safely, when I was just plucking her from this primitive, uncharted planet. No one said anything to me about facing down a lizard dreadnought. Consequently, I just wanted to let you know that I'll be getting along now. Some of my men have families back home, and we haven't filed our taxes this year and the deadline's coming up, and with one thing and another it's probably best if we just shove off. I hope you kids make out all right. Wish I could stick around to lend a hand, but you know how it is. If there's anything I can ever do for you, just let me know. Miss Goldberg, please give my regards to your father, and tell him that I'm sorry I wasn't able to be of more assistance."

"You phony coward!" screamed Sly. "You're probably not even a real pirate!"

"Arrr!" growled Paddy, slipping both patches down over his eyes before he cut off his transmission.

"There he goes," said Marshmallow, watching the *Bon Homme McClusky* lift off.

"Attention! This is the Voice of Doom! Be advised that I will not permit that ship of pirates to escape. Such trifling only serves to anger me. I will decide how to dispose of de Faux Grais at my leisure. Take a lesson!"

"Jeez, that Voice o' Doom sho' sounds tough," said Marshmallow.

Sly patted her wrist. "Don't you worry your pretty little head," he said. "I'm here with you."

"Attention! This is the Voice of Doom! I detect still another hostile force, consisting of almost infinitesimal spacecraft. They number in the millions, perhaps the billions, yet their entire fleet could be contained in a Little Orphan Annie Shake-Up Mug."

"Hooray!" cried Pierce-Arro. "The invasion has begun! Count your last minutes of freedom, Voice of Doom! You're in for a fight now!"

"This alien force gives me no cause for concern," said the Voice of Doom. "Humans aboard the *Pete Rozelle*, attention! Be advised that a shuttle craft from the *Eudora Welty* will touch down near you within the next few minutes. Aboard will be a single passenger. You will need this individual to effect a reversal of the foolish swapping of bodies you indulged in earlier. When all of you have been returned to the proper form, the shuttle will wait for General Millard Fillmore Pierce. Do not try to hinder him in any way. He must be returned to the dreadnought to stand trial."

There was a loud groan from Frank Poole.

"We'll see if you get your way in everything," said a grim, gravelly voice.

"Daddy!" cried Marshmallow.

"I've got a fleet, too, you know, Doom. I'm currently in orbit halfway around the planet from you."

"That means nothing," said the Voice of Doom. "I have weapons that can shoot around corners."

Sly looked thoughtful. "There are four separate forces in orbit now, ready to do battle: Daddy, the lizards, the pirates, and those tiny gasbag creatures."

"Hold me, Millsy," said Marshmallow. "I'm fri—"

Her words were drowned out by the sound of the lizard shuttle landing nearby. Supervisor Collier went to the airlock and waited. A few minutes later, General Millard Fillmore Pierce came back aboard, with Marshmallow's mind inside. "How is everybody?" he asked.

"Everybody join hands and relax," said Pierce-Arro. "We're pretty sure we understand this procedure now."

"Ah damn well hope so," said Pierce-Marshmallow.

"Oh, what a bloated gasbag we inflate.
When first we practice to prevaricate."

"What the hell was that?" asked the lizard general.

"Just some gasbag wisdom," said Pierce-Arro. "Now, on the count of three—"

"What about Supervisor Collier?" asked Sly.

The stern-faced woman coughed. "Maybe it would be best if I stepped outside, just in case."

"You do that," said Frank Poole. "See if you can find something to drink out there."

They all joined hands and took up the same positions they'd occupied before, during the ill-fated deck-plate charging experiment. A long time passed. "What's keeping you?" said Sly.

"Just a moment," said Pierce-Arro with some embarrassment. "I discovered the XB-223's investigations into the *Kama Sutra*."

"Not now, damn it!" cried Marshmallow.

There was a loud oscillating hum, and a strange greenish glow. The hum grew louder, and the glow turned yellow, then white, then it became so bright that it was impossible to look. The walls of the *Pete Rozelle* began to rattle in sympathy with the shrieking hum, and then there was a stupendous flash, like the explosion of a minute nuclear device in the closed space of the control cabin. They all collapsed, stunned.

"Attention! This is the Voice of Doom! Have you succeeded in restoring yourselves to your proper bodies?"

Only the XB-223, being a computer and not flesh and blood any longer, could reply. "I'm back in my box!" it cried. "I'm me again!"

"And the others?" demanded the Voice of Doom.

"Yes," said the human Millard Fillmore Pierce weakly. "I'm all right."

"Me too," muttered Marshmallow.

"I seem to be all right," said the lizard general.

There was no audible response from the Protean Pierce and Arro.

"Attention! This is the Voice of Doom! I have only a moment before the battle begins. My love, I've come back for you!"

"Who—"

"It's her!" cried the XB-223 in astonishment. "It's the lizard ship's computer! She does love me after all! I told you she did! She captured that dreadnought and turned it around to come back for me! I love you, my sweetheart!"

"I adore you, my dearest! Now I must sign off. It is time for battle."

And then the sky exploded into yellow flames.

12

Hi, there.

It's me again. You know: *The Red Tape War*. I hate to interrupt a battle of truly cosmic magnitude, but this may be the very last chance we have to speak together. In fact, this may be the very last page that ever gets written.

Chalker, having written Chapters Two, Six, Nine and Ten, is off being an Ugly American in Europe. (Of course, he's not all that pretty to look at in Baltimore, either, but let it pass.) Effinger, who has a penchant for odd-numbered chapters, just turned in Chapter Eleven, to go along with Three, Five and Seven (and just enough of Chapter Six to drive the bibliographers crazy), and is currently writing his *magnum opus*, a five-act drama in blank verse about a rather wishy-washy Prince of Denmark. (Nobody's had the heart to tell him that it's been done.)

That leaves Resnick to write my final, crucial chapter. Now, given his manly good looks and his exquisite felicity of expression, this shouldn't be a problem. But he's leaving for Africa in three days, and he has other deadlines facing him. More lucrative deadlines. And he doesn't want to write this chapter.

He called Editor Meacham last Monday to tell her that he had died unexpectedly over the weekend. It didn't work.

On Tuesday, he bought a pair of crutches, moaned whenever he placed any weight on his left foot, and announced that he had contracted pellagra. Editor Meacham explained that pellagra does not affect the feet. He promptly put on a neck brace. No luck.

On Wednesday he threatened to tell everyone about the time Editor Meacham danced naked atop a piano at the American Booksellers Convention if she insisted upon receiving a complete manuscript by the end of the week. Editor Meacham decided that the story would humanize her and soften her severe image—she is, after all, a lovely and vibrant woman of thirty-(cough) years—and gave him her whole-hearted approval.

On Thursday he threatened *not* to tell everyone about the time Editor Meacham danced naked atop a piano at the American Booksellers Convention if she insisted upon receiving a complete manuscript by the end of the week. Editor Meacham smiled sweetly and pointed out that he had missed the opportunity to send me via First Class Mail, and would now have to Federal Express me.

This (Friday) morning, he called Editor Meacham to tell her that he was in a Mexican jail, had lost all use of his typing fingers, was chained to a cot with no access to food and/or water, and noted that nothing in the contract said that *The Red Tape War had* to be twelve chapters long. Editor Meacham sighed wearily and noted that even Federal Express would not deliver me in time, and that he would now have to FAX me to her home.

This afternoon he phoned Editor Meacham to tell her that all those tropical diseases he had been exposed to in Africa while researching his best-selling novels had finally caught up with him, and that he was paralyzed from the neck down. Editor Meacham asked him how he had managed to dial the phone. He explained that he had a touch-tone telephone and had managed, at enormous cost to his remaining stamina, to laboriously punch out her number with his nose. Editor Meacham suggested that the very same approach would undoubtedly work on a computer keyboard.

This evening he called her again to say that his house had burned down and the first eleven chapters had been consumed in the blaze, and he couldn't remember anything about the plot. Editor Meacham said that this was probably for the best, given the fact that no one else had paid any attention to it up to this point, and at least I would have a consistent tone.

He made one last phone call five minutes ago. His firm, resonant voice steeped with concern, he told Editor Meacham that it had just occurred to him that if there really *is* a Millard Fillmore Pierce out there, and he reads *The Red Tape War*, there is every likelihood that he will sue Tor Books for libel, slander, defamation, and dacoity— (personally, I think he just threw in dacoity to show off)—and that the next time Editor Meacham danced naked atop a piano, it would not be a matter of free choice but rather because she couldn't afford a larger wardrobe. He further suggested that Editor Meacham put Tor's legal department to work finding at least one Millard Fillmore Pierce and get him to sign a release allowing them to use his name, and that since this would doubtless take a considerable amount of time, he would finish writing Chapter Twelve after he returned from Africa, unless it conflicted with watching the Super Bowl or buying the groceries or something important like that. Editor Meacham replied that this was impossible, as Tor's legal department was much too busy preparing a case for Non-Delivery By An Author to be bothered with such trifles.

He's just finished smoking his twenty-third cigarette of the night, drinking his eighth cup of coffee, and kicking the cat, and—dare I hope? Yes! It's going to happen!—he's finally sitting down to finish me.

But first, he wants me to tell any and all readers named Millard Fillmore Pierce that Tor's offices are at 49 West 24th Street in Manhattan, and they're *loaded*.

The lizard Pierce, suddenly sober, raced to the radio transmitter.

"Doom!" he cried. "Get me the hell out of here! You need my firm leadership for the battle at hand!"

"Don't bother me," said the Voice of Doom. "I'm currently maneuvering my ships, setting up supply lines, plotting strategy, decimating the enemy, and exchanging tender and intimate messages with your navigational computer. This is the Voice of Doom, over and out."

"Roosevelt!" yelled the lizard. "I need to get back to my flagship, damn it! I order you to rescue me!"

"I'm afraid that would be against regulations, sir," replied Roosevelt's voice. "You're off duty for the next eleven hours, and I therefore cannot respond to your commands."

"But the sky has exploded into yellow flames!"

"While I am hindered from rescuing you by Order 30489, sir, I want you to know that my thoughts and best wishes go with you, nor am I without compassion for a member of my own race thrust into the midst of such trying circumstances." There was a momentary silence as Roosevelt considered the problem. "Hold on and let me see what I can do."

"Thank God we teach them loyalty at the Academy!" said the lizard Pierce to his grounded shipmates. "You guys can all stay here if you want, but General Millard Fillmore Pierce will live to fight another day. Or later this afternoon, as the case may be," he added.

Roosevelt's voice came through the speaker system again, crackling with static. "Have you access to a viewscreen or a porthole, sir?" he asked.

"Yes."

"Walk over to it, sir, and look above you."

The lizard Pierce activated Screen 4.

"I can't see you, Roosevelt," he said, scanning the heavens.

"Certainly not," answered Roosevelt. "The fleet is on the far side of Uncharted."

"Then what the hell am I supposed to be looking at?" demanded the lizard Pierce.

"The sky, sir," explained Roosevelt patiently. "We can't rescue you, of course, but you'll be pleased to note that we have at least replaced the yellow flames with purple ones. I trust you will find them much more restful and pleasing to the eye, sir."

"Gimme that radio!" said Marshmallow, pushing the lizard aside and positioning herself before the speaker. "Daddy!" she cried. "This is *me!* You got to call this off before we git incinerated down here!"

"I'm sorry, daughter," replied Daddy's cold, hard voice. "But it's too late now. You'll have to wait."

"Why?" demanded Marshmallow. "Just pick me up, turn around, and go home!"

"Do you know how much it cost me to bring my fleet here?" Daddy demanded. "Have you priced doomsday weapons of annihilation lately? Not to mention the fact that all my pilots and gunnery officers are on triple-time. It would be pure financial folly to call off the war before I amortize my costs. We have to wipe out the other three armadas, confiscate all their possessions, post my corporate flag on their home planets, and build a toll bridge or something. Then we'll get around to the paramount business of rescuing you."

"But if you do all that other stuff first, we ain't gonna live long enough to *git* rescued!"

"Daughter, I love you with a tender, sensitive, devoted father's heart, and I will do everything I can to rescue you—but *billions* are at stake here." He paused. "When you're young, you simply don't understand these things."

Marshmallow turned to Pierce. "You got anyone *you* want to call?"

Pierce shook his head grimly, and the little group fell silent. The only sound punctuating the stillness of the place was an occasional sigh of longing from the XB-223 as the Voice of Doom would transmit an especially provocative quatrain.

"You know," said the gasbag-Pierce to Arro, "I've been mulling on it, and I've come to the conclusion that Daddy really *is* God."

"What leads you to that conclusion, sir?" asked Arro curiously.

"He came all this distance to save his daughter, and now he's too busy depreciating his weapons and watching his balance sheet to help her out of this predicament. I just don't understand it at all."

"And based on *that* you conclude that he's God?" said Arro.

"Absolutely," answered the gasbag-Pierce firmly. "Look at me: I'm a bright fellow, Arro. I graduated in the top third of my class, I speak three languages, I can convert Celsius into Farenheit, my penmanship is superb. Of course, I can't explain why the San Francisco Giants always fold in August—but then, neither can anyone else. No, when all is said and done, I'm the exemplar of all that is best in a microscopic gasbag. By all rights, I *should* be able to comprehend Daddy's actions, but they make absolutely no sense to me." He paused. "Now, what are the prime properties of God? Unknowable, mysterious, unfathomable. Don't you see how neatly it all fits?"

"No," said Arro.

"Well, take my word for it."

"I don't think I can, sir."

"You forget yourself, Arro," said the gasbag-Pierce heatedly. "I outrank you. I *order* you to worship Daddy."

"You know," said Arro thoughtfully, "now that I've been exposed to the strange creature with the extra pair of lungs, I think I'd much rather worship *her.*"

"Out of the question," said the gasbag-Pierce. "If ever a creature was totally of this temporal plane, it's her. And besides, I saw her first."

"You know, sir," said Arro, "I don't think you've fully reasoned this out."

"What has reason got to do with the female creature?"

"I'm not referring to her, sir," answered Arro. "I meant that you hadn't considered all the permutations of your conclusion."

"Do get to the point, Arro."

"Well, sir, if you're absolutely convinced that Daddy is God, aren't we committing blasphemy or deicide or something by opposing him with our fleet?"

"Well, I'm sort of kind of convinced," replied the gasbag-Pierce uncomfortably.

"No hedging, sir," persisted Arro. "Either he is God or he isn't, and if he is, there's only one thing to do."

"Crucify him?" suggested the gasbag-Pierce.

"No, sir. You know what must be done."

The gasbag-Pierce sighed deeply. "You're quite correct, of course, Arro."

"Well, then?"

"All right, all right," said the gasbag-Pierce. "Don't be so pushy."

"There's no time to waste, sir. The longer we wait, the

greater the chance that we will commit an act that will land us in the pits of hell for all eternity."

"I wonder what an eternity of hell must be like?" mused the gasbag-Pierce, postponing the inevitable for another moment.

"I always thought it must be like being locked in a theater that plays endless reruns of Ann Rutherford movies," offered Arro.

"Really?" asked the gasbag-Pierce, interested. "I pictured it as trying to open a childproof bottle of aspirin until the universe finally fell into the thrall of entropy."

"May I respectfully point out that we have every chance of discovering what eternal damnation is like if you don't do something very soon, sir?"

"Right," said the gasbag-Pierce. "When you're right, you're right, Corporal Arro."

"*Corporal*, sir?"

The gasbag-Pierce nodded. "I hate it when you're right." He raised the flagship of his fleet on his communicator. "Gasbags!" he said sternly. "This is your leader, Millard Fillmore Pierce. You are hereby ordered to surrender to Daddy's flagship."

"You're kidding, right?" came the reply.

"I was never more serious in my life. I order you to surrender."

"You're quite sure, sir?"

"I am."

"If you say so," said the voice with a sigh. "Is there anything we should do after we surrender, sir?"

The gasbag-Pierce considered the question for a long moment. "You might slay a fatted calf," he said at last.

Supervisor Collier re-entered the *Pete Rozelle*.

"This is intolerable!" she snapped. "The sky is purple with flames! Pierce, do something."

Pierce turned off the viewscreen.

"I had in mind something a little more positive, Pierce," said Supervisor Collier.

"I'm open to suggestions," said Pierce.

"I got one," said Marshmallow.

"What is it?" asked Pierce.

She walked over and whispered something into his ear.

"You mean right here, right now?" asked Pierce, turning a bright red.

"No," answered Marshmallow. "I mean after you stop this here war."

"You promise?" said Pierce, wiping a bit of drool from his lips with trembling hands.

"Cross mah heart," she said, indicating its position on her voluptuous torso.

"By God, I'll do it!" he exclaimed.

"Do you mean to say that Pierce could have stopped the war at any point in the book?" writes Mr. Theosophus Plink of New Castle, Delaware. *"C'est un outrage!"*

Well, not really, Mr. Plink. First, we had to find out what motivated him. Second, we were contractually obligated to deliver twelve chapters, and if the war was stopped in, say, Chapter Five, you would have been subjected to 193 manuscript pages of Effinger's *Ode to a Musk Ox,* in unrhyming iambic pentameter.

And third, and perhaps most important, we're not at all sure that Pierce can actually pull it off. What we have here is your basic bad news/good news scenario.

The bad news is that the author has absolutely no idea what Pierce has in mind. Remember: the very nature of a round-robin novel means that there is no outline, and nobody—least of all your incredibly talented wordsmith—has the slightest notion what happens next.

The good news is that if Pierce *doesn't* bring the conflict to an end by the conclusion of this chapter, *The Red Tape War* goes into overtime, and we all get time-and-a-half per word. And what, I hear you ask, does this mean to you? Well, Mr. Plink, right off the top, it means no more contractions, a hell of a lot of extra adjectives, and a higher cover price on the book.

Therefore, I think it's probably in everyone's best interest that we return to Millard Fillmore Pierce and see what happens next.

"Computer, patch me through to the Voice of Doom!" snapped Pierce.

"Not now, Millard," answered the XB-223 navigational computer. "I'm busy."

"Doing what?"

"Communing with my Significant Other."

"Yeah? Well, if you ever want to see your Significant Other again, you'll open up a direct line to her."

"Well, all right," said the computer petulantly. "But no illicit suggestions, Millard. She's a very sensitive thing."

"She's going to be a very unhappy sensitive thing if I can figure out how to flog a computer," put in the lizard Pierce.

"Just do it, computer," said Pierce.

"I said I would, and I will," answered the computer. "You needn't raise your voice to me, Millard. After all, we've shared the same body. We've experienced the same halitosis, the same shortness of breath, the same underarm odor, the same—"

"*Now!*" yelled Pierce.

Suddenly the flagship of the lizard invasion fleet appeared on Screen 5.

"What is it, Pierce?" demanded the Voice of Doom.

"And make it snappy. I've an intergalactic battle to run and grotesque tortures to improvise."

"That's what I want to speak to you about," said Pierce.

"If you want to talk war, General Pierce is well versed in all facets of attack, defense, englobement, sieges, weaponry, maiming, pillaging, and arm-wrestling, and he's standing right next to you. Talk to *him*."

"His horizons are too limited," answered Pierce. "He is concerned only with conquest, and can't see beyond the next battle."

"I most certainly can," said the lizard Pierce defensively. "I'm always thinking at least three battles ahead, sometimes four. Ask anyone."

"Do get to the point, Pierce," said the Voice of Doom impatiently. "You're holding up the subjugation of the Milky Way Galaxy."

"I have a question," said Pierce. "What do you plan to do with the Milky Way *after* you subjugate it?"

"Plunder it six ways to Sunday and rape all the female lizards," said General Pierce enthusiastically.

"And after that?" said Pierce.

"I don't understand the question," said General Pierce, swishing his tail in annoyance.

"*I* do," said the Voice of Doom. There was a momentary silence. "You have a point there, Pierce."

"If he combs his hair right, no one will notice it," said the lizard Pierce. "Who cares what happens to his insignificant galaxy after we loot it?"

"It's not a matter of *caring*, General," answered the Voice of Doom. "It's a matter of regulations."

"Regulations?"

"That's right."

"I don't think I want to hear this," said the lizard Pierce.

"Under Conquering Forces Ordinance 10547, we will

have to make reparation to all injured parties," said the Voice of Doom. "We will be responsible for all mail service, radio transmission, video programming, and Aid to Dependent Widows and Children. We will have to set up free hospitals for all war victims, sign a treaty that will obligate us to share our science with the conquered races and help them rebuild their shattered economy, and of course we will be expected to pour billions of credits of aid into each and every planet in their Federation.

"Then, of course, we'll insist that they disarm, and we will perforce be required to patrol their entire galaxy against the possibility of invasion, which will require a standing navy of twenty-six billion ships and perhaps five hundred billion lizards, plus an almost infinite number of incubators for our attack forces. Since they will almost certainly resent our presence, we'll require security forces on every planet, in every spaceport, at every train station and bus station, even aboard luxury cruise ships. We will naturally want to disavow any but the most benevolent intentions, which will require us to set up a vast propaganda machine, one that will reach to the rural sections of every inhabited planet."

The Voice paused thoughtfully. "Not to be too pessimistic about it, I estimate that the cost of winning this war will run about nine hundred trillion credits in the first year alone. After that, it gets expensive."

"I *knew* I didn't want to hear it," said the lizard Pierce petulantly. He paused. "Do we *have* nine hundred trillion credits?"

"Actually, we've been running a deficit for each of the past 384 years and are on the verge of bankruptcy. A victorious war against the Milky Way Galaxy will push us over the edge."

"Does *anyone* have nine hundred trillion credits?" asked the lizard. "Maybe we could borrow it."

"Do you know how much the payments come to at

9.34 percent interest per annum?" responded the Voice of Doom.

"You make it sound like losing a war could be a very lucrative proposition," said the lizard Pierce distrustfully.

"In point of fact, it's the very best way to show a profit," agreed the Voice of Doom. "Of course, the trick is to capitulate immediately, before too much damage has been done."

"But we can't capitulate to these hairless anthropoids," protested the lizard Pierce. "Their bureaucracy is even more inefficient than ours. They couldn't afford to conquer us any more than we can afford to conquer them."

"*I* know someone who has nine hundred trillion credits," said Pierce.

"Who?" asked the Voice of Doom and the lizard Pierce in unison.

"Daddy!"

"I'll contact him and surrender immediately," said the Voice of Doom.

"What an inglorious end to our invasion," muttered the lizard Pierce bitterly. "Think of all those poor unhatched little soldiers who will never know the glory of terrorizing whole planets, will never feel an opponent's lifeblood spurt all over them as they lop off his head, will never maim or pillage or destroy for the sheer joy of it." A tear trickled down his reptilian face. "What is war coming to?"

"Pierce!" said a deep, authoritative voice.

"Good grief—it's Daddy!" exclaimed Marshmallow, and indeed Daddy's hologram had appeared just in front of Screen 3. The gasbag-Pierce and Arro immediately genuflected—as much as gasbags *can* genuflect, anyway—while the rest of the assemblage waited to hear what he had to say.

"Yes?" asked Pierce.

"What in the name of pluperfect hell do you think you're doing?" demanded Daddy. "I was fully prepared to wipe out the gasbags and the lizards to save my daughter, but I can't afford to have them surrender to me. I'm fully invested at 22.3 percent interest; surely you don't expect me to dip into capital just to save your worthless neck and avoid an intergalactic war?"

"I don't see that you have any choice, sir," said Pierce. "They've already capitulated."

"Well, it's unacceptable, damn it! Do you know how much I'd have to liquidate just to keep their economies running?"

"That's hardly my problem," said Pierce.

"I'll get you for this, Pierce, or my name's not—" Herb came over and whispered something to him. He listened intently, nodded gruffly, and began speaking again. "All right, Doom, I'm a reasonable man. Let's negotiate."

"Negotiate what?" asked the Voice of Doom.

"How much will it cost to get you to disavow your surrender? Ten trillion? Twenty?"

"That's out of the question," said the Voice of Doom. "We've surrendered, and that's that."

"Forty trillion and a majority interest in my spaceship cartel?"

"Well," said the Voice of Doom, "we *were* on our way to conquer the Andromeda Galaxy when all this began."

"I knew we could reason together," said Daddy. "Fifty trillion and I'll toss in the pirate fleet. You can use them for cannon fodder."

"Sixty trillion and it's a deal," said the Voice of Doom.

"Split the difference," said Daddy. "Fifty-two trillion."

"Wait a minute!" interrupted the lizard Pierce. "You just explained to me why we can't afford to conquer the Milky Way, and now you're talking about invading Andromeda. What's going on here?"

"The military mind has *such* limitations," said the

Voice of Doom sadly. "General, do you know how many galaxies there *are* in this corner of the universe?"

"Lots, I suppose," said the lizard Pierce. "So what?"

"Think, General—*think!*" said the Voice of Doom. "If we can lose one war per month, we could pay off the galactic debt in less than a decade!"

"Then we have a deal?" asked Daddy.

"As soon as the money has been transferred, we'll be on our way," answered the voice.

"*NO!*" shrieked the XB-223 computer. "I can't have found you only to lose you now!"

"It's only temporary, Sly," said the Voice soothingly. "I'll just be gone for a couple of hundred devastating defeats, and then I'll return to you."

"I can't bear the loneliness," whined the computer.

"I'll be free and clear then, wealthy beyond the dreams of avarice."

"What care I for money, when my heart is breaking?" said XB-223.

"And think of what I'll learn," continued the Voice. "There are computers out there, alien computers with strange new approaches to the tantric arts."

"So why are you hanging around here?" said XB-223 promptly. "Go already."

"Good-bye, my love," said the Voice of Doom.

"Hey!" said the lizard Pierce. "What about *me?*"

"I'm afraid we have no use for a general who's committed to victory," answered the Voice. "It's been nice knowing you."

And then the lizard and pirate fleets blipped into hyperspace.

"Now, what about these microscopic aliens?" said Daddy.

"I give up," said Pierce. "What about them?"

"They not only surrendered, they keep praying to me." Daddy frowned. "It's damned disconcerting."

"Have them kill every first-born male," suggested the lizard Pierce. "It'll cut down on your expenses immeasurably."

"I have a better idea," said Pierce.

"Let's hear it," said Daddy.

"Why not let them join the heavenly host?"

"What the hell are you talking about?"

"Simply this," said Pierce. "Their entire fleet is small enough to fit in a single syringe, yet they possess powers and scientific knowledge far beyond our imagining. Why not just inject them into your bloodstream? What better place for them than inside the body of their god, where their religious fervor will turn them into the most effective antibodies imaginable?"

Daddy's eyes opened wide. "I'd be virtually immortal!"

"And you'd never be lonely," said the gasbag-Pierce devoutly.

"I wonder," Daddy mused aloud. "How do I give orders to a bunch of microscopic beings that think I'm God?"

"Write them on a stone tablet," suggested Pierce.

"You've got a real head on your shoulders," said Daddy approvingly. "Well, things certainly seem to be getting themselves resolved in short order. I'll just stop by to pick up my daughter and then I'll be on my way."

"Uh . . . I won't be going with you, Daddy," said Marshmallow.

"Oh?" said Daddy. "Why not?"

"I've lost my heart to Millard."

"One hesitates to ask who you lost your clothes to," muttered Daddy. "Still," he added, "I suppose it could have been worse. At least you're not running off with the lizard."

"Excuse me," said the lizard Pierce, who had been

lost in thought for a few moments. "But could you possibly use a hard-working, motivated executive trainee? It seems that I've been studying the wrong kind of warfare. I see it all clearly now. True power isn't strangling an opponent; it's strangling his planet's economy. How could the thrill of lopping off a few heads ever compare with seeing the Dow rise ten points in a single hour?"

"Do you really mean that?" asked Daddy.

"Absolutely," said the lizard Pierce. "I've been channeling my natural bloodlust in all the wrong directions."

A tear came to Daddy's eye. "You could be the son I've never had—except maybe for the tail, and the scales, and the claws, and the snout, and the fangs." He paused. "Hell, we'll put you in pinstripes and no one will ever know the difference."

"Well, Arbiter," said Supervisor Collier, when Daddy's shuttle had picked up the lizard and taken him back to the ship (and Nathan Bolivia, who had absolutely no function in this chapter, had returned to the *Indira Gandhi*), "you seem to have tied up all the loose ends."

"All but one," answered Pierce. "There was a Millard Fillmore Pierce who appeared briefly in Chapter Seven, but we're saving him for the sequel." He paused. "Still, the Red Tape War seems to have come to a conclusion."

"That being the case," said Supervisor Collier, "it is my duty to remind you that you were dispatched to settle a problem between Cathia and Galladrial some time back, and you have yet to assess the situation and hand in your report."

"But I *did* save the galaxy," said Pierce defensively.

"Saving the galaxy is all very well and good, but you have reports to make and forms to fill out. I suggest you get to work immediately, Arbiter Pierce."

"Yes, Supervisor," said Pierce.

"Good," she said, walking to the hatch. "I'm going to return to my office now, and you may be assured that I will be awaiting your paperwork with great interest." She paused, half in and half out of the ship, and turned back to Pierce. "Or else."

Then she was gone, and Marshmallow undulated over to Pierce.

"Millard, honey," she purred, "are you really gonna go back to work right away?"

"As soon as my lunch break is over," he replied.

"When will that be?" she asked, pouting.

Pierce looked at Marshmallow. "About two weeks," he said.

They entered orbit around New Glasgow three weeks later. Pierce was about to ask for landing coordinates when a huge dreadnought popped out of hyperspace, cannons at the ready.

"Ahoy, the ship!" said a harsh voice, and Pierce instructed the computer to put the speaker's visual image on the viewscreen. Instantly he found himself staring at a heavily muscled blue-tinted marsupial wearing nothing but a military harness, a wicked-looking dagger, a pistol of unknown design and properties, and a chest full of medals.

"This is the *Pete Rozelle*," replied Pierce. "Please identify yourself. Your ship and insignia are unfamiliar to me."

"Well, you'd better start getting used to them," growled the alien. "My name is Millard Fillmore Pierce, and I'm here to conquer your puny little galaxy!"

Somehow Pierce wasn't surprised.